D1158043

CHINESE CLASSICS

Journey to the West
with the
Stone Monkey

———————

Retold by
Yun-Chong Pan

Illustrated by
Serena Chen

 CHINA INTERCONTINENTAL PRESS

中国国家版权局著作权合同登记号：图字01-2009-602号

图书在版编目(CIP)数据

西游记故事：英文／（加）Pan Yun-chong编.—北京：
五洲传播出版社，2010.1（2014.7重印）
ISBN 978-7-5085-1729-2

Ⅰ.①西… Ⅱ.①潘… Ⅲ.①故事—作品集—加拿大
—现代—英文 Ⅳ.①Ⅰ711.45

中国版本图书馆CIP数据核字(2009)第202545号

JOURNEY TO THE WEST WITH THE STONE MONKEY

First published 2009 by Bayeux Arts, Inc. (www.bayeux.com)

Retold by Yun-Chong Pan
Illustrated by Serena Chen
Executive Editor: Zheng Lei

Published and Distributed by China Intercontinental Press, 25th Floor, Huatian Plaza, 6 Beixiaomachang, Haidian District, Beijing 100038, China, (86) 10-58891281, http://www.cicc.org.cn
First Printing: January 2010
Printed by Beijing Picture in Picture Printing Co, Ltd

ISBN 978-7-5085-1729-2
08800

CONTENTS

PART 1

Part 2

Part 3

PART ONE

◙ CHAPTER 1 ◙
The Birth of the Magic Monkey

Long, long ago, in the land of the East, there was a high mountain, on top of which was a large stone. The stone had the dimensions corresponding to the universe, and cavities that corresponded to those of living beings: seven for the eyes, ears, nostrils, and mouth; and three for the navel, urinal and anal orifices.

Over thousands of years, this stone received the spirit of the universe, and started to show the characteristics of a living being. One day the stone exploded, and a stone monkey leaped out of it. The stone monkey quickly learned to walk and leap and its eyes emitted golden rays, which shot all the way up to the sky and was seen by the Jade Emperor in Heaven, who was the head of all gods. The Jade Emperor said, "This is a newly-born creature, and as long as he remains harmless, let him be."

◙ CHAPTER 2 ◙
The Stone Monkey Becomes King

The stone monkey joined the other monkeys in the mountain, playing, cavorting, feeding on the fruits, jumping from tree to tree, and having great fun. One day, as they roamed around their mountain, they came upon a waterfall. The monkeys cried in unison, "Wow, what is this? We have never seen this before. What could be behind the water?"

The waterfall was very wide and there was a huge torrent of water rushing down the cliff. The monkeys said, "Well, we don't

One day the stone exploded, and a stone monkey leaped out of it.

know what is behind this waterfall. If one of us is brave enough to go find out, then why don't we accept him as our King?"

When the stone monkey heard this, he said, "I will go there." So he closed his eyes, and leaped through the screen of water, and landed in a dry cave behind the waterfall.

The stone monkey found stone tables and chairs, and other furniture. There was also a big sign at the entrance of the cave, saying 'Water Screen Cave'. The stone monkey was delighted, and he leapt out of the cave through the waterfall, and shouted, "Hey! I found quite a nice living place for us!"

Now that the other monkeys had seen the stone monkey go through the water and return unscathed, they all followed his example and leapt into the cave. The cave was large enough to accommodate everyone. Everyone was happy, and they decided to accept the stone monkey as their king. Now the stone monkey called himself the 'Magnificent Monkey King'.

◙ CHAPTER 3 ◙
Monkey King is Struck by the Notion of Mortality

Those in the monkey kingdom, with the Magnificent Monkey King at its head, were living in comfort and happiness for a long time. Then one day, after a few hundred years, the Monkey King realized that all living things must die, and that he was no exception. He became sad and depressed, and the other monkeys asked him what was troubling him.

He replied, "I realize that I must die one day, but I don't know how to escape that fate. I have decided to leave you and go search for a way to be immortal." Everyone was saddened, but they agreed that their King should have the opportunity to look for immortality. So they helped their King prepare for his voyage.

◎ CHAPTER 4 ◎
The Monkey King Seeks Immortality

The Monkey King embarked on his voyage, and after a few months, he hit the shore of a magic continent. He went into the town, asking for the master who can teach him immortality, and eventually came to an ashram (hermitage). He asked to be accepted as a disciple.

He was admitted as a novice, and was given the name Sun Wukong. As a novice, he had to take on a servant's work, such as cooking, sweeping, woodcutting, washing, and serving the master and the higher disciples. After a few years, he was able to learn some of the teachings by listening to the lectures while sweeping outside of the classrooms.

A few years later, he was slowly admitted to the lectures. When he heard the first lecture, and understood its profound meaning, he was overjoyed, and jumped with joy. The Master chided him for frivolity, but Sun Wukong explained that he was so happy to hear the truth that he could not contain himself. The Master then asked him what he wanted to learn. Sun Wukong said he wanted to learn the way to achieve immortality.

The Master said, "How about 'Shu' (craft)?" Sun asked what it does. The Master said it involves witchcraft and medicine. Sun asked if this would help with immortality and the Master said, "No." Sun said, "Then I do not wish to learn it."

The Master said, "How about 'Liu' (scholarship)? It would enlighten you on many schools of thought such as Confucian, Taoist, Sophist, Political Scientist, and so on." Sun said he wondered if it would help gain immortality and the Master said, "No." Sun said, "Then I do not wish to learn it."

After a few more suggestions, the Master was fed up, and he hit Sun with his rod three times and left the classroom holding the rod behind his back.

That night, Sun went to the Master's house at 3 a.m., entering through a backdoor. The Master was still up, and Sun knelt in front of him. The Master asked, "Why did you come at this hour?"

Sun replied, "You hit me three times, and held your rod behind your back, so I knew you wanted me to come to you at 3 a.m. and enter through the backdoor."

◉ CHAPTER 5 ◉
Sun Wukong Learns Immortality

The Master was impressed by Sun's understanding of the riddle, and decided to teach him the way to achieve longevity. The Master gave him the secret mantra (invocation) and instructions to follow through. This, said the Master, would make him immune to sickness and ageing. Sun gratefully accepted these, and worked very hard to memorize and to follow all the instructions.

After a few months, the Master asked Sun how he was doing. Sun said he was pretty sure he had succeeded in achieving immortality. The Master chuckled, and said, "You have achieved longevity, but not immortality. Because there will be three shocks that will come upon everyone who has lived for several hundred years. They all kill, and no one can avoid them, unless one knows the way."

Sun asked what these three shocks would be. The Master said, "The first one is a thunderbolt that visits you after five hundred years. It is not a natural thunderbolt. It comes from the depth of the universe, and unless you can avoid it in advance, it will burn up your bones and cause you to explode." Sun was frightened, and begged to hear about the second shock.

The Master said, "After another five hundred years, there will be the fire, which will burn your soul." Sun was in deep distress, and asked the Master to tell him about the third shock.

"The last shock, after another five hundred years, is the death wind. Again, it is not a natural wind, but it comes from the depth of being. Unless you know how to avoid it, it will blow you into pieces."

Now Sun was in a real panic. He knelt in front of the Master and begged him the save his life. The Master said, "Very well. There are two sets of supernatural tricks that you can learn that will counter the effects of the three shocks. One is a set of thirty six tricks, and the other is a set of seventy two."

Sun thought about it and, and decided, "I prefer more tricks to less, so please let me learn the set of seventy two." The Master agreed, and taught him the tricks.

Sun worked very hard, and over the period of a year, mastered the seventy two tricks. He was so good that now he could manage to levitate and fly about. The Master asked him how he was doing. Sun told him that he could now fly. The Master told him to show how he flew. Sun levitated himself and moved about in the air.

The Master laughed, and said, "This is not flying! You know that fairies can fly thousands of miles in an instant. What you are doing is just crawling around in the cloud."

Sun begged, "Master, please do not leave me imperfectly trained. Please teach me how to fly for real."

The Master said, "Well, you are a monkey, so I will show you a flying technique that befits a monkey. It is called 'somersault fight'. It will enable you to fly one hundred and eight thousand miles with one somersault." The Master gave the magic chant that enabled the flight, and Sun diligently memorized it. After a while he was able to fly in a flash.

One day Sun was talking with his fellow disciples, when they asked him to show what he had learned. Sun said, "Just tell me what you want me to be." One of his friends said, "Why not turn yourself into a pine tree?" Whoosh! Sun turned himself into a huge pine tree.

His friends were very impressed and they applauded loudly. When the Master heard the commotion, he came out to see what was going on. He scolded everyone for the noise, then took Sun aside and told him, "You should now leave here. What you have done is not good. It inspires envy, and envy can lead to jealousy. You will no longer be safe here."

Sun protested, "But Master, I have spent more than twenty years here. Where can I go?"

The Master said, "Remember where you have come from? Go back there."

Sun suddenly remembered his mountain and his cave and his kingdom. He knelt to the Master to thank him for all he had taught, and took one somersault to return to his mountain, crossing two continents in a second, a distance that earlier took him several months to travel.

◙ CHAPTER 6 ◙
SUN WUKONG REESTABLISHES HIS KINGDOM

When Sun arrived in the mountain, and reached the Water Screen Cave, he noticed the place was in disorder. He shouted, "Everybody! I am back."

The monkeys came out of the cave and from behind trees to greet him. "Sire, you have been away for so long, leaving us unprotected. There is a monster king in the north that raids us, and has taken many of our monkeys hostages," they said.

Sun replied "I am now immortal, and have learned 72 supernatural tricks. Let me go north and fix everything."

Sun took one somersault to get to the cave where the monster king was living, and shouted, "I am the king of the Monkey Kingdom. Return the hostages and all you have robbed from us, or I shall destroy you."

The monster king came out of the cave, and started to laugh. "Look at you, only four and a half feet, and you talk as if you were a giant."

Sun pulled a few strands of his own hair, and blew it towards the monster king, shouting, "Get".

The strands turned into hundreds of monkeys who descended on the monster king and pinned him to the ground. Sun then took the monster king's sword, and chopped him into half. He then sucked in his breath and all the monkeys turned back into strands of hair, and came back to him.

Sun said to the several hundred monkey hostages in the cave,

Sun Wukong pulled a few strands of his own hair and
blew them towards the monster king, shouting "get!"

The strands turned into hundreds of monkeys...

"I am going to take you home. Close your eyes while I fly with you." He flew back to the Water Screen Cave and said, "Now you can open your eyes."

Everyone was delighted, and said, "Wow, we are so lucky to have our King back, with such amazing supernatural skills."

◎ CHAPTER 7 ◎
Sun Wukong's Kingdom Thrives

In organizing his kingdom, Sun wanted to have a good army, but he did not have weapons for his monkey soldiers. One of his monkey advisers suggested, "Why not go and buy some swords and bows and arrows from the kingdom nearby? Sun thought it was a good idea and decided to go to the neighboring kingdom and see.

Once he was there, he saw big towns and small villages. The capital had a big population, and streets were filled with people going about their business. He decided to play a trick; he took a deep breath, and blew out in the direction of the Wind God, and there was a huge gale that churned up a sand dust which sent everyone scurrying inside their houses.

With the streets deserted, Sun went to the armory, where there were thousands of swords, spears, bows, arrows, armors, saddles, and many other weapons. He pulled out his hair and, once more, said, "Get." The hair turned into hundreds of monkeys who promptly went and gathered up various weapons and followed Sun as he flew back to the Water Screen Cave.

The weapons started to drop from the sky as Sun retrieved his hair, and the monkeys excitedly collected the weapons and played with them. Now the kingdom was well armed, and the monkeys trained avidly under the instruction of Sun, whose supernatural tricks included martial arts.

The monkey kingdom grew stronger with good government under Sun, and with military training for his monkey army. The other animals in the mountain and around became aware of this, and they all came to Sun, wanting to be on a friendly terms with his kingdom. These included other monkey species such as gorillas, chimps, baboons, as well as owls, sparrows, eagles, falcons, snakes, lizards, deer, bears, wolves, leopards, tigers, even lions. Soon, Sun was presiding over not only his own kingdom, but a large alliance of many smaller kingdoms.

◎ CHAPTER 8 ◎

SUN WUKONG ACQUIRES THE WEAPON OF HIS CHOICE

But Sun did not like any of the weapons: they were too flimsy and lightweight. One of the old monkeys told him that the Dragon King of the Sea had the most wonderful treasures in his palace, no doubt including some super excellent weapons. "But can you go into the water?" asked the adviser.

Sun said, "I have achieved immortality, and have seventy two supernatural tricks that allow me to get into the heavens, the sea, into the earth, everywhere. Of course I can go into the water."

So Sun decided to pay the Dragon King a visit. From his cave, the waterfall flowed down to the sea. Sun went downstream, and when he arrived at the sea, he used his trick to part the water, and went down to the depths of the sea. There he ran into the Dragon Patrol, who asked who he was.

Sun said, "I want to see the Dragon King. Take me there."

When the Patrol asked, "Who are you?" Sun replied, "I am the Divine Fairy, King of your neighboring kingdom. You ought to know me."

The Patrol took Sun to the palace and presented him to the Dragon King. The Dragon King said, "Respected Divine Fairy, is there anything I could do for you?"

Sun said, "Yes. I am looking for a weapon that is suitable for me, as the ordinary weapons are too light and flimsy. I hear you have some excellent weapons, so I would like to request one such weapon."

The Dragon King decided not to be rude, so he ordered for

a large sword to be given to Sun. Sun brandished it around and said, "No. This is too light, too."

The Dragon King, surprised, then ordered for a trident. Again, Sun said it was too light. The Dragon King was now truly frightened by Sun's strength. He said, "But, Divine Fairy, this trident weighs three thousand six hundred kilograms."

Sun said, "You must have something better than this. Then, the Dragon King's wife remembered something, and said to the Dragon King, "You see, this Divine Fairy must be someone special. Remember the magic stick in our special vault? It has been giving out a strange light the last three days. Maybe this Divine Fairy is destined to have it."

The Dragon King explained to Sun that the stick was used by the Emperor Yu, long time ago, as the measuring rod when the rivers of China were flooding the country, with millions drowning, and no one able to do anything about it. Yu took on the task of regulating the rivers and bringing them under control. Yu was so successful, and the people of China so grateful, that he was enthroned as the Emperor of China. When Sun heard the story, he asked for the rod to be brought to him. The Dragon King replied, "No. It is too heavy and no one can move it. I am afraid you are going to have to go where it is kept."

So the Dragon King took Sun to the special vault where the magic stick was housed. It had a note attached to it: "The stick that complies with the wishes of its rightful owner. Weight: 13,000 kilograms."

Sun took the rod in his hand and said, "It's a little too fat," and to everyone's astonishment, the stick immediately became thinner. Then Sun said, "It would be nice if it is a little shorter," and to his delight, the stick shortened.

The Dragon King felt resigned over the prospect of giving up the stick to Sun. Sun was the only one who could handle it, and, even more remarkable, the stick obeyed Sun's commands, just as the note said it would. When Sun commanded the stick to shrink to the size of a needle, so he could put it inside his ear, the stick obeyed.

Sun then asked the Dragon King for armor. The Dragon King said, "I have nothing in my storage to offer, but I am only the Dragon King of the Eastern Ocean. My brothers, the Dragon Kings of the Western, Northern and Southern Oceans might have some treasured armor that you might like." Sun said, "It is better to bother one host than two. Why don't I stay here, and you can ask your brothers to come and offer their wares."

The Dragon King had no choice, so he sounded the magic bell to summon his three brothers, who came in an instant. They could each fly and swim at supernatural speeds. They asked, "Brother, what has happened that's so urgent?"

When The Dragon King of the Eastern Ocean explained what happened, the three brother Dragon Kings said, "This is outrageous. Why don't we arrest him and put him in the dungeon?" Their Eastern brother shuddered at this. "No, no, no," he said. "He is very strong. He can wield the Magic Stick like a bamboo staff. It would be impossible to fight him." The three brothers said, "All right. Why don't we offer him what he wants, and then go to the court of the Jade Emperor to complain. That way we will have some satisfaction."

So decided, the Dragon King of the Northern Ocean offered a pair of magic boots, the Dragon King of the Western Ocean offered a set of golden armor, and the Dragon King of the southern Ocean offered a golden helmet. Sun was satisfied, and he put on the paraphernalia and shouted, "Hooray!" as he left the palace of the Dragon King.

When Sun emerged from the water at the shore, his monkey advisers were waiting for him. Seeing him emerge without getting wet, and dressed in brilliantly shining armor, they all applauded.

Sun said, "Look at the weapon I got." He pulled the magic stick out of his ear. It was the size of a sewing needle. He commanded, "Longer, longer, and thicker." It grew to be 8 feet long and 2 inches in diameter. He planted it on the ground, and the monkeys all tried to pick it up. Of course no one could budge it. They marveled. "How come we could not even budge it?" they asked. "It is so heavy." Sun replied, "No wonder. It weighs thirteen thousand kilograms." Then he pulled it up and showed them the art of manipulating the stick. Everyone gazed with fascination, delighted that their King was now so well equipped.

◙ CHAPTER 9 ◙
SUN WUKONG RAIDS THE UNDERWORLD

Sun's kingdom thrived and many neighboring kingdoms paid Sun tributes. There was feasting everyday. The time of peace and prosperity lasted for decades and decades.

One day, after one of the feasts, Sun was dozing off when he saw two messengers approaching him. They quickly put handcuffs on him and started dragging him. Sun was surprised, and asked, "What are you trying to do?" At this, one of the men showed him a document that read, "Warrant for taking Sun Wukong, whose time of death has come."

Sun said "How dare you? I have achieved immortality and have the supernatural ability to counter anything that might harm an ordinary and even an extraordinary man. You cannot take me to the Underworld." The two dispatchers ignored him and continued to drag him towards the Underworld.

Sun was sleepy and drunk and did not put up a fight for a while. But when they arrived at the gate of the Underworld, he realized that this was the entrance into the realm of the dead. He protested, "No. I am not going in," but the two dispatchers continued to tug at him.

This time, Sun was really angry. He tore apart the handcuffs like he was shredding paper, pulled out his magic stick from his ear, shouted, "Longer," and beat the two dispatchers into pulp. Then he decided to confront the King of the Underworld and settle the issue once and for all.

He entered the gate, beating up all the guards into meatballs, and came to the main palace building. He shouted, "Where is the King of the Underworld!! How dare you come to take me into the realm of the dead!! I am an immortal. Explain why you sent for me."

Sun had been causing such havoc by this time, killing hundreds of angels of death, that the King was well and truly scared. He came down from his throne, trembling, and said: "Please, there must be a mistake."

Sun said, "No. You must have a record book. Bring it to me so I can examine it". The King reluctantly showed Sun the Book of the Dead, and Sun was able to find entry No.1350 which read: "Sun Wukong, stone monkey, life span 342 years."

Sun took a big brush, and obliterated his entry by brushing over it, and he obliterated all the entries on the monkeys he could see. Finally, Sun threw down the brush, saying "Now we are out of your control." He then took out his magic stick, and smashed the furniture and the walls on his way out.

As he returned to the Water Screen Cave, he was met by his four senior advisers. They said, "Sire, you have slept for a long time. What was going on?" Sun explained what happened, saying, "From now on we are no longer subject to the inevitability of death."

Down in the Underworld, there was chaos and commotion, and the King of Underworld decided to report this disturbance to the Jade Emperor.

◙ CHAPTER 10 ◙
Sun Wukong Gets a Job in Heaven

At the Heavenly Palace, the Jade Emperor received two complaints, one from the Dragon King of the Eastern Ocean complaining about Sun's behavior and his taking of the magic stick and armor, helmet, and boots. The other was from the King of the Underworld complaining about Sun's raid.

The Emperor said, "This kind of unruly conduct cannot be tolerated. We should send an army to capture him and bring him to justice."

The God of the North Star advised, "Your Majesty, why not

summon this monkey to come here, and give him a small position in the Heavenly Palace. This would save bloodshed, and keep him under control, without too much expense." The Emperor decided to take this advice, and asked the God of the North Star to be his envoy and bring Sun to the Heavenly Palace.

The God of the North Star left the Heavenly Palace, and came down to the Water Screen Cave. He told the guards, "I am God of the North Star. I come from Heaven. Your king has been invited to come to Heaven. Take me to him."

When Sun heard of this, he came out to greet his guest. "I have always wanted to visit Heaven," he said, "so your invitation is very welcome. Let us proceed at once."

In the Heavenly Palace, Sun was presented to the Emperor. Instead of kneeling, as everyone else did, Sun only gestured with his hand in greeting, scandalizing everyone in the court by his behavior. The Emperor asked where a minor position could be found, and he was told that there was one at the Imperial Stable looking after the Heavenly Steeds. So Sun was offered the position of the Imperial Stabler. Not knowing the status or significance of the position Sun was happy, and started to work at the stable. He was by nature hard working, and the Heavenly Steeds were very well looked after.

Everything was good, and everyone was happy, till one day, about half a month into his job, when Sun was having a drink with his colleagues. Sun asked them how exalted his position was. They laughed and said his position was so low it did not even appear in the register of officials. When he heard this, Sun was furious. "I am a King, and I am an Immortal. How dare they put me to work as a horse servant?" He took out his magic stick, made it to its usual size, and charged out of the Heavenly Gate, damaging a lot of fixtures on his way. With one somersault he returned to his Water Screen Cave.

His monkeys said, "You have had quite a visit, fifteen years. You must have had a very good time." Sun said, "I was only there for half a month, not fifteen years." He did not realize that a day in heaven is a year on earth. When he explained his humiliating experience, his monkeys were outraged. They said, "Sire, with your ability and your position, it would not be too much if you were to be given the title of Heavenly Grand Fairy."

Sun liked that title, and had banners made with that title on them, and the banners fluttered all over his kingdom.

◙ CHAPTER 11 ◙
Sun Gets his Title of Heavenly Grand Fairy

In the Heavenly Palace, they reported to the Emperor that Sun had left his job, smashing things as he left. This time, the Emperor decided that a harsher approach was needed, and assigned the famous father-and-son heroes named The Tower King and Vedic Prince to lead an army to capture Sun.

The Heavenly Army came down to the Water Screen Cave, surrounding it. The Tower King shouted, "Hey, Stabler, come out and surrender." Sun put on his armor, helmet and boots, took out his magic stick, and came out.

One of the Heavenly centurions said to the Tower King, "Let me go and capture this monkey," and he took on Sun. Within a few seconds, Sun hit the Centurion's shoulder, and forced him to retreat in pain. Vedic Prince then volunteered to fight Sun, and he used his supernatural trick to turn himself into a monster with three heads and six arms, wielding six different weapons to attack Sun. Sun saw this, and also turned himself into a three-headed, six-armed monster, with three magic sticks, to fight. They were fighting for a while, when Sun decided to play a further trick. He pulled one of his hairs, turned it into the three-headed and six-armed monster, while he himself sneaked behind Vedic Prince and hit him on his arm with the magic stick. The prince also retreated in pain.

The Tower King decided to report the situation. He told the Emperor that Sun was really very strong, and it might be difficult to subdue him. He also reported that Sun wanted the title of Heavenly Grand Fairy.

It was the God of North Star again, who advised, "Why not give him the title. It is just an empty name without any power or responsibility. Give him the title, a nice mansion, and he would be happy. If you agree, I will go and talk him into accepting this Heavenly offer." The Emperor agreed, and the envoy was on his way.

The envoy arrived in Sun's cave and said, "I managed to persuade the Emperor to offer you the title of Heavenly Grand Fairy. Why don't you return to the Heavenly Palace with me to receive this title?" Sun was happy, and together they went back to the Heavenly Palace.

The Emperor told Sun, "I will confer upon you the title of Heavenly Grand Fairy, with a nice mansion in the palace complex. Be at peace." Sun said, "All right," but did not kneel.

From that time on, Sun was content. He lived in the Heavenly Palace, making friends with other gods and fairies.

◙ CHAPTER 12 ◙
Sun Steals the Heavenly Peach and Longevity Pills

After a few months, Sun was roaming around the Heaven carefree and happy, but some of the fairies and gods were a bit worried about Sun's idleness. They suggested to the Emperor that Sun be given a job to occupy him, so he would not be driven by boredom to create mischief.

The Emperor summoned Sun, who came happily, asking whether the Emperor had good news for him. The Emperor said, "I see that you have work to occupy you, so I have decided to give you an assignment. You should be in charge of the Heavenly Peach Orchard."

Sun happily accepted the job, and went to the orchard. He summoned the god in charge of the orchard and told him of his new assignment. The god bowed, and asked what instructions Sun might have for him. Sun said, "Explain to me what the orchard has."

The god said, "There are three thousand six hundred trees of Heavenly Peach. The first twelve hundred trees bear smaller fruits, and they ripen every three thousand years. If one eats the fruit, one would achieve health and longevity. The second twelve hundred trees bear larger and sweeter fruits, and they ripen every six thousand years. He who eats the fruit is immune to illness and ageing. The last twelve hundred trees bear super purple and red fruits, which ripen every nine thousand years. If one eats it, one would live as long as the universe."

Sun was delighted to hear this, and proceeded to inspect the orchard as well as the pavilions and landscapes surrounding the garden. He would come to the orchard every other day or so to inspect the work of the gardeners, and everyone was happy.

Sun felt tempted to try eating the peaches. One day he told his gardeners that he was a little tired, and wanted to take a nap in one of the pavilions. After they had left, he climbed up the trees – as a monkey he was expert in tree climbing – and picked some of the peaches and ate them. He had all three varieties, and felt very good.

This continued for some time, and the ripened fruits were beginning to get scarce. One day, there came the occasion of the Heavenly Empress's annual Peach Party. The Empress sent a team of fairies to fetch the peaches. When they arrived at the orchard, the god in charge of the orchard told them that now the Heavenly Grand Fairy was in total command and his permission had to be obtained. The god went into the orchard and informed Sun of the visitors, and Sun was nowhere to be seen. The fairies said they could not wait for Sun, and started to pick the peaches.

Sun was awakened from his sleep by the commotion and, jumping down from a tree, shouted, "Who dares steal my peaches?"

The fairies said the Empress had sent them to fetch Heavenly Peaches for her annual peach party. Sun asked if he was invited. They said they were not aware of it. Sun decided to find out, so he told them, "Ladies, wait a while here." Whereupon he cast a spell

Sun Wukong picked some of the peaches and ate them.
He had all three varieties and felt very good.

to freeze them, leaving them standing stiff like logs.

Sun flew to the garden of the Empress, where he ran into the Barefoot Grand Fairy. Sun told him that the party would start soon, but not at the usual garden; instead, it would open at the palace and then move on to the garden.

The Barefoot Grand Fairy, being a straightforward person, believed Sun, and turned towards the palace. Sun then used his trick to turn himself into the Barefoot Grand Fairy and went into the garden.

Inside the garden, he saw preparations going on for the party. There were sumptuous food, wine, and sweets. He smelled the wine, and was immediately intoxicated by the aroma. But the wine vats were guarded by the workers. Sun then took a few of his hairs and blew them towards the workers. The hair turned into sleeping bugs, and bit the workers, who fell asleep. This allowed Sun to get to the wines, which he drank to his heart's content.

After eating and drinking and making a mess of the preparations, Sun suddenly realized that he was in trouble. He decided to get out of the garden, but in his drunken state he lost his way, and ended up at the Temple of Tao, where Laotse, the founder of Taoism, lived.

Sun thought to himself, "I hear that Laotse makes longevity pills. Maybe I can find some to eat." He wandered into the oven room, where the pills were made, and found five jars of pills. He ate them like one would eat peanuts.

Then, suddenly, Sun was alarmed by the enormity of his offence. He groped his way out of the Heavenly Palace complex, exiting through the gate. The gate keepers were well-known to him, and did not prevent him leaving.

Sun returned to his Water Screen Cave, shouting, "Hey, everyone, I am back."

CHAPTER 13

HEAVENLY ARMY ATTACKS SUN

Meanwhile, there was commotion in heaven. The frozen fairies in the peach garden unfroze after an hour. They immediately reported on Sun's activity and the fact that there were very few ripe peaches to be picked. The Barefoot Grand Fairy went to the palace and was told by the confused guards that the party was indeed to start at the garden and not in the palace, exposing Sun's deception. The workers at the garden told that Sun, disguised as the Barefoot Grand Fairy, had stolen the wine and the food. Then Laotse reported the loss of longevity pills, but could not identify the culprit.

It was clear that it was Sun who had done all this, and this time there was no question about the need to bring Sun to justice.

The Tower King again commanded the army, this time with greater numbers. They were now aware of Sun's strength and very wary. The army numbered one hundred thousand. As the army arrived and surrounded the Water Screen Cave, Sun led his own army of monkeys, wolves, tigers, bears, and others to confront them. The God of the Nine Planets led the Heavenly Army, and the fighting was fierce.

While the two leaders battled each other, the Heavenly Army attacked, capturing the wolves, tigers, bears, and other allies of Sun. While engaged in fighting the God of the Nine Planets, Sun was startled to notice the capture of his allies. So he took out some of his hair, turned them into an army of monkeys, and chased his opponents back to their camp. By now, the two sides were exhausted, and decided to call it a day.

As the battles were going on, the Jade Emperor was anxiously waiting for reports from the front. Just then, the Bodhisattva Kuanyin arrived at the Heavenly Palace, accompanied by her senior disciple, Hui-an, to attend the annual peach party. Instead of the party, she saw the place in disarray, and asked what had happened. The Emperor explained, and Kuanyin offered to send Hui-an, who turned out to be the second son of the commander-in-chief, the Tower King, to help. Hui-an went down to the army's camp, and reported to his father.

After being briefed about the situation, he decided to go out and challenge Sun. Sun took one look at Hui-an, and said, "You look young and delicate. Why don't you go home? I have nothing against you and do not wish to hurt you."

Hui-an said, "You insolent monkey. Here comes my sword!" This annoyed Sun, and he used his magic stick to attack Hui-an. After an hour or so of fighting, Hui-an started to feel weak in his arms, and decided to retreat. He went to his father, the commander-in-chief and said, "This monkey is really very strong. Even with my level of strength and skills, I am no match." This was duly reported to the Heavenly Palace, and the Emperor started to grow very anxious.

Kuanyin suggested that the famous hero, the Emperor's nephew, the Second Prince, be asked to come and deal with Sun. An envoy was immediately sent to the Second Prince with the Emperor's request, and he proceeded to the scene of battle.

When Sun saw the Second Prince, he said "Hello, who are you?" The Second Prince said, "You ignorant and blind monkey. Don't you know the great hero, the Second Prince? Surrender quickly and you may be spared." Sun scoffed at this, and the two engaged in a very fierce fight.

The Second Prince turned himself into a towering giant a thousand feet tall, with arms like huge trees, attacking Sun. In response, Sun also turned himself into a giant of the same size. The fight was dramatic and heroic. As it was going on, the Heavenly Army moved in on the Water Screen Cave, capturing thousands of monkeys.

Sun wanted to save his monkeys, so he stopped his fight, and tried to go back to his cave. The Second Prince chased after him, so Sun turned himself into a sparrow perching on a small branch. Everyone thought Sun was lost, as no one could see where he was.

The Prince, however, had superior supernatural power, and his eyes could distinguish the real and the unreal, so he was able to see where Sun was hiding.

The Prince then turned himself into a falcon, and charged towards Sun. Sun quickly jumped into the water, and turned himself into a catfish. The Prince then turned himself into a pelican, and diving into the water, attempted to catch Sun. Sun turned into a snake, hiding in the grass. The Prince turned into a crane, pecking at Sun, who then turned into a partridge. The Second Prince then returned to his own form, and took a bow and arrow to shoot at Sun. Sun then turned into a temple, with two windows and a door.

The Prince said, laughing, "You think you can fool everyone. Not me. I will smash your eyes by shooting at the windows, and I will tear our mouth by pulling apart the door." Sun quickly changed himself and, flying over to the Prince's own home temple, turned himself into the Prince and sat on the Prince's seat in the temple. But the Prince quickly came to his temple, and Sun had to escape again, flying back to his cave. The Heavenly Army surrounded the cave very tightly.

In the Heavenly Palace, the Emperor was getting impatient over Sun's capture. Kuanyin said, "Well, the Second Prince did defeat Sun. Now all that remains is his capture. Why don't I throw my jade vase at him? It would at least knock him out, if not kill him." Laotse, who had come to join them, suggested that he had a platinum bracelet with magical abilities, which would be sturdier. So it was decided that Laotse's bracelet should be tried.

Laotse went to the Heavenly Gate, and threw down the bracelet at Sun, hitting him in the head, knocking him out. The Heavenly Army swarmed over him and captured him, tying him with the magic rope to prevent him from playing any tricks.

Sun was taken to the Heavenly Palace, where the Emperor decided to execute him. He was taken to be beheaded, but because he had eaten the magic peaches and the pills, swords could not harm his body. Then they decided to burn him at the stake, but again, fire could not burn his body. They were at their wit's end, when Laotse suggested that maybe his pill-making oven could destroy Sun because the wind blowing in the oven was not ordinary wind but a wind of special magic power, which would probably burn Sun into ashes. So Sun was taken to the oven, and put inside it. Laotse then started the fire, and kept it burning for seven times seven days, forty nine days in all. At the end of that, convinced that Sun could not survive this, they opened the oven door. Sun, who was hiding in the corner of the oven near the wind intake and where the fire was not very strong, had survived, and he leapt out of the oven as they opened the door, dislodging a red-hot pile of bricks which fell on earth to form the Flaming Mountain of Xinjiang, China.

◙ CHAPTER 14 ◙
THE BUDDHA VANQUISHES SUN WUKONG

When Sun broke out of the oven, he took out his magic stick and started attacking everything in sight, smashing things and injuring the Heavenly Horde as he went. No one could stop him, and soon he was approaching the Emperor's Palace. The Divine Guardian God came forward to confront Sun, and they were engaged in a violent fight. The thirty-six Thunder Gods also came to fight Sun, but Sun was undaunted. He became three-headed and six armed, with three magic sticks, to take on all his adversaries. Other gods and heavenly warriors joined, surrounding Sun in a tight, heavy circle. They were able to confine him, but could not subdue him.

The Emperor decided to request the assistance of the Holy Sage Buddha. An envoy was sent to the Western Heaven where the Buddha resides and teaches his great truth, and the envoy presented the message from the Emperor. The Buddha came to the Emperor in an instant, flying one hundred and eight thousand miles. The Emperor explained the situation, how Sun had robbed from the Dragon King, messed up the Underworld, abandoned his job, stolen the peaches and longevity pills, and finally broken out of Laotse's oven. The Buddha said, "Let me speak to this monkey and see what should be done."

The Buddha went to the battle site, and said, "Do not fight. Speak to me." Sun asked, "Who are you?" The Buddha replied, "I am Siddhartha Buddha, the one who achieved ultimate enlightenment and Nirvana. Tell me, why are you fighting like this?" Sun said, "I believe that I am great enough to replace the Emperor. If he abdicates, and gives me the throne, there will be peace."

The Buddha laughed and said, "The Emperor has achieved his position by going through one thousand seven hundred and fifty trials, each lasting one hundred twenty nine thousand and six hundred years. What merit do you have to even dream of taking over from him?"

Sun said, "I have seventy two supernatural tricks and vast strength. I can match anyone in the universe."

The Buddha said, "I tell you what. If you can fly out of my palm, I will ask the Emperor to let you have a turn with the throne. If not……"

Sun interrupted, "Ha, I can fly one hundred and eight kilometers with one somersault. Fine, I agree." With that, Sun leaped onto the Buddha's palm, and somersaulted away. After a few somersaults, he saw five pillars ahead of him, each in the color of flesh. He thought this must be the end of the universe. So he stood at the foot of the pillars, and pulled out one of his hair, turned it into a paint brush, and wrote, "Sun Wukong was here." He relieved himself at the foot of one of the pillars, then flew back to the Buddha.

Sun proudly declared, "I not only flew out of your palm, I was at the end of the universe where there were five pillars. I left a note on one of the pillars." The Buddha showed him his hand. On one of his fingers, there was Sun's note, "Sun Wukong was here." And it still smelled of Sun's urine.

Startled, Sun tried to escape, whereupon the Buddha grabbed him with his hand, and put him down on earth, turning the hand into a mountain weighing down on Sun. The Heavenly Horde,

He stood at the foot of the pillars and pulled out one of his hairs, turned it into a paint brush, and wrote "Sun Wukong was here."

led by the Emperor, applauded this feat.

One of the gods of the land reported that Sun's hands and head were sticking out. The Buddha said, "Do not be anxious. He will not be able to leave this mountain till the time when his master comes to get him. Meanwhile, feed him iron balls and molten copper. It will be five hundred years before his master comes by."

The Emperor thanked the Buddha, and the Buddha went back to his Tranquil Western Heaven.

⊙ CHAPTER 15 ⊙
The Buddha Wishes to Save the Souls of Mankind

After the great commotion caused by Sun, there was peace for hundreds of years. The Buddha, giving his sermons to the exalted sages, bodhisattvas, gods and disciples said, "People are constantly fighting, scheming, robbing, and killing each other. I am saddened by that. I want to save their souls. There are three collections of documents that contain my teachings, which, if followed, would bring about bliss and tranquility to the world. These documents, or sutras (literally, thread or rule), fill three sam zong (warehouses), dealing with the truth of the universe, life, and eternity. There are altogether thirty five collections, fifteen thousand one hundred forty four volumes. I would be happy to give these away freely, but they must want to obtain these documents. I wonder if any of you would be willing to go to China and persuade a man of superior morality and learning to come to me for the documents."

Kuanyin, the Goddess of Mercy, said, "I would be willing to volunteer for that task."

The Buddha was very pleased. "You are the best qualified for this task," he replied. "I cannot be more pleased. Now I have five magical gifts for you. One is a monk's robe with gold brocade; the second is a monk's walking stick which has the magic power of helping the holder's walk. Then there are three rings, made of gold, platinum, and diamond. The robe and the stick should be given to the monk who would undertake the journey from China to my residence in the western Heaven, but the three rings should be kept by you. When you encounter someone you wish to recruit for the cause of obtaining the documents, you could put one of the rings on his head, and it would immediately take root on the flesh and he would not be able to remove it until you release it by saying the magic words. So, off with these, and I shall see you after your job is done."

◎ CHAPTER 16 ◎
KUANYIN'S RECRUITMENT TOUR

Kuanyin took the five gifts and left, with Hui-an accompanying her. On her way to China, she saw a wide, dark river of quicksand, which would swallow anything and anyone that tried to cross it. It was flowing with high waves and splashing quicksand sky high, menacing even those standing away from its banks.

Kuanyin was looking at the river in fascination, when a monster with fiery eyes and fangs leaped out of the river, charging towards Kuanyin, wielding a stick with a half-moon tip. Hui-an shouted, "Monster, get a taste of my sword." And the two started to fight.

The monster could not win over Hui-an, and he shouted, "Who are you, so strong?"

Hui-an said, "I am Hui-an, the senior disciple of Kuanyin, the Goddess of Mercy."

The monster said, "Oh, I am sorry, I did not know. Can you take me to her?"

Hui-an pointed to Kuanyin who was standing above a cloud in the sky. The Monster went to her in the sky, knelt, and said, "Forgive me; I did not know it was you. Now I would like to beg for your mercy. I was a fairy serving in the Heavenly Palace, in charge of the heavenly screens. One day I smashed a crystal lamp by mistake, and after receiving eight hundred lashes, I was exiled to this place. They also send sword every seven days to stab me a hundred times. There is nothing to eat, so I came out of the river to capture a man or two to eat. I have been here for hundreds of years, and have been punished enough. Can you have mercy and save me from this ordeal?"

Kuanyin said, "I am on my way to China to recruit a holy monk who will go and obtain the true teaching of the Buddha. He will be passing through here, and you should offer yourself as one of his disciples and escort him to the Western Heaven. This would gain you forgiveness. Will you be willing to do that?"

The monster said, "Yes, but what if the holy monk never shows up?" Kuanyin assured him that the holy monk would definitely pass by.

Before leaving him, Kuanyin gave him a new name, Sha Wujing - Sha meaning Sand (family name, based on the fact that he was from the river of quicksand); Wu meaning to know; and Jing meaning Serenity. Wujing together means 'to understand serenity'. He would be known later as Sandy.

Kuanyin continued on her way, and came to a craggy and deep mountain. Suddenly, a monster with a pig's head came charging, wielding a rake with nine teeth. Hui-an again stopped him and they fought for a while. Seeing that he could not win, the monster asked Hui-an who he was.

When the monster discovered that Hui-an was Kuanyin's senior disciple, he also said, "Oh! I am so sorry. I did not know. Can you please take me to her?" They flew up to where Kuanyin was standing, above the clouds, and the monster knelt down, saying, "I beg for your forgiveness. I am not a monster from birth. I was a fairy in the Heavenly Palace in charge of the heavenly canopy. One day I was caught teasing one of the female fairies, and as punishment, I was hit two thousand times with a hammer, and banished to the world below. By some mistake, I was put inside the womb of a sow, and was born with the head of a pig and the body of a man. I killed the mother pig, and am living here eating animals and man. I would like to ask for your mercy to relieve me from this predicament."

Kuanyin asked, "Will you be willing to escort a holy monk

on his way from China to the Western Heaven to obtain the true teachings of the Buddha? If so, the merit of such action would redeem whatever offence you've committed."

The monster said yes, but he too was worried that the holy monk might not pass by his mountain. Kuanyin assured him the monk would come by, and gave him a new name, Zhu Wuneng - Zhu meaning Swine (surname, based on the fact he had the head of a pig); Wu meaning Know; Neng meaning Capability. Wuneng together means 'to know the potentials'. Kuanyin also gave him the nickname Bajie, ('of Baggai') in Taiwanese. He would be known as Zhu Bajie, Di Baggai in Taiwanese (Pig Eight Taboos), or Swiney.

Kuanyin continued on her way, riding the clouds and mists. On their way, they came upon a jade dragon hanging in the air. The jade dragon pleaded with Kuanyin for mercy. He cried, "I am the youngest son of Dragon King of the Western Ocean. One day I burned the palace and a crystal ball. My father reported my unruly disobedience, and I was whipped three thousand times and left hanging here. An execution will soon follow. I beg for your mercy. Please save my life."

Kuanyin said, "If you are willing to serve as the animal of burden for the holy monk on his journey to the Western Heaven, I would ask the Jade Emperor to spare your life." The dragon promised he would be willing to turn himself into a horse to carry the holy monk to the Western Heaven. Hearing this, Kuanyin went up to the Heavenly Palace to ask the Emperor for a special dispensation.

As Kuanyin and Hui-an continued to fly east, they noticed brilliant lights of many colors shooting up from a mountain that looked like a clenched fist. Kuanyin stopped at the mountain, where all the gods of the soil came to kneel in front of her. They told her, "Some five hundred years ago, the Buddha imprisoned a trouble-making monkey here. It has been pretty quiet here, but for some reason in recent days these lights have started to shoot up from the chamber where the monkey is imprisoned."

Kuanyin said, "It must be because the time has come for me

to offer him a chance to be free." She went down to where Sun Wukong was imprisoned, and heard him shout, "O Goddess of Mercy! Help me get out of this. It's been almost five hundred years." Kuanyin said, "If you are willing to serve as a disciple to the holy monk and escort him faithfully all the way to the Western Heaven, you may get out of this predicament. He will come by and lift the spell that has kept you imprisoned here."

"Yes, but how can I be sure that he will come by?"

"He will come by, all right."

Sun swore that he would serve faithfully. Kuanyin was going to give him a new name, but Sun said he already had one - Sun Wukong. Kuanyin was delighted, because she had given the letter Wu to the two sworn disciples before. Sun means grandson, but is also part of the word 'husun' which means monkey. Wukong (Gokong in Taiwanese) means 'to understand the vanity of all things worldly'.

◙ CHAPTER 17 ◙
BIRTH OF THE HOLY MONK

A young man named Chen, who studied very hard, left his mother at home to take part in the Imperial Examination for scholars and won the first place. The prime minister was impressed by him, and decided to marry his daughter to Chen. Chen was then given a post as a Magistrate in South China.

Before his departure, Chen wanted to have a banquet, and so he purchased a carp. He noticed that the carp had an extraordinarily brilliant eye that emitted a golden glance. Deciding to let the fish live, he released him where he was caught. On his way back, a pirate killed him, tossing his body into the river. The pirate then took over his household, masquerading as Chen.

The river where Chen's body had been dumped was the one where Chen had released the carp with extraordinary golden eye. It turned out that the carp was the Dragon King himself, and he wanted to repay his savior.

Chen's bride, grief-stricken, was pregnant. She wanted to give birth to the child, so she did not kill herself. After the baby boy was born, to prevent the pirate from killing him, she cast him into the river in a basket, with a letter explaining the whole story, begging whoever found the baby boy to care for him.

The baby was picked up by the resident monk of an old temple, and raised as a monk. When the boy was about eighteen, the old monk gave him the letter, whereupon he asked for leave to go and seek out his mother. He found her living in the Magistrate's mansion, and went to see her and explained who he was, showing the letter she had written.

The mother had written another letter to her father, the prime minister, who was shocked to learn of the crime. He organized an army to capture the pirates. These pirates were executed at the riverside. As they gave their final offerings to the spirit of Chen, in repentance, Chen's body floated up from the bottom of the river, and he woke up and rose, to everyone's amazement. He explained that he had once saved the life of a Dragon King of the River, and in return he had been saved.

The young monk Chen grew up to become a famous scholar and a virtuous sage. He had a temple in the capital.

◎ CHAPTER 18 ◎
CHINESE EMPEROR TOURS THE UNDERWORLD

In China, it was a period known as the Tang Dynasty (618 – 907), during which China had extended its territory beyond the Great Walls and South China Sea. This was also the period during which China opened itself to a vast number of foreigners and accepted their cultures.

During the early Tang Dynasty, the most illustrious period was when Emperor Taizong was on the throne (626 – 649). The entire Chinese Empire was at peace, and people enjoyed unprecedented prosperity.

At the time, there was a wood-cutter and a fisherman who

were friends. They would meet every evening when the fisherman came back from the sea and the wood-cutter from the mountain. They enjoyed their drinks and conversations together. One evening, as they were about to part after the daily drinks, the fisherman said, "Well, good night and have a nice day tomorrow, though I know your mountain is not quite as nice a place as my sea."

The wood-cutter replied, "Why! I think your sea is not as nice as my mountain."

The fisherman said, "My sea is beautiful, where one can see the sun rise and set on the horizon, and the moon casting its romantic rays; where one can feast on fish and shrimps and octopus; where the scenery is wide open and makes one forget the trivial things of the world."

The wood-cutter said, "But my mountain is infinitely variable; in the summer's heat, it provides cool respite; the sun gives life to the trees, and the moonbeams inspire one's meditative mood; the meats of animals taste better than fish, shrimps or octopus; and the cloud-shrouded mountain tops make one feel other-worldly."

The two continued arguing about the virtues of their places for another hour. And at the end, the wood-cutter said, "All right, my friend, we just agree to disagree. Good night and take care. I don't want to experience 'one less friend's face amongst the crowd'. The fisherman said, "What an inauspicious thing you say! But don't fear, I am fully informed about the weather so there is no danger of being struck by unexpected storms."

The wood-cutter asked, "How so?"

The fisherman replied, "There is a fortune-teller of great wisdom who can predict the weather precisely, so I consult him every morning before putting out to the sea." And the two parted.

This conversation was overheard by one of the retainers of the Dragon King of the River Jing. He went and reported it to his master, who decided to teach the fortune-teller a lesson.

The Dragon King went to the fortune-teller's stall and asked for the forecast for the next day. The fortune-teller gave him 3,348 points of rain at 3:00 p.m. The Dragon King was taken aback. He himself did not know about it. He asked the fortune-teller, "Are you quite sure?"

The fortune-teller said, "Of course." The Dragon King answered, "I will come and take down your sign if your forecast is wrong." And he went back to his river palace.

As he arrived, there was an imperial instruction ordering him to provide 3,348 points of rain at 3:00 p.m. the next day. He was in a panic. One of his advisors suggested that he provide 3,340 points at 2:00 p.m., so he would have carried out the instruction but with a slight alteration. He took that advice and provided 3,340 points at 2:00 p.m.

The next day he went to the fortune-teller and tore down the sign, saying, "You are a charlatan. I am here to teach you a lesson."

The fortune-teller answered, "I am not worried. You are the one that should be worried. I know you are the Dragon King of River Jing in disguise. You have modified the imperial instruction and will be beheaded in a few days."

The Dragon King was terrified, and begged the fortune-teller to save his life. The fortune-teller told him that the minister Wei would be designated to execute him, so if he begged the Emperor Taizong, maybe his life could be saved.

The Dragon King appeared in the Emperor Taizong's dream, and said to him, "Your majesty, you are the real dragon, while I am only an animal dragon. I have violated the instruction I received from the Jade Emperor and am about to be executed. Your Minister Wei will be designated to behead me tomorrow at noon. I beg you to save me."

Taizong said, "Very well, I will invite him to my palace at noon. That should prevent him from beheading you?" The Dragon King thanked Taizong, and left.

The next day Taizong invited Minister Wei to the palace and proposed they play a game of chess. During the game, Minister Wei dozed off. But then he started to perspire.

Taizong knew how hard working Minister Wei was, so he did not mind that he was dozing off. When he saw Wei perspiring, he took a fan to help Wei cool off.

Suddenly, Wei shouted, "Kill!" And then he woke up. He was mortified that he had dozed off in the presence of the Emperor, and apologized. Taizong said, "Don't worry." Then the palace guard reported that a dragon's severed head had dropped from the sky. It was the head of the Dragon king of the River Jing, beheaded by Minister Wei even as Wei had dozed off and completed his task in his dream.

When Taizong went to bed that night, he dreamed of the Dragon King of the River Jin coming to him and accusing him of breaking his promise. The dead Dragon continued to haunt him every night, and nothing the Emperor could do would help. He even arranged to have Minister Wei stand guard at his bed chamber door, but nothing helped. Finally, exhausted, the Emperor died and went to the Underworld.

Yanlo, the King of the Underworld, received Taizong and introduced him to the Keeper of the Book of the Dead. The Keeper turned out to have been one of the Emperor Taizong's ministers, and when he saw Taizong, he decided to help. He added twenty years to Taizong's life by changing the entry in the Book of the Dead. Yanlo saw that the book entry allowed another twenty year of life to Taizong, apologized for his 'mistake' and sent Taizong back.

Having seen the Underworld and how large numbers of people were suffering there because of the evil deeds they had committed, Taizong decided to organize a religious service to console those suffering souls but also to try to teach civility to the living so they could avoid a similar fate.

◙ CHAPTER 19 ◙
MONK CHEN VOLUNTEERS TO GO WEST

Meanwhile, Kuanyin had arrived in China's capital, Chang-an. The gods of the city paid her homage, and put her up in their palace. When Taizong's religious service took place, Monk Chen was asked to preside over it.

Kuanyin decided to test the sincerity of the Emperor's devotion. She and Hui-an changed their shapes into two leprous beggar monks and, going to the main street near the place of the religious service, announced that they were selling the two items that the Buddha had given Kuanyin as the gift for the monk that would make the journey – the robe and the walking stick. People felt quite revolted at their sight, but the beauty of the robe and the walking stick attracted them.

When asked the price for the items, Kuanyin, the older leprous monk, said, "Five thousand ounces of gold for the robe, and two thousand for the walking stick." Everyone laughed, saying, "This is crazy. How can anything like these be worth so much?"

Kuanyin said, "These could cost as much as I said, or they will be given away for nothing to the right person."

The Emperor's guards heard the commotion and came out to see what was going on, and they were struck by the magnificence of the two items. They asked the two monks to come into the hall of religious service and present themselves to Taizong the Emperor. Taizong saw the beauty of the two items, and decided to give them to Monk Chen.

He asked for the price, and Kuanyin again said, "It could cost five thousand ounces of gold for the robe and two thousand ounces of gold for the stick, but it could also cost nothing, for I am prepared to give them away to the right person."

Taizong said, "I want to give them to Monk Chen, who is presiding over this religious service." Kuanyin then said, "In that case, I will be happy to present these two items to him free of cost." Taizong said, "I will pay you. Do not think that I am the Emperor and therefore you should not ask for money or gold."

Kuanyin said "No, I am presenting these items to Monk Chen, that's all. Whether or not you are the Emperor has nothing to do with that." Kuanyin then put down the two items in front of the Emperor and left.

The day of the service arrived, and Kuanyin and Hui-an went to attend. Monk Chen was clad in the robe Kuanyin had given him, and he started to give a sermon which was very profound and enlightening. Suddenly, Kuanyin, still in the shape of a leprous old monk, jumped up and shouted at Monk Chen, "What you are preaching is the Hinayana, the Small Vehicle. That is not good enough. You need the teaching of the Mahayana, the Great Vehicle."

The Monk was very pleased to hear that, and asked, "Thank you for your suggestion. But where can I get the Mahayana?" By this time Taizong had recognized the old leprous monk, and said, "Are you not the monk who gave the robe and the walking stick?" Kuanyin said yes. Taizong said, "You spoke about Mahayana. Can you explain it?" Kuanyin said yes.

Taizong then asked her to get up to the podium to lecture the congregation. Kuanyin went up and, on the podium, she revealed her true form, the Goddess of Mercy, with her full regalia and brilliant halo emanating from her body. Disciple Hui-an, also in all his princely grandeur, wielded his magic golden sword.

Everyone was filled with awe and everyone, including Taizong, knelt and said, "Praise the Goddess of Mercy!"

Kuanyin then said, "The true teaching of the Great Buddha, the Great Enlightened One, is available. But someone must go to the Western Heaven to get it. These documents fill three warehouses dealing with the truth of the universe, life, and eternity. Altogether there are thirty five collections, fifteen thousand one hundred forty four volumes. It would be given freely by the Buddha himself. But someone has to go there to get them. The journey will be arduous and perilous, with many monsters hindering the way. But for the truly devoted, it is possible to complete the journey." With these remarks, Kuanyin and Hui-an rode the cloud and rose to heaven, leaving behind the congregation in a trance.

After everyone had recovered their senses, Monk Chen said to Taizong, "I would like to volunteer to journey to the West and obtain the sutras." Taizong said, "I shall be grateful if you do so. I will recognize you as my own brother."

All the provisions, food, money, escort and horses were given, and Monk Chen went off on a long, hard and perilous journey.

Before leaving, Monk Chen was given a new title – Sanzang, meaning Three Warehouses (full of sutras). He said farewell to his staff at the temple, telling them that it might be ten years before he came back, but they were to keep the temple open.

Sanzang left the capital of Chang-an with two able-bodied young men to serve as his escort and servants, and headed west. Soon they were in a thick forest where there was no clear paths, so they had to slowly grope their way forward. Suddenly, they fell into a trap, and heard a shout, "Get them, get them."

A group of a dozen or so little monsters came and grabbed the three, bound them up, and took them to their cave. Once there, they said to their master, "We got three men who look like they are travelers." The master, with a thunderous voice coming out of his red mouth from which protruded white fangs and his face covered with wiry hair, said, "Good. We can have a feast tonight."

As they were unbinding the three captives, there arrived two visitors, Bear Spirit and Buffalo Spirit. They and their captors decided to eat the two young men first, leaving Sanzang for the next day. After they had eaten the two young men, feeling full and drunk, they went to bed. Sanzang was kept in a cage and, resigned to his fate to be eaten the next day, he prayed all night.

Near dawn, he heard a voice, "Sanzang, I have come to your rescue. Come with me." He walked out of the cave, and the voice said, "Your luggage is there, along with your horse. You were captured by a tiger monster, and the two guests of his were a bear monster and a buffalo monster, but you are now free." Sanzang thanked him. The voice continued, "As you are on a holy mission to obtain the sutras, I will be watching over you. I am the Golden Star of the Dipper." Sanzang knelt in the direction of the Dipper to thank the god, and continued his journey, alone with his horse.

Sanzang was still in the mountain, traveling as quickly as his horse would go. Suddenly, there was a gale of wind, and a huge tiger appeared, roaring and menacing. Sanzang realized that there was no escape and, once again prepared to accept his fate, he started to pray. But soon the tiger became fearful, turned around, and ran away. From the other side of the forest, a fierce-looking man with weapons on the ready emerged. Sanzang pleaded, "Please, I am a poor monk. Take whatever I have, but spare my life so I can fulfill my duty."

The man smiled and said, "Please do not be alarmed. I am neither a monster nor a bandit. I am a hunter. My name is Liu. Since I have been hunting here for a long time, the tigers, leopards, boa constrictors and other wild beasts are scared of me. That was why the tiger ran away when I came."

Sanzang explained who he was, that he was going to the Western Heaven by order of the Emperor. Liu showed his respect, and invited Sanzang to his home for the evening. Liu's wife offered him meat, but Sanzang said, "I have been a vegetarian since my infancy. I have never tasted meat in my life. Please do not worry about me. I can fast for a few days."

Liu's mother said, "We have some vegetables and fruits. So please have them." Then she said, "Today is the anniversary of my husband's death, Liu's father. Will you be kind enough to say a few prayers for him?" Sanzang put on his magic robe and prayed for the soul of Liu's father.

The next morning, Liu's mother said, "Last night, in my dream, my husband showed up and told me that he had been saved by your prayer. Yanlo, the king of Underworld, revealed that you are a sage of the highest order, and your prayer carries special power. He is now going forward to be reincarnated in a well-to-do family in China. Thank you very much."

Sanzang was glad to have helped, and bid the Liu family farewell. Liu said, "The way forward is still teeming with wild beasts. I will escort you to the border between China and Tatary." Sanzang thanked the family, accepted some provisions, and departed with Liu.

CHAPTER 21

SUN WUKONG JOINS SANZANG

They came to a mountain called Two Border Mountain. Liu said, "This is as far as I can go. Let me wish you good luck for your journey ahead." Almost before he could finish his sentence, they heard a loud cry, "Master, Master, let me out, Master!" They were startled, and Liu said, "This mountain was formed some five hundred years ago, and it imprisons a magic monkey. I have heard people say that this monkey disturbed the Heavenly Palace and was imprisoned here by the Buddha himself."

Sanzang asked, "Where is the monkey? Let's go and see him." Liu was afraid that the monkey would get out and harm both of them. Sanzang said, "If he was imprisoned by the Buddha, he will not be able to get out. Let's go." So, the two went down to the prison.

There they saw Sun Wukong who stuck his head and hands out of the cell. He said, "Master, aren't you the sage on your way to the Western Heaven to obtain the sutras? What took you so long to come? But it is good to see you. Please get me out of this prison so I can serve you as a disciple and protect you on your journey to the Western Heaven."

Sanzang said, "But I don't know how to get you out." Sun answered, "It is easy. You have only to go to the top of this mountain and you will find a sign with the magic command of the Buddha. No one can destroy or remove that sign. Only someone who is properly designated by the Buddha can lift it. You are that person."

Sanzang believed Sun to be sincere. So he climbed to the top of the mountain. As he approached the top, suddenly he saw a wondrous rainbow of light. He went to where the light was, and saw a sign, which had been left by the Buddha to imprison Sun Wukong.

The sign said 'Om Mani Peimeihong (magic chant). Sanzang knelt in front of it, saying, "Holy Buddha, your humble disciple

Sanzang is here on his way to you. If Sun Wukong is indeed destined to be my disciple and escort, let me lift this sign. If not, let me not."

Thus he stretched his hand to lift the sign, when suddenly there came a whiff of fragrant wind, blowing the sign off into the sky. Sanzang saluted and came down to the cell where Liu was still waiting. He told Sun, "The sign that imprisoned you for five hundred years is no longer there now. You are free. Now you can get out and be my disciple."

Sun said, "I am going to burst out of this cell. You should go some distance away so my breaking out will not hurt you."

Liu and Sanzang rode away from the cell. They stopped at about five miles, but Sun shouted, "Further, further!" At ten miles, Sun still cried, "Further, further!" Finally, they travelled for twenty miles, when Sun said, "All right, I am getting out!"

There was a huge explosion, and Sun flew out of the cell, leaping thousands of feet high, eventually landing in front of Sanzang. Sun knelt in front of Sanzang, calling him Master. Sun also saluted Liu and thanked him for having escorted the Master. Liu took leave of Sanzang, and Sanzang told him, "Please give my regards to your mother and wife. I shall see you on my way back."

Sun took charge of Sanzang's luggage and horse and they continued on their journey. Suddenly, a big tiger appeared and charge at them. Sanzang was frightened, but Sun said, "Don't worry. Here comes my clothing."

He took out the magic stick from his ear, changed it into his preferred size of three inches in diameter and six feet in length, and went up to the tiger and shouted, "Don't you dare move!" The tiger trembled in fear and froze. Sun hit it over the head, killing it instantly.

Changing his magic stick into a sharp knife now, Sun skinned the tiger and cut the skin to make his loin cloth. Once he had cut the skin to size, he changed the magic stick into a needle, and sewed up the skin into a pair of trousers.

Sanzang asked, "Why did the tiger suddenly become so afraid? What did you do?"

Sun said, "My power is such that not only tigers, but even dragons are scared of me. Not only that, no animal or monster can be my match." Sanzang was very happy to hear that, feeling that he was now able to journey to the West with good protection.

They continued their journey for another few days, and one evening six bandits suddenly blocked their path, shouting, "Stand and deliver. If you leave everything here, we will let you go."

Sanzang started to shake with fear, but Sun said, "Don't worry. These bandits have brought their money and treasure for us."

Sanzang asked, "Are you hard of hearing? They want us to give them our money and treasure, and you say they were bringing us theirs?"

Sun went up to the six bandits, and said, "You scum, you cannot harm me. Come and try your hands on me." The six came up to him, and started to cut and spear him, but they could not harm even a hair. They were incredulous, and Sun said, "Now let me try my magic stick on you."

He pulled the needle-shaped stick out of his ear, changed it to his favorite size, and beat the six into meatballs as they tried to flee in panic. Sun then took their wallets and chests, and gave them to Sanzang.

Sanzang was not pleased. He said, "Even though these were bandits, their crime did not merit death. What you did is cruel and contrary to the virtue of mercy as taught in our religion. With such conduct and such temperament, you will not make a good monk, and neither will you make it to the Western Heaven."

Sun was annoyed. He said, "You and your mercy business. If I did not kill them, they would have killed you." Sanzang replied, "I would rather die than commit such a grievous sin. Unless you change your ways, you will not make it."

Sun said, "Very well. So I don't qualify. Then I quit. I am gone!" In an instant he flew off, leaving Sanzang all by himself, frightened and lonely.

Sanzang thought to himself, "This little monkey! He cannot take a little criticism and advice. Well, maybe I am not destined to have a disciple. In that case, I shall go it alone if necessary." Still, he felt miserable, tired, frustrated and confused.

Then an old woman appeared, and she asked Sanzang who he was. He explained who he was and told her what had just happened. She said, "I am sure he will come back, as his error were serious and he will not be permitted to forget."

She had a package of handsome clothing and a hat with a golden rim. She said to Sanzang, "When your disciple comes back, give this to him to wear. The golden rim will attach itself to his skull, and only the Buddha or Kuanyin, the Goddess of Mercy, can remove it. I will teach you a 'ring-tightening mantra'. When you say the mantra, the ring will squeeze the skull with excruciating pain. This should help keep your disciple in line." So she taught Sanzang the mantra, and flew off with a breath of fragrant wind. Realizing that this was Kuanyin in disguise, Sanzang knelt and paid his homage in the direction of Kuanyin's abode.

After he flew off from Sanzang, Sun planned to return to his kingdom of Water Screen Cave. On his way he passed the Dragon King's palace and decided to pay him a visit. The Dragon King said, "I heard your ordeals were over. Congratulations. But why are you roaming around like this? Are you not supposed to be escorting the Sage on his journey to the West?"

Sun said, "Yes, but I killed six bandits who were trying to kill him, and he said such action was not acceptable and that I would never make a monk. Also, that I would never make it to the West. So I left him."

The Dragon King said, "But you are mistaken. Killing should be avoided if at all possible, and the teaching of mercy is one of the most important principles of Buddhism. If you do not escort the Sage to the West, you would end up being just another monkey monster. This is your chance to achieve true salvation. You should go back to the Sage."

Sun was impressed by the argument. He sipped some tea with the Dragon King, then took leave of him and started to fly back. Along the way, he ran into Kuanyin in the sky. Kuanyin asked, "What are you doing here, flying around?" Sun told her about his dispute with the Sage, and the advice of the Dragon King, and that he was on his way back to the Sage.

Kuanyin said, "Go back quickly. And do not leave again. Be steadfast." Sun saluted her and went back to the Sage. He said, "Master, I am back. We had a bit of a tiff. Let bygones be bygones. I will never leave you again."

Sanzang asked him where he had been, and Sun said he was having tea with the Dragon King in the Eastern Sea. Sanzang said, "Wukong, we are monks. We must be truthful and not exaggerate or boast. The Eastern Sea is thousands of miles away. You had been away for only an hour. How can you have gone that far and back?"

Sun said, "I am not boasting. I can fly one hundred and eight thousand miles in an instant, so it is nothing for me to go that far in a very short time. I also know seventy two supernatural tricks that allow me to do all kinds of impossible things." Sanzang was very glad that he now had a super hero as a disciple.

They decided to eat their supper, provided by the hunter Liu and, during the process of unpacking, Sun noticed a robe and a very smart hat with golden rim. He asked Sanzang what these were. Sanzang said they were given him by an old woman, but if they fit him, he could have it all. Sun put them on himself, and when Sanzang saw the hat securely fitting on Sun's head, he started to say the 'ring-tightening mantra'.

Immediately, Sun started suffering a crushing pain in his head, and began rolling on the floor in agony. Sanzang stopped saying the mantra, and the pain was gone.

Sun saw this and realized that he had been tricked. Furious, he took out his magic stick to attack. Sanzang quickly started saying the mantra again, and Sun rolled on the floor in pain once more. After a while, Sun said, "Master, I've learnt my lesson. Please do not say the mantra, and I will be obedient."

Sanzang told him that the robe and hat had been given to him by Kuanyin. Sun said, "The old foxy Goddess! All right, I am committed to escorting you to the Western Heaven. So I will stick it out with you no matter what."

◉ CHAPTER 22 ◉
Sanzang Collects More Disciples

Sanzang and Sun entered a valley and arrived at the Falcon's Anguish Pond, so called because the pond's water was so smooth and clear that birds, attracted by their own reflected images, would fall into the water. They were enjoying the beautiful landscape when a dragon leaped out of the pond and charged at the two.

Sun quickly helped Sanzang down from the horse and tried to hide him away from the dragon. The dragon could not catch up with them, instead he swallowed the horse that they had left behind.

Sun then rushed to face the dragon, taking out the magic stick and attacking, and in a matter of moments, the dragon was defeated and it crawled back into the pond. Sanzang looked around and asked, "Where is the horse?" Sun went up to the sky, and cast his magic eye to look for the horse, but could not see it anywhere. Sanzang said, "It may be behind a hill or a rock, and you cannot see it."

Sun replied, "Master, you do not know my abilities. My eyes have supernatural vision and, within a radius of a thousand miles, I can see everything, even a dragonfly opening its wings. A big animal like a horse cannot escape my eyes. I suspect the dragon ate it." Sun said he would go back and find the horse, but Sanzang was afraid. "If you leave me here alone, and if the dragon should attack me, what would I do?" he asked. But there were voices in the sky, saying, "Sanzang, we will protect you while Sun goes about his task. We are the heavenly officials and minor gods sent by the Goddess of Mercy to watch over you. Do not be concerned, let Sun go."

Sanzang knelt down, hearing the voices, but Sun said, "Cha! These minor characters! I was going to punish them for not coming sooner. Master, you need not kneel to them. They are like my servants."

So Sun went back to the pond, and using his magic stick as a huge stirring stick, muddied the water so much that the dragon could not breathe, and had to come out again. Sun shouted, "You miserable little snake. Give me back the horse!"

The dragon said, "So I did eat your horse. How do you expect me to spit it out?" Then, afraid of Sun's powers, he turned into a small grass snake and hid under a rock.

Sun was exasperated, and he summoned the gods of the area. They came to pay him obeisance, and Sun said, "You bunch of useless little gods. Let me hit you with my magic stick to amuse myself." They trembled, and begged for mercy. Sun said, "The dragon in the pond has eaten my horse. What do you know about the dragon?" The chief god said, "A few years ago, Kuanyin, the Goddess of Mercy saved the life of a dragon, who was the third son of the Dragon King of the Western Oceans, and told him to await the Sage on his way to the Western Heaven to collect sutras. If you asked Kuanyin to come you would resolve all problems."

Sanzang said, "But Kuanyin is so far away. How long will it be before she arrives?" One of the gods protecting Sanzang volunteered to go and ask Kuanyin to come, and in an instant, there were beautiful, mysterious rays of light, and Kuanyin arrived.

When he saw Kuanyin, Sun asked, "What kind of Goddess of Mercy are you? You have tricked me into wearing this golden crown on my head that causes me unspeakable pain!"

Kuanyin said, "You ignorant, red-buttocked wild monkey. You don't know what a favor I granted you. With this crown you are assured an orderly conduct, and also success in your task of escorting the Sage to the Western Heaven. The crown will liberate you from being an ordinary monster with some supernatural abilities and place you in the ranks of the holy gods."

Sun understood, and knelt to thank Kuanyin. Kuanyin flew over with Sun to the pond, and the local god called out, "Third son of the Dragon King of the Western Ocean! Come out. The Goddess of Mercy is here." The dragon immediately showed up, and paid his homage to Kuanyin.

Sun asked the dragon, "If you were given the task of escorting the Sage to the Western Heaven, why did you attack us?"

The dragon said, "But you never mentioned anything about the Sage." Kuanyin removed the magic crystal ball from the dragon's chin, and commanded, "Change!" The dragon turned into a white horse, and followed Sun back to Sanzang.

Sanzang said, "Oh, our horse is back, and it now looks even sturdier than before."

Sun said, "Master, this is not our horse. This is the dragon that the Goddess of Mercy turned into a horse to take you the Western Heaven. An ordinary horse would not be able to sustain the hardship, but this horse has supernatural strength and would have no problem going through the hardships."

Sanzang knelt in gratitude, and before she left, Kuanyin pulled Sun aside and told him, "Now you must do your duty without wavering or hesitating. To help you in especially difficult situations, I will give you three special hairs. When you are in a truly difficult situation, use them." She took three leaves from the willow branch she was carrying and planted them at the back of Sun's head. Sun thanked her, and she parted. Sun then dismissed the gods, and the two continued on their journey.

They came upon a river, and were wondering where to find a ferry, when they saw an old man coming down the stream. Sun called out to him, and he came ashore to take Sun, Sanzang, and horse on board to cross the river.

After they had crossed the river, Sanzang wanted to pay the old man, but he declined to accept, and sailed away. Sun said, "Don't worry about thanking him. He is the god of this river. If he had not come, I would have punished him."

Then they traveled through the mountains, and as the sun went down, they saw a cluster of houses ahead of them. They decided to ask for a night's lodging, and Sun went and knocked at the door.

An old man came to the door and invited them in. He saw their horse, and said, "Your horse looks as though he was stolen, because there is no saddle on him."

Sun said, "No. this is the changed form of the dragon from

the Falcon's Anguish Pond. He ate our original horse, saddle, strap and all. But then Kuanyin appeared and brought him in line." The old man said, "We have a saddle that no one is using. I would offer it to you when you depart tomorrow morning." Sanzang thanked him, and the next morning, they received the saddle, which fitted the horse as if designed for it. They took leave.

When they looked back, there was no house where they had spent the night. A voice in the sky said, "We have been sent by the Goddess of Mercy to offer you a saddle. Have a good journey." Sanzang wanted to pay homage, but Sun said, "These little gods! I was going to punish them for not coming forth sooner. They are lucky that I didn't beat them up. Don't pay them homage."

◎ CHAPTER 23 ◎

The Theft of the Robe and the Submission of the Black Bear

Now the three of them traveled through several forests and countries, and a few weeks later they came upon a temple. It looked like a shrine for Kuanyin, so they decided to ask for a night's lodging. The chief monk received them, and Sanzang explained his journey and how he had adopted Sun and the dragon as his companions.

The old monk told them that he was two hundred seventy years old, and Sun said, "You are just a young lad. I have been around for a thousand years." The old monk said that he had lived all his life in the temple, unlike Sanzang who had traveled so far. He said that one of his pleasures was the collection of robes. And he showed his one hundred twenty pieces of superior quality robes. Then he said, "Since you are from the capital of China, you must have wonderful treasures. Can you show us some?"

Sanzang replied, "No, we are sworn to poverty. Besides, we are traveling. Even if we had treasures, we could not carry them." But Sun added, "Well, we do have a robe that makes your robes look like rags."

At this, Sanzang said sternly, "Sun, do not show off. It is no good to tempt people. You might invite jealousy and greed which could harm everyone." Sun said, "Nah! Don't worry. I can handle it." And he opened the package to reveal the robe given to Sanzang by Kuanyin.

The old monk was struck by its magnificence. He started to weep, saying, "I am so unfortunate. I have never seen anything so wonderful." He begged to borrow the robe overnight so he could have a good look. Sanzang could not say no, and blamed Sun for all this. Again, Sun said, "Don't worry. I can handle it."

The old monk took the robe back to his room, and sighed and lamented that he could not have it to himself. One of his junior monks said, "Why not set fire to the pavilion where they are sleeping, and you can keep the robe." The old monk decided to follow that advice.

The junior monks then piled up dry wood around the pavilion, and the sound aroused Sun's curiosity. Sun, as an immortal, slept with his consciousness intact. So he was aware of the goings-on around him. He realized that there was a conspiracy afoot to burn the pavilion. He took one flight up to Heaven Gate, where the guardian gods, startled, cried, "Look who is here! The big trouble maker!"

Sun said, "I am not here to make trouble. I simply want to see Big Eye Fairy King." They let him in, and he went to the palace of the Big Eye Fairy King and asked to borrow his fire repellent net.

The King was concerned that this well-known trouble maker would take off without returning the net, but Sun assured him, "I am now a disciple of the Sage. I will of course return it as soon as I am done with it." So the net was given to Sun, and he flew back to the pavilion and covered it with the heavenly fire repellent net just before the monks set fire to the dry wood.

Sun sat at the top of the pavilion, and to add to the commotion, he used one of his supernatural tricks to cause a gale of wind to blow the fire over to the rest of the temple complex. The fire was fanned by the wind, and the flames rose hundreds of feet up. This caught the attention of a monster that lived some twenty miles away. He decided to go and help.

When the monster flew over to the temple, he saw Sun sitting on top and blowing a gale of wind at the fire. He then went to the old chief monk's pavilion to see what he could do to help. But then he saw a package that was emitting a rainbow of brilliant rays, and he promptly forgot about helping.

The monster grabbed the package and flew back to his cave. After a few hours, the fire burnt out, and Sun took the net and flew back to Heaven and gave the net back to the Big Eye Fairy King, who was relieved to get it back.

The next morning, Sun woke up Sanzang, who said he had had a good sleep. Sun said, "Aha, you were oblivious to what went on last night! The old monk decided to steal the robe, and kill us by setting fire to our pavilion. But I got the heavenly fire repellent net to save us. Let us go and ask for the robe back."

They went to the main complex and found the chief monk, and asked for the robe back. The old monk was distraught because the robe was nowhere to be found. In desperation, the old monk said, "I have not only committed a sin, I do not have the robe. I am truly damned." Then he rammed his head against the stone wall to kill himself. Sun addressed the rest of the monks, "Now tell me, where is the robe?" But nobody knew where the robe was.

Sun then asked if there was any monster living nearby, and the monks said, "Oh yes, there is a Black Wind Cave in the Black Wind Mountain where there is a monster who calls himself the Black Wind King." Sun said, "This must be the one who took away the robe," and he immediately flew off to the cave. The monks saw Sun fly, and were awestruck and said, "We never knew that you were supernatural. Our chief monk was ignorant. No wonder he had to die."

Sun arrived at the cave, and saw a monster servant carrying a message on his way down the mountain. He killed it in one stroke, and read the message, which said, "Dear chief monk, I want to invite you to a party to celebrate my acquisition of a magnificent robe.' Sun realized that the monster was a friend of the chief monk, so he decided to go to the cave in the form of the chief monk. He was invited in, and the Black Wind King was about to offer him tea when one of his little monsters came reporting that the messenger had been found dead on the roadside.

The Black Wind King realized that the chief monk in front of him was someone else, so he challenged him to a fight. Sun took on his actual form and the two started to fight. The fight lasted till dusk, when the Black Wind King decided to call it a day. So he turned into a black wind and disappeared to his cave.

Sun returned to the temple, narrated what had happened, and decided to go back the next day. The fight continued, and Sun found out that the Black Wind King was as strong as him. He told Sanzang, "I should ask Kuanyin to help. After all the theft happened in the temple dedicated to her." Sanzang asked how long he would be gone, and Sun said, "No more than a few minutes."

He flew quickly over to Kuanyin's abode at South Sea Mountain and asked her to help. Kuanyin said, "This monster is the spirit of a black bear. He has achieved immortality, like you, and he is not evil. So I will tame him and have him come and serve me. Kuanyin then flew with Sun to the Black Wind Mountain, where Sun went ahead to challenge the monster to a fight.

The monster came out, and Kuanyin took out a gold crown and threw it at the monster, saying, "Change! And attach!" The crown changed into five crowns, and attached themselves to the monster's head and four limbs. But the monster disappeared.

As they approached the cave, they saw a Taoist priest walking towards it, with a small plate carrying two pills. Sun hit him with his magic stick, turning him into a meatball. Kuanyin scolded him for such cruelty, and Sun said that this is a friend of the monster. Upon his death, the Taoist priest turned into a wolf.

Sun suggested that Kuanyin take on the form of the Taoist priest, and he, Sun, would turn into one of the pills. "And offer the pills to the monster," said Sun. "I will turn myself into the larger pill which you should offer to the monster. I will then rip apart his guts from inside. We can take it from there."

Kuanyin agreed and turned herself into the form of the Taoist priest. Sun said, "Ah! The Goddess of Mercy, you look just like the Taoist Priest!"

Kuanyin said, "Goddess, Monster, Sun Wukong. In the end, all is an illusion." Sun felt a sudden enlightenment upon hearing this, and he kowtowed in gratitude.

Now, Kuanyin, as the priest, went to the cave and met the monster. After greetings, she offered the pills to the monster. He thanked her and took the larger pill, which was Sun's disguise. Sun quickly went into the monster's stomach and started to jump around, causing the monster great pain. As the monster rolled on the floor in agony, Kuanyin revealed her true form and took out one of the golden crowns and placed it on his head. Then she told Sun to get out of the monster's body.

Sun leapt out through the nose, and revealed his original form. The monster got up to attack when Kuanyin chanted the mantra and the monster rolled on the ground in pain. Sun laughed in glee as the monster was writhing in agony, and said, "Now will you submit to the Goddess of Mercy and return the robe?"

The monster cried, "Yes, yes. Save me!"

Sun went into the cave and recovered the robe, and the monster followed Kuanyin back to her abode in the South Sea Mountain.

◙ CHAPTER 24 ◙
ZHU BAJIE (DI BAGGAI) JOINS

Sun and his Master traveled for a few days in sunny and warm weather and they came upon a village. They decided to seek lodging there, and Sun went to the village square to find a suitable place for the night.

He saw a young man hurrying on, and asked him if there was a devout household. The young man ignored him and hurried on. Sun, a bit annoyed, grabbed his arm. He tried to get away, but of course he could not escape from the magic grip of Sun. In desperation, he asked, "What do you want? I am on my way to find a good witch doctor so I can avoid being punished by my employer.

*Sun Wukong quickly went into the monster's stomach and started to
jump around, causing the monster great pain.*

Now you have stopped me. I am going to be in trouble."

Sun said, "We are on our way to get the Buddha's sutra, and want to find a place to stay the night. You only need to tell me where I could find a devout family. But why are you looking for a witch doctor?"

The young man said, "My employer is a devout man, so you can go to his place. His name is Gao, and his place is well known. I am looking for a good witch doctor because my boss wants to get rid of his third son-in-law."

Sun said, "But why do you need a witch doctor?" The young man replied, "My boss has three daughters, and the first two were married out. The third daughter was intended to have a husband marrying into the Gao family. They were seeking a suitable man, and one day a man came, claiming to be single without family burdens. Old Gao was impressed and took him in as son-in-law. At first he was behaving himself, working hard on the farm. But soon he started to show his true colors, eating vast amounts of food, coming and going as he rode on a cloud. Eventually, his face turned into that of a black pig. Old Gao decided to get rid of him, but this person was very resourceful and powerful. No witch doctor could do anything. So I am being dispatched to look for a really good witch doctor to deal with the situation."

Sun said, "Ha, that is just what I am very good at. Take me there and I will help get rid of the pig monster." The young man was delighted, and offered to lead Sanzang and Sun to the Gao home.

Old Gao invited them in, and scolded the young man for not going about his task. The young man explained what had appened, and Old Gao bowed to Sanzang and Sun, saying, "I will be eternally grateful to you if you can rid me of this monster."

Sun said, "Tell me more about this son-in-law of yours." Old Gao said, "When he came to us, he looked like an ordinary young man and he worked very hard at the farm, more than doubling the production. But soon he started to change his looks, and now his head is that of a pig, with large ears and a long snout. He eats mountains of food, and treats my daughter like a prisoner, locking her in a room and not allowing her to have any contact with us. He can fly, rides clouds. I persuaded several witch doctors to exorcise him, but all of them were killed and eaten by him. We are at our wit's end. If you can help us, we shall be eternally in your debt."

Sun said, "This is right up my alley. Let me help you. First, let me take a look at the room your daughter is imprisoned in. Meanwhile, look after my Master well." Old Gao ordered his servants to prepare for food and bath for the Sage, and took Sun to the room. Sun said, "It seems your son-in-law is not in. Take your daughter back home. I will stay in the room to deal with the monster."

Sun turned himself into the daughter and lay in bed. After a few hours, the pig monster came in the room and tried to kiss Sun who had assumed the appearance of his wife. Sun grabbed the snout and threw him on the floor. The pig monster said, "Hey, what's the matter? I just wanted to show my affection."

Sun used the woman's voice and said, "There's bad news. They will try to get rid of you." The pig monster said, "Your father is being unreasonable. After all, I work very hard at the farm and production is up. Sure, I eat a lot, but nothing to put a dent in the overall production. But don't worry. They have tried many times but no one is my match because I am not an ordinary monster. I am the reincarnation of the Heavenly official."

Sun said, "But this time, they've got someone called Sun Wukong, who was a great trouble maker in Heaven, to come and deal with you." The pig monster was startled, saying "That is bad news. I know this Sun to be very strong and resourceful. Maybe our days as a married couple are over and I should return to my mountain cave."

As he rose to go, Sun returned to his original form and shouted, "Stop, you miserable monster. Here I am, the Heavenly Grand Fairy Sun Wukong. Surrender and you will be forgiven."

The pig monster ran out and started to fly away, riding a cloud. Sun chased him to the sky. The pig monster said, "Why are you meddling in my business? Here is my trusty rake!" Sun said, "That weapon of yours! You are not going to do any damage to me. Why don't you try it. I will stand still and let you have a swing at me."

The pig monster hit Sun's head hard with his rake. There was a loud noise and sparks flew, but no damage was done to Sun. Startled, the pig monster commented, "What a tough head. Is it made of some supernatural material?"

Sun said, "Now you see. My head has been tempered in the magic oven of Laotse and with my eating of the heavenly peaches and Laotse's pills."

The two resumed their fight, Sun using his magic stick and the pig monster using his rake of nine teeth. The pig monster was no match for Sun, and turned into a gale of wind and escaped into his cave.

Sun went back to the Gao home and reported what happened. Old Gao said, "He may have run away, but if he is not gotten rid of, there will be no peace for us. Please go tomorrow to finish him off." The next morning, Sun went to the cave and hit the door, smashing it to pieces. The pig monster came out and said, "I have done nothing to you. Why do you want to trouble me like this? Besides, I thought you were mostly living in the east. What are you doing here?"

Sun said, "So you don't know everything. I am now the disciple of the Sage who is going to the Western Heaven to collect the sutra of ultimate teaching of the Buddha." When the pig monster heard this, he threw his rake away, and knelt down, saying, "I am sorry. I did not know you are now working for the Sage. I was converted by the Goddess of Mercy and had sworn to follow the Sage when the time came, escorting him to the Western Heaven."

Sun said, "If that is the case, let me bind you up and take you to the Master." Presently Sun took the pig monster, pulling him by the ear. They went to the Gao home where Sun presented the pig monster, explaining what happened. The Sage asked, "Are you sure you want to escort me all the way, fighting the monsters and demons who will surely try to harm us?" The pig monster replied, "Yes, yes. Please accept me as your disciple."

Sanzang then shaved his head, and said, "I should give you

a name." The pig monster replied, "The Goddess of Mercy has already given me a canonical name. It's Zhu Wuneng." Sanzang was delighted. He said, "That is good. Sun Wukong and Zhu Wuneng. Both with 'wu' as the common signature. Very fitting."

Old Gao suggested a farewell send-off, offering wines and food. Sanzang said, "I cannot drink, even if the wine is not related to meat." Sun also said he would not drink. But Zhu Wuneng said he would like permission to drink. Sanzang agreed. "All right," he said, "as long as in moderation. I will give you another name, a name to be used as a daily reminder of the need for moderation and virtue. It is Bajie (Baggai in Taiwanese, meaning Eight Taboos)." Thus, Zhu Wuneng joined in the journey, with the informal name of Bajie.

The quartet continued their travel to the west, and the season turned pleasant. It was spring, and as they went on they came upon a large house, where they asked to stay the night. An old man invited them in, and offered them food and accommodation. Before Sanzang could finish saying his grace for the meal, Bajie swallowed a fowl full of rice. Before Sanzang and Sun could finish their first bowl, Bajie finished three more bowls. The old man realized Bajie's extraordinary appetite, and brought out more food. In all, Bajie finished more than a dozen bowls.

They then chatted about their mission to go west, and Sanzang asked the old man how far the Western Heaven was and how hard it would be to go. The old man said, "It is very far, and very difficult because there are many demons and monsters on the way. Just some thirty miles from here, there is a Yellow Wind Cave occupied by a monster who calls himself the Yellow Wind King. He eats people."

The next day, they approached the mountain, where they ran into a blowing gale. Sanzang said, "This wind is strange, not at all like the natural wind. Could this be the so-called Yellow Wind?" Sun said, "Let me catch the wind and smell it." Bajie asked, "How will you catch the wind?" Sun said, "One of my seventy two skills is to capture wind. Let me now try it."

So Sun stretched his arm and grabbed at the wind. Then he

brought his fist to his nose and smelled it. "Hum, it is fishy. I believe it is not a natural wind. It must have come from the monster. Let's be careful." Suddenly a tiger charged at them, and Bajie said, "I've got him," and charged at the tiger.

The tiger stripped his skin, revealing a human form. He shouted, "I am the vanguard for the Yellow Wind King. Who are you to attack me?" Bajie said, "You ignorant beast! We are the monks on our way west to get the sutras. Do not obstruct our way, and we will leave you alone."

A fight was unavoidable, and went on for a while. Sun, becoming impatient, said to Sanzang, "Let me see how Bajie is doing. Just wait here." And he went to help Bajie. The tiger was no match and quickly started to run away. The two pursued him closely. The tiger then used the trick of 'leaving a cocoon and letting the cicada escape', putting his tiger skin on a rock, while his real body slipped away from it. The two attacked the tiger, but they hit the rock. They smashed the rock, but did not see any tiger.

Meanwhile, the tiger went over to where Sanzang was resting, grabbed him, and took him back to the Yellow Wind Cave. He reported to his master what happened. The monster sounded a bit worried. "I only wanted you to go and catch some ordinary people to eat," he said. "Now you've got this Sage. I believe he now has Sun Wukong as a disciple. That fellow is very powerful. Let's not eat the Sage for a while. We'll wait to see whether Sun will come looking for him."

Sun and Bajie went back to where their Master was resting and found him missing. They knew right away it was the tiger who had grabbed the Sage. Hurriedly, they went to the cave and shouted, "You insolent monster! Return our Master or else."

The monster sent his tiger vanguard out to fight, and he was hit by Bajie with his rake, leaving nine holes in his head, and died. Next, the monster himself came out and, after trading insults, started to fight.

The monster was no match for the two, and blew a whiff of yellow wind at them. Sun got hit by the wind head on, and his eyes started to burn. The two retreated, decided to rest overnight and continue the fight the next day.

They went to a small house nearby and asked for a night's lodging. Their host asked what was troubling them, and they explained the day's events, with Sun complaining about his eyes. The host said, "I have a magic drop that will cure you, but you must keep your eyes shut for the rest of the night, opening it only tomorrow morning."

When Sun opened his eyes the next day, he marveled at the effectiveness of the drops. They decided to go for another fight and left the house. When they looked back, there was no house. They worked their way towards the cave. This time, Sun decided to play a trick. He told Bajie to wait. Turning into a mosquito, Sun flew into the cave. He saw Sanzang bound to a chair, flew to his ear and said, "Master, I am Wukong. Don't worry, I will get this monster."

The monster was talking to his underlings. "I believe the monkey was either killed by my wind, which does kill, or is going somewhere to ask for help. But no one can help him, except the Bodhisattva of Auspicious Spirit."

Sun immediately flew out of the cave. Changing back into himself, he told Bajie, "Now I know whom to seek help from! But where is the Bodhisattva?" As they were wondering, they saw an old man coming by. Sun greeted him, and the old man said, "You seem to be in some kind of a trouble. What is troubling you?"

Sun said, "I would like to pay a visit to the Bodhisattva of Auspicious Spirit, but I do not know where he lives." The old man said, "I'll tell you where he is - due south three thousand miles." Sun thanked him, and he disappeared in a whiff of fragrant wind, and a sheet of paper fell from the sky, which bore a note: 'I am the God of the North Star. You are cured, so go forward to save the Sage'. Bajie wanted to kowtow, and Sun said, "Go ahead! He was the one who brought me to the Heavenly Palace in the first place."

Sun now flew to the abode of the Bodhisattva, who received him very pleasantly, and Sun told him of the trouble they were in.

The Bodhisattva said, "This monster! He is the spirit of a mink. I was supposed to supervise him to ensure he does not harm innocent people. Now he has broken his promise. I will go and take care of him. I have two instruments; one, a 'wind-stilling pill' and the other, a 'golden dragon stick'. These will be enough to take care of him."

The two flew back to the Yellow Wind Cave, riding on a cloud. The Bodhisattva said to Sun, "This monster is afraid of me. So I will wait here in the cloud. Why don't you go and lure him out?"

Sun went down, joined Bajie in approaching the cave, and shouted, "You perverse monster! Here I am back. Return my Master or else."

The monster came out, but before he could fight, the Bodhisattva threw the golden dragon stick at him. The stick turned into a golden dragon and grabbed the monster, which turned into a mink rat. Bajie wanted to kill him, but the Bodhisattva said, "Spare him. I will train him into a good servant for the Buddha." Sun and Bajie then entered the cave, killed all the small monsters, and rescued the Sage.

◙ CHAPTER 25 ◙

SHA WUJING (SANDY) JOINS, COMPLETING THE PILGRIM TEAM

The quartet proceeded in a mild weather with sunshine and soft wind caressing their faces. After a few days they came upon a dark, ominous river of quicksand. They were taken aback, and wondered how they could cross this strange river.

Sanzang said, "This looks much more difficult than any ordinary river of water. I wonder whether there is a boat that can cross this quicksand without being swallowed by the quicksand?" Sanzang wondered how wide the river was, and Sun used his supernatural vision to size up the width.

Sun guessed, "It looks like about eight hundred li (about one hundred kilometers) to me." Bajie said, "I could fly over this in an instant, but I cannot fly while carrying the Master. His body is still that of an ordinary human, and is not suitable for carriage on a flight." Sun also said, "I have the same problem. I cannot carry the Master across. Now what shall we do?"

As they were talking, a fierce-looking monster wearing a big necklace of nine skulls jumped out of the sand and approached them. Bajie shouted, "You ugly monster! Here comes my weapon!" They fought for several hours. Finally, Sun could not contain himself and, taking his magic stick out of his ear, joined the fight.

The monster was already feeling overwhelmed by Bajie, so he turned into a wind and went into the river. Sun said, "Bajie, you were the former Heavenly officer in charge of the Heavenly River (the Milky Way). So you will be better at fighting in a river. Why don't you go in there and lure him out? I will then finish him off."

Bajie went in the river and found the monster's hiding place, where the monster was still panting from the fight. He challenged the monster again and they fought. Bajie pretended to be losing and began retreating to the surface of the river.

As soon as Sun saw them out of the river, he attacked the monster with his stick. But the monster was quick in response, and immediately withdrew back into the river. Now he would no longer respond to Bajie's challenge and come out of his hiding.

Sun asked, "What can we do now? I think we should ask the Goddess of Mercy to come and help." Bajie asked, "Why should Kuanyin come and help us?" Sun reasoned, "Because this business of getting the sutras was her idea, and she was the one that got us all into this journey together. So I hold her responsible for any of our troubles. Let me go and ask her to come." And Sun turned a somersault and, in an instant, was at the South Sea Kuanyin Mountain.

The black bear which stole Sanzang's robe and was tamed by Kuanyin met him and asked, "Now what is your problem?" Sun replied, "Aha, so you are now an apprentice. How do you like your life here? Anyway, take me to the Goddess of Mercy."

They went to the Goddess together. The Goddess, who was all-knowing, said, "Wukong! Why did you not tell the Quick Sand River Monster that you were helping the Sage in his quest for the sutras? That would have immediately solved your problem. Very well, I will send Hui-an with you, and he will take care of your difficulties."

She gave Hui-an a red gourd, and said, "When the monster surrenders, use the nine skulls from his necklace and them put around this gourd. This should serve as the ferry to take the Sage and his team across the quicksand river." Hui-an saluted and left with Sun.

While still in the sky, Hui-an called out, "Wujing! Come out." The monster recognized Hui-an's voice, and came out of the river. He saw Sun and started to retreat in fear, but Hui-an said, "Do not fear. This is the first disciple of the Sage who is on the way to the Western Heaven to get the sutras. You should join them as a member of the pilgrim team."

The monster threw away his stick and knelt before Sanzang, saying, "I am sorry. I did not know you were the pilgrim to the west. Please accept me as your disciple."

Sanzang said, "Very well. I should give you a name." And the monster replied, "The Goddess of Mercy has already given me a canonical name of Sha Wujing." Sanzang said, "That's great. We have Wukong, Wuneng, and now Wujing. You three should work and help each other like brothers. Since Sha means sand, we shall call this new member Sandy."

Hui-an took the nine skulls from Wujing's neck and put them around the red gourd, which then formed a boat. Sanzang and the horse went on it first, followed by Sun, Bajie and Sandy, and the boat sailed smoothly across the river, without incident. When the crossing was done, Hui-an collected the gourd, and the nine skulls disappeared into the air amidst bright light, having found their own peace after serving their divine task. The pilgrims thanked Hui-an, who then returned to the Kuanyin Mountain.

CHAPTER 26

Gods Test the Team's Integrity and Resolve

Now the team was complete. The Sage had three disciples and the dragon horse. Sandy and Bajie carried the luggage, and Sun walked the Master on horseback. They journeyed for a few weeks, and one evening they came upon a mansion and decided to seek a night's lodging.

The owner turned out to be a middle-aged woman, who invited the four of them in. The hostess said, "I welcome you. This must be our good luck night. I am a widow. My name is Mu. We own this mansion and quite a substantial piece of land, orchards and forests. I have three daughters, all of marriageable age, named Zhenzhen, Aiai, and Lianlian. Now you seem like decent people. I think it may be a good idea if each of you were to marry one of us."

Sanzang was horrified, and did not reply. The hostess continued, "Our holdings are quite large, and we have been hiring people to work them. But sometimes it is hard to trust people. If we can have our own husbands work on the farms, orchards and forests, that would be infinitely better."

Sanzang remained unresponsive, and the hostess said, "I am forty five, so perhaps I can marry you, Master, and since all my daughters are quite pretty, I believe your disciples would be happy to marry them." Sanzang remained silent, but Bajie could not contain himself any longer, and said, "Master, our hostess is addressing you." Sanzang scoffed at Bajie, and said, "My resolve to go west and complete my task is unshakable. But if you want to remain here and marry one of the pretty ladies, you can stay."

Sun joined in and suggested that Bajie marry, but Bajie said, "Well, let's discuss it further." The hostess, annoyed, said, "Well, if not all of you will marry us, at least one of you should."

Sanzang turned to Wukong and said, "How about you, Wukong?" Sun said, "No, I am not very good at this marriage thing." Sanzang then asked, "And what about you, Bajie?" Bajie answered, "This has not been discussed further." Sanzang finally asked Sandy, "Wujing, how about you?" Sandy said, "I am seeking to release myself from the unending cycle of reincarnations, and I joined you only a couple of months ago. Since then, I have benefited from your teaching. Now how can I give all that up and get married here?"

Seeing she was not likely to get any of them, the hostess shut the door and went back into the house. Bajie said, "I think I want to take the horse to find grass." Sun decided to find out what Bajie was up to, so he turned into a dragon fly and followed Bajie.

As Bajie took the horse to the back of the mansion, he saw the hostess and her three daughters sitting and having tea. The hostess called on Bajie and invited him in, saying, "You really should consider marriage, even though you are quite ugly." Bajie said, "I may be ugly, but I am more useful to you. Some people may be handsome, like my Master, but they are useless."

The hostess said, "Good, then why don't you go back and discuss with your team about your decision." Bajie said, "I am an independent person, and I can make my own decisions." The hostess said, "Still, it is more proper for you to let them know, rather than just disappear."

So Bajie took the horse back to the Master, but before he could do that, Sun the dragon fly flew back and reported to everyone what had happened. They were laughing when Bajie came back with the horse, saying there was no grass. Sun said, "Ah! But instead of grass, you found a new wife." Sanzang and Sandy also teased him, and Bajie felt embarrassed. But then the door opened and the hostess came out to invite him in. Once inside, Bajie said, "Mother, I cannot choose from amongst the three beautiful ladies. Why don't all three of them marry me?"

The hostess said, "No. I will tell you what. I will blindfold you, and put the three shirts of my three daughters on the table. You take one and put it on you. The owner of the shirt will be your wife." Bajie agreed and, blindfolded, he groped around, grabbed a shirt and put on himself. The shirt turned into thick ropes and bound Bajie tightly, leaving him hanging on a branch of a tree.

The next morning, Sanzang, Sun and Sandy woke and saw the mansion had disappeared. They heard Bajie crying out loudly, "Master, Wukong, help me." When they looked around, they saw Bajie hanging on a tree, tightly bound. There was a note on the tree, saying: 'Goddess of the Pear Mountain, invited by Kuanyin and accompanied by two Bodhisattvas, have tested the integrity of the pilgrim team. All proved faithful and committed, except Bajie.'

Sanzang kowtowed to the Goddess of Mercy. Sun took the note and teased Bajie before taking him down. Bajie said, "I have learnt my lesson now. I shall never stray again."

◙ CHAPTER 27 ◙
Encounter With Baby-Shaped Fruit Tree

The pilgrims traveled cheerfully, and the weather was very agreeable. They came to a mountain wrapped in a serene atmosphere. There was a large, elegant temple from where magnificent light was emanating. Sanzang said, "This is so beautiful and serene. Could this be the Buddha's abode in the Western Heaven?" Sun said, "Not a chance. We are not even a tenth of the way. Sanzang asked, "In that case, how much longer do we have to go?" Sun said, "If Bajie or Sandy were to go, they could do it in a day, and if I were to go, I could complete fifty return flights before dusk. But you are still a human and have to go on foot; it would take you years." Sanzang said, "All right. But this place looks noble. It must be the abode of some exalted being. Let us meet him and stay a night." Sun said, "You are right. This looks like the residence of a very noble and exalted god."

The temple belonged to God of Universe's Origin, who was absent that day, having gone to the Heaven to attend a gathering of gods. He had a garden in which there was a divine tree which bore thirty fruits in the shape of human babies, which took three thousand years to flower, three thousand years for fruition, and three thousand years to ripen. Anyone who so much as took a whiff of its smell would gain three hundred sixty years of life, and anyone who ate one fruit would live for forty six thousand years. Before his departure, the God of Universe's Origin told the two junior fairies that he was expecting an old acquaintance to visit. He said, "The Sage on the way to the Western Heaven is the reincarnation of the elder in front of the Buddha, the Reverend Golden Cicada. He was one of the senior disciples, but was found sleeping during one of the Buddha's sermons, and was made to redeem his sin by reincarnating as a monk and seeking the sutra. When he and his three disciples come, treat them with courtesy and offer two of the Rensheng fruits, one for the Sage and the other for three disciples to share among them."

When the pilgrims arrived at the temple and knocked on the door, the two junior fairies opened the door and invited them in. Sanzang asked about the temple, and the two junior fairies said, "This belongs to our master, the God of Universe's Origin. Unfortunately, he is not here today, but he has left instructions for us to receive you. Please make yourselves comfortable, and we would like to offer you our hospitality."

Sanzang thanked them, and the junior fairies went to the garden and picked two of the Rensheng fruits and offered them to him and the three disciples. Sanzang was taken aback, because the fruits looked exactly like human babies. He said, "I've heard of people eating babies during a famine, but what is this? I adhere to the principle of no killing. How can I eat this?" The fairies said, "Please do not be alarmed. These are not babies but fruits in the form of babies." Still, Sanzang would not touch them.

The two junior fairies took the fruits back to their quarters and started to eat them, saying, "Well if he is so ignorant, we might as well enjoy them." Sanzang sent Bajie into the kitchen to prepare their food, and he overheard the fairies' conversation. He told Sun, "Hey, what the Master refused to eat is apparently a rare, very magical fruit. You are a master at stealing fruits. Why don't you find out where they are, and get us some?"

Sun happily obliged. He went to the garden where he saw a

tree a thousand feet tall with a trunk fifty feet in diameter, with baby-shaped fruits hanging on its branches. He used his magic stick to hit one of them, which fell to the ground and promptly disappeared. Sun could not see where it had gone and, feeling frustrated, he summoned the local god who was in charge of the area. The god came to him saying, "Local god reporting. What is your command?"

Sun said to him, "How dare you steal the fruit? I could not find it after I knocked it down." The god protested, "No, no. I did not steal. These fruits are formed in accordance with the qi (energy flow) of the universe. They obey the qi and respond to the five elements. They fall when they meet gold, that's why the fruit fell when you hit it. They wither when they meet wood; melt when they meet water; sublimate when they meet fire; and disappear when they meet soil. That's why the fruit disappeared when you let it fall to the ground." Sun understood. He dismissed the god, and went back to the tree.

This time Sun received the fruits with his sleeve and, picking three of them, went back to the kitchen. He asked Bajie what it was, and was told it was Rensheng fruit. Sandy was also familiar with it, as he had seen it when working in the Heavenly Palace.

The three of them enjoyed the fruits, but their conversations were overheard by the fairies who went to the garden to check. They found out that there were only twenty two left. They were alarmed. "There were thirty," they cried. Our Master gave two for us to share, and offered two for the Sage. So there should be twenty six left. The monkey stole four."

They went to Sanzang to complain. Sanzang did not know anything about it, and asked, "Wukong, what happened? If you stole the fruits, it's not such a grievous matter. Why don't you apologize and be done with it?" Sun replied, "Yes. I apologize. I am sorry I stole the fruits."

But the two fairies were not content. They continued to call Sun names. Sun became annoyed, and pulled out one of his hairs and turned it into himself. Then he slipped away to the back garden and pushed the tree down, uprooting it. The fairies noticed that Sun was strangely quiet, and decided to go and see what was happening in the garden. They were appalled to find the tree uprooted and destroyed. They decided to pretend that they knew nothing, and offered the pilgrims supper and allowed them the night's lodging.

After supper, when the pilgrims bedded down, the fairies closed the doors and locked them in. They were to keep them for the return of their master. Next day, they woke up and found themselves locked in. Sanzang said, "Now how do we get out?" Bajie said, "I know Wukong can get out. He has only to turn himself into a fly and get out. But we are stuck." Sanzang warned, "Wukong, if you get out alone, I will chant the ring-tightening mantra." Sun said, "No, no, no. I will open the door for all of us. I can unlock these locks." He pointed his finger at the lock and it opened. The four of them took the horse and left the place in a hurry.

Soon the God of Universe's Origin returned. He asked the fairies if the Sage had visited. They said, "Yes, and we offered them two fruits. But the Sage would not eat it, because he thought it was a baby. Then Sun Wukong stole four fruits. When we complained, Sun went and uprooted the tree. Now the tree is dead, and we don't know what to do."

"Where are they now?"

"We locked them up," replied the fairies, "but somehow they opened the lock and now they are gone."

The God then took off, to find the fleeing four. He flew a thousand miles but could not find them. When he looked around, he saw the pilgrims moving slowly, barely a hundred miles from his temple. He laughed. "I see that they are proceeding at human speed. This must be because the Sage is a human without supernatural abilities." He went back to meet up with them, and said, "I offered you hospitality and you damaged my treasure. Come back with me, and I shall punish you."

Sun and his two fellow disciples raised their weapons against the God, but the God just lifted his sleeve, and with a trick called 'universe within a sleeve', he captured everyone inside his sleeve and flew back to his temple. "Now I shall punish you with 100 lashes of iron sticks," he said.

Sun thought that Sanzang would be too frail to sustain such punishment. So he said, "Do not punish my Master. I am the one who stole and then destroyed the tree. Punish me."

The God was impressed by Sun's loyalty, and instructed his fairy to give Sun the lashes. Of course it did no harm to Sun's hardened skin. After that, the pilgrims were kept in a room, all bound up. That night Sun again said, "I can unbind us. Let's go." He pointed at each of his team, and the ropes fell down, and they escaped from the temple once more.

It was to no avail. The next day the God again caught up with them, and again brought them back to the temple in his sleeve. This time he decided to put Sanzang into boiling oil. Sun again said, "Please, my Master is innocent. Put me into the oil." The God said, "You are a loyal disciple. I respect that. All right," he told the fairies, "put him in the wok."

When the fairies tried to lift Sun to drop him into the wok, the wok shattered and oil splashed all around. It turned out that Sun had escaped but turned the stone lion next to him into himself. The God said, "You still want to play your little tricks with me. You will never leave this place until the tree is revived." Sun replied, "Ah! Why did you not say so in the first place? For me it's nothing to revive a tree. I will revive it if you will let us free." The God said, "I respect your courage and loyalty. If you can restore my tree, I will not only let you all go, I will acknowledge you as my brother."

Sanzang asked, "How are you going to revive a dead tree?" Sun said, "I will get help." Sanzang said, "Very well. But do it in three days. Otherwise I will chant the ring-tightening mantra." Sun flew off to the south, seeking help.

First, Sun came to the mountain where the three gods – the Gods of Luck, of Prosperity, and of Longevity – resided. They greeted Sun courteously, asking why he was there instead of escorting the Sage. Sun explained his problem and asked if they could help. They did not know how.

Sun said, "You see, I am trouble. If I don't find the tree-resurrecting formula within three days, my Master will chant the ring-tightening mantra and my head will be squeezed in great pain." The three gods volunteered to go and accompany Sanzang and ask Sanzang not to chant the mantra when the three days were up. Then they went off to the temple, where they were received the God of the Universe's Origin. Sanzang kowtowed to them, and they said, "Please do not kowtow. We came at the request of Sun, and would like to ask you not to chant the mantra when the three days are up."

Sanzang said, "I obey you. I will not." Meanwhile, Sun went to a few more gods and fairies, and no one could help. Finally, he found himself near the Kuanyin Mountain. Again, he met the bear spirit, who, after some friendly banter, took him the see Kuanyin. She said, "You are a trouble maker. Why did you waste your time looking for the tree-resurrecting formula?"

Sun thought he had now found his salvation, and quickly kowtowed and asked Kuanyin to help. Kuanyin agreed, and flew with Sun in divine brilliance towards the temple.

The God of Universe's Origin greeted the Bodhisattva, as did the three gods of Fortune, Prosperity and Longevity. Sanzang kowtowed piously, thanking her for her gracing the place. Sun said, "Please, let's not delay. Let's go and revive the tree." They went to the garden, where the tree lay dead, roots exposed and withered away.

Kuanyin commanded, "Wukong, open your palm." She wrote a mantra of resurrection on it. Sun then grasped the roots, and Bajie and Sandy pushed the tree to an upright position. Kuanyin then dipped her willow branch into her jar, and sprinkled the tree. In a few moments, the tree revived, with leaves growing back and twenty three fruits hanging on its branches. The two fairies said, "Strange! We counted twenty two the last time. Where does the extra one come from?" Sun said, "I believe this was the one that disappeared into the ground when I dropped it."

Delighted, the God of Universe's Origin threw a party and plucked five fruits to offer Kuanyin, the three gods, and Sanzang.

This time Sanzang was familiar with the fruit, and he ate it without hesitation. Kuanyin and the three gods then took their leave. After a few days, the pilgrims left to continue their journey.

◎ CHAPTER 28 ◎
WUKONG IS BANISHED AFTER KILLING THE DEMON OF BLEACHED SKELETON

Their journey took them through open fields and towns and cities. Then they came to a mountain. Bajie said, "This mountain looks ominous. Maybe there is a monster here." Sun flew up and looked around from the sky, but did not see anything. He then uttered a howl, which sent the tigers, bears, wolves and other animals running for cover.

Sanzang said, "I am famished. Wukong, why don't you go and find some food from devout donors?" Sun took the begging bowl and left. But Sun's howl had aroused the curiosity of the demon in the mountain, who decided to find out who had come into his domain. She saw a monk on a white horse, accompanied by two rather fierce-looking warriors escorting him.

She found the monk appealing to her appetite, but she felt a bit intimidated by the two escorts. So she decided to play a trick. She turned into a pretty young woman, holding a bowl of food, and approached the three.

Bajie was immediately infatuated by her, and said, "Hello, young lady. It is dangerous for a young woman to be travelling alone in this terrain. Who knows what wild beasts and bandits are lurking there?" She replied, "I live in this neighbourhood, and I am used to walking around here. My mother is a devout person, and she prepared this pure vegetarian bowl to offer to monks. Since you are monks, I offer it to you."

Bajie told Sanzang, "Well, this is fortuitous. Wukong is not back yet, but why don't we accept this." Before Sanzang could respond, Sun came back with his bowl of food. When he saw the young woman, his supernatural vision recognized her as the demon. So he flew down, and hit the young woman with his stick.

The demon left behind the corpse of the young woman, and escaped by shedding that body. Sanzang was upset. He said to Sun, "This is outrageous. She was offering us food, and you just killed her." Sun explained, "No, no, no: this was a demon playing tricks on you." Bajie was also upset because Sun had killed the pretty woman. He said, "Master, Sun is just lying. Look, here is the corpse of that lady. Where is the demon?"

Sun said, "But look at the food in the bowl. It is all maggots and rotten meats." Sanzang took a look, but Bajie said, "Aha! This is another of Wukong's tricks. He has turned the food to this state to deceive you." Sanzang was naïve and so he believed Bajie. He said, "I do not condone this violence" and started to chant the ring-tightening mantra. Sun was rolling in pain, and cried, "All right, all right. I will never do this again." Sanzang relented, and they ate the food Sun had brought.

The demon then turned into an old woman, walking slowly towards the pilgrims. Bajie said, "Now we are in real trouble. The young lady's mother is looking for her daughter. What are we to do?" Sun again saw that this was the same demon. He said, "No, this is the same demon." He hit her with his magic stick again. The demon escaped once more, shedding the body of the old woman.

Bajie said, "Wukong is playing his tricks again." This time too, Sanzang naively believed Bajie, and started to chant the mantra. Writhing in pain, Sun swore he would not do it again, and again Sanzang relented.

The demon next appeared in the form of a man.

This time Sun was careful. He summoned the gods of the area, and asked them to prevent the demon from escaping. Then he told Sanzang that this was the demon, and this time it would not escape." He hit the demon again with his magic stick. With the gods surrounding the demon, she was trapped. She could not escape and died, turning into a bleached skeleton, bearing the sign 'Lady White Bones' on its skull.

Sun said, "See, this is indeed the demon. Look at her skull."

Bajie continued to insist that this was another of Sun's tricks, and Sanzang said, "Wukong, you are incorrigible. Despite my admonitions, you have killed three people. Such violence cannot be tolerated. I can no longer accept you as my disciple." And again he chanted the mantra, leaving Sun in agony. Sun cried, "All right, if you want to banish me, I will leave. But do not chant."

Sanzang said, "I will not chant it again if you leave." Sun kowtowed to Sanzang and said to Bajie and Sandy, "I am now banished. The two of you must now escort the Master to the best of your abilities. If there are monsters or demons that cause you trouble, tell them Sun Wukong is the first disciple of the Master. That should scare them." With that he flew off to the Water Screen Cave.

◙ CHAPTER 29 ◙
SUN GOES HOME

When Sun arrived home, he saw the mountain denuded and desolate. There was no one around. He called out, "I am home. Where is everybody?" Hesitantly, the monkeys came out and said, "Your majesty. We need your protection." They explained that in recent years, hunters had been raiding the mountain and capturing the monkeys. Some were eaten, some made to play in circuses, and some used as slaves.

Sun was furious, and asked, "Where are they from, and when do they come?" The monkeys said they were from the north, and they came every day. As they were talking, a monkey came and told them that the hunters were approaching. Sun told the monkeys to collect rocks on top of the hills. As the hunters drew near, he blew a breath which created a hurricane-force wind, blowing the rocks on the hunters and killing them all. Sun then ordered the monkeys to tidy up everything, planting trees, fixing the living quarters, and generally make the place comfortable. Soon the monkey kingdom was prospering again, and the other animals again came to pay tribute. These included tigers, bears, deer, wolves, buffalos, snakes, lizards, and birds of all feather.

◙ CHAPTER 30 ◙
Yellow Robe Demon Defeats
Bajie and Sandy

After Sun's banishment, the three of them proceeded onwards. One evening, Sanzang asked Bajie to go obtain some donated food. He went off, but he felt lazy, as usual, so he lay down to take a nap on the roadside. Sanzang and Sandy waited for some time, and when Bajie did not return, Sanzang sent Sandy looking for him.

Left all alone, Sanzang felt bored and lonely. So he decided to take a walk, and walked in a southerly direction. Ahead of him, he saw some light, an agreeable golden colour. He thought to himself that this must belong to a highly virtuous monk, so he decided to pay his respect.

As Sanzang approached the gate, he noticed someone lying there asleep. It was a monster, clad in yellow robe, with blue face, red mouth, yellow hair, and white fangs. Frightened, Sanzang tried to withdraw, but by then he had been noticed by the monster's followers. He was captured and taken inside the cave, named 'Broken Moon'.

The monster was happy to get Sanzang and asked him his identity. Sanzang explained who he was and what he was doing, and the monster asked if he had any disciples. Sanzang was an honest man, so he told the truth. The Monster was happy. "So you have two escorts?" he said. That would be enough for us to fill our stomachs for a while. Let me get them both before I eat you."

Sandy had gone looking for Bajie and found him sleeping on the roadside. He awakened him and said, "The Master sent you to collect food, and look at you. This is negligence and irresponsibility. It's been quite a while since I left the Master. Come, let's go see whether he is safe. Then you can go get some food."

When they went back, they found only the horse and no Master. Startled, they looked around to see where he could be. They noticed the golden rays in the southern direction, and surmised that the Master might be there worshipping. When they arrived at the Broken Moon cave, they realized that this was not a temple, but a monster's nest. Bajie shouted, "You monster, give us back the Sage, or else."

The monster came out and said, "I do have the monk. Now you two have come to join him on my dinner table." They fought, and Bajie and Sandy could not win. They kept fighting for a long time.

There was a princess in the cave, captured by the yellow robe monster thirteen years before and had borne two boys by him. The princess saw Sanzang and decided to release him. She went to him, and said, "Your reverence. I am princess Baihuaxiu (envy of a hundred flowers). I am the third daughter of the king of Baoxiang kingdom (Precious Elephant). Thirteen years ago this monster kidnapped me and has kept me here since. I will let you go, and would ask you to take my letter to my parents."

Sanzang was happy to oblige. So she unbound him, wrote a letter for him to take, and let him out of the backdoor. Then the princess went to the front where the yellow robe monster was still fighting and called on the monster to come. He abandoned the fight and came to his wife. She said, "I had a dream in which god told me to save the life of a holy man. I see that you have captured such a holy man. Why don't you let him go? This would also save you the trouble of having to fight these two."

The monster said, "All right. I will let him go." He turned to Bajie and Sandy. "It's not that I am afraid of you," he said. "But since my wife asked me to let your Master go, I will let him go. Collect him and go away." They went to the backdoor, found Sanzang, and proceeded to the Baoxiang kingdom.

Once in the kingdom, they sought audience with the king, presenting him with the imperial edict from Taizong, and were treated to a Buddhist dinner of all vegetables. Sanzang gave the king the letter from the princess, which said, "My dear royal parents. I write this letter in great sadness. I have been kidnapped by a monster in yellow robe who has imprisoned me for thirteen years. I have been forced to be his wife and now have two children by him. Fortunately, here is the Sage who is going to the Western Heaven to obtain the sutras. He has agreed to carry this letter to you. I hope you are both in good health. Your suffering daughter, Baihuaxiu."

This caused the king and queen great distress. The king said, "Thirteen years ago my third daughter disappeared, and I mobilized the whole kingdom to look for her. Many heads rolled because no one could find her. Now we know where she is. But my army is no match for the monster with supernatural powers. What am I to do?"

Bajie said, "Your majesty need not worry. I can beat this monster. I have thirty six supernatural tricks, and my weapon is powerful." He stretched, and he grew to be twenty feet tall. Then he called a cloud and rode away towards the monster's cave. The king was amazed. Sanzang told Sandy, "I think you should go and give Bajie a hand." Sandy also stretched himself to a height of twenty feet and flew away. Together, the two went to the Broken Moon cave and called out to the monster, "Now you have kidnapped the princess. Return her or else."

The monster came out and the three started a fierce fight. Half way into the fight, Bajie saw that they could not win, and decided to slip away. He said to Sandy, "Brother, I have to relieve myself. I will be back if you just carry on fighting with this monster. The Heavenly Contingent of gods and fairies assigned to protect the Master will be with you." And he quietly went away.

Sandy, left alone, was not strong enough to fight the monster. After a while, he was captured. The monster took him back to the Broken Moon cave, and went to the princess's room and pulled her out. "How did these pilgrims know that you are here?" he asked angrily. " You must have written a letter for the monk to take to your father when I agreed to let him go." She denied it, and the monster asked Sandy about it. Sandy thought to himself, "I am going to be killed here anyway. So I might as well protect the princess." He replied, "Don't talk nonsense. There was no letter. My Master was invited by the king and, during their conversation my Master told him about the princess he had seen here."

The monster was quietened. He apologized. "Sorry for the misunderstanding," he said.

With Sandy captured, Bajie delinquent, and the princess still a prisoner, Sanzang felt helpless.

Back in his cave, the monster decided to visit the princess's parents, the king and queen. He turned into a handsome young man and proceeded to the palace, introducing himself as the royal son-in-law. The king and queen could not see through the monster's disguise but, remembering what the princess had said in her letter, they asked about their daughter and why she was kidnapped.

The monster replied, "I did not kidnap her. We met when she was out picnicking. We fell in love with each other and she decided to come with me to my home. We now have two boys together, and she is living happily." The king had his doubts but, seeing the handsome man, he relented and decided to welcome him into the palace.

When the monster saw Sanzang, he said, "This monk is not really a monk. He is a tiger who has changed his appearance into that of a monk." The king said, "But this is the Sage who is on his way to get the sutra from the Buddha."

The monster then played a trick, changing the Sage into a huge, fierce tiger. Everyone was terrified. The royal guards slashed at him with their swords and spears. Luckily for the Master, the Heavenly Contingent was protecting him, so none of the swords or spears could harm him. Still, Sanzang was now caged as a tiger.

Seeing that both Bajie and Sandy were no longer around, and that the Master had been tricked into the shape of a tiger, the pilgrim's horse felt that he had to do something to help. So the horse changed into a lady-in-waiting and approached the monster, offering to pour wine for him. The monster was taken by this pretty woman, and asked if she could dance. She, now the horse dragon, agreed to do a sword dance. She used the sword to attack the monster. Unfortunately for the horse dragon, the monster was alert and moved quickly. He shouted, "Who are you to dare attack me like this?"

The lady-in-waiting revealed her real form, that of a dragon, and they fought. The dragon was no match for the monster. He was hit in the leg and escaped from the battle in the shape of a small fish in the stream.

◉ CHAPTER 31 ◉
Sun Wukong Rejoins the Pilgrim Team

Meanwhile, Bajie woke up from another of his naps and went back into the king's palace. He noticed that the horse was all wet, and wondered what happened. The horse suddenly said, "Bajie, Sandy has been captured, and the Master is in trouble because the monster changed him into a tiger. You have to do something to help."

Bajie was startled. "How come you are talking like a human? I thought you were a horse."

The dragon said, "I am a dragon, the third son of the Dragon King of the Western Ocean."

Bajie said, "The monster is quite strong. I don't think I can rescue Sandy." The dragon then suggested to Bajie, "Brother, now we are in a desperate situation. I believe you should go and ask our Senior Brother Sun Wukong to come and help."

Bajie said, "I don't see why he would help. The Master chanted the mantra to torture him three times before expelling him. Besides, I was the one that distorted the truth about the Bleached Bone Demon that caused the Master to expel him. I am sure he hates me and if he sees me now he will beat me up."

The dragon said, "No, I know Sun is not a small minded person. He will forgive you. Besides, his devotion for the Master is unyielding. So I believe if you told him the trouble the Master is in, he will immediately come to the rescue."

Reluctantly, Bajie agreed. He flew to the Water Screen Cave and, as he approached the cave, he saw Sun sitting high up on the mountain, surrounded by thousands of monkeys and other animals. He felt guilty about the lies he had told to cause Sun's expulsion, and did not want to go directly to him. He hid amongst the monkeys, but he could escape Sun's sharp eyes. Sun called out, "Who is out there, with big ears?"

Bajie stood up and said, "Greetings, brother. Look at you. Living so well and having so much fun. No wonder you don't miss us." Sun laughed. "What are you doing here, not escorting the Master?" Bajie said, "The Master sent me for you because he misses you. Come back and join us."

Sun said, "I do not believe you. The Master chanted the mantra three times and expelled me with a curse. I am sure he does not want me back." Bajie did not want to beg for his help, so he insisted that the Master did miss him. Sun remained adamant in his unwillingness to return and Bajie had no choice but to explain that they were in trouble.

Sun said, "Very well. I will help. But only this one time. Afterwards, I am coming back here." The two of them then rode their cloud, and returned to the monster's cave. Sun said, "Let me go in to see what's what." Bajie said, "But the monster is not here."

Sun went ahead anyway and saw two boys playing in front of the cave. He snatched them and was about to throw them down, when the princess, hearing them crying, came out and called to Sun, "Do not harm them. Their father is very powerful. You will regret it if you hurt these children."

Sun said, "I will deal with him." He then went into the cave and told the princess to release Sandy, who was overjoyed to see Sun. Sun told the princess that she should hide herself while he fixed the monster. The princess agreed and went to hide, while Sun turned himself into the princess's form, awaiting the monster's return. Bajie took the two kids to the palace and, from the sky, threw them down onto the front gate of the throne room, shouting, "These are the two monster kids. We have come to get rid of the monster who is deceiving you by taking on the form of a handsome young man."

The monster was drunk and in a stupor, but he heard this and came out to see. When he found his two boys dead, he was angry and flew back to his cave to see what was going on. When he saw his wife, who was really Sun in disguise, he asked, "What happened to our kids?" Sun replied, "They were taken away by your enemy." The monster said, "These pilgrims are no match to me. Let me fix them."

Sun said, "But now they have someone called Sun Wukong who has come to join them." This alarmed the monster. "That is bad news," he said. "This Sun is the trouble maker who made a big mess of the Heavenly Palace. Now I have to be careful."

Sun suddenly revealed his original form, and threw the monster to the ground. Then he pulled out the magic stick, made it into a stick two inches in diameter and eight feet long, and started to beat the monster. The monster also grabbed his weapon and they fought.

Sun managed to hit the monster on his shoulder, and he disappeared. Sun went up to the sky, looked around with his supernatural vision, but he could not find the monster. He concluded that the monster did not belong to the earth. So he flew up to Heavenly Gate where the guardian god and others hurriedly greeted him. He asked them to check and see which one of the heavenly horde was missing. They went through the registers, checking the stars, fairies, and gods of all description.

The register of the 28 Milky Way Stars showed one of them missing, so they sent the head of the 28 to go looking for him. The monster, hearing the call of his boss, came out of his hiding, and was duly arrested. He said, "The princess is not a human. She was one of the Heavenly Ladies-in-Waiting, with whom I fell in love. To be together, we decided to leave Heaven and come to the earth."

Sun thanked the gods, and returned to the king's palace. There, he saw Bajie, Sandy and the horse. They took him to the Master, who was still in the form of a tiger. Sun said, "Ah! Master, how do you feel?" The tiger roared, but rather plaintively, for it was the Master and he could understand what was said. Sun said, "Do not worry, I will help you." He took a sip of water and blew it on the tiger, and the tiger immediately changed back into Sanzang. It was like awakening from a bad dream, and Sanzang said, "O Wukong, thank you for your help. And welcome back. When we succeed in getting the sutras, your merit will be the highest."

Sun said, "Never mind that. I will be happy if you just stop chanting those damned mantras." The pilgrim team was now complete again, and they proceeded on their journey.

◙ CHAPTER 32 ◙

Troubles With Gold Horn and Silver Horn

The pilgrims proceeded through mountains and rivers, plains and fields, and came upon a massive, craggy mountain. Sanzang said, "This looks like a mountain that might harbour a monster. Bajie, why don't you go and investigate." Bajie was not very keen, but had to obey the Master. So he went ahead of the team to check things out.

Knowing how untrustworthy Bajie was, Sun said to Sanzang, "Bajie may do his usual thing, just go for a nap instead of performing his task. Let me follow him and see what he does." He changed into a dragon-fly and flew right behind Bajie.

Sure enough, Bajie was grumbling to himself, "This old fool of a monk. Why didn't he get the monkey to do it? Well, I am going to have a good nap." He lay down to sleep.

Sun changed into a woodpecker and pecked at Bajie's nose. Bajie groaned, "These days everyone is out to make trouble for me, even the woodpecker. Go away, let me sleep." He hid his nose under his sleeve, and tried to sleep.

But Sun the woodpecker was not going to let him sleep. He pecked away at his ears. Bajie gave up. "Ay ay ay, all right! It's not in my luck to have a nice sleep." He saluted a big rock nearby, as if it was his Master, and said, "Master, I have finished my task.

This mountain is known as the Stone Head Mountain. There is a cave called Stone Head Cave, in which a monster lives, with some forty or fifty small elves." Sun quickly flew back to the Master and reported what happened. When Bajie returned, Sun asked him mischievously what his finding was. Bajie said, "This mountain is known as the Stone Head Mountain." Sun added, "And there is a cave named Stone Head Cave? And there is a monster in it, along with forty or fifty small elves? I saw you saluting a rock to rehearse this."

Bajie was mortified and embarrassed. He promised to go again and this time would do an honest investigation. Sun did not follow him, but he was afraid that Sun was somewhere behind following him. Bajie was muttering, "All right, all right, I will not cheat again." So he went, this time in earnest, and soon ran into a monster.

The mountain was occupied by two brother monsters, Gold Horn and Silver Horn, living in a cave named 'Lotus Flower Cave'. They had heard that the pilgrims were on their way to the Western Heaven and that their mountain was on their path. Gold Horn said, "I hear that the Sage is a holy man who is of perfect virtue, and his flesh could bring infinite longevity to whosoever that eats it. Let's not let them pass. We have to catch him and eat his flesh."

Silver Horn was out that day looking for a quarry to hunt and, when he saw Bajie, decided to catch him. Bajie fought him off, but after some time, found it difficult to keep up, and started to run away. The small elves chased after him and, tripping on a root, Bajie fell and was captured and brought into the cave.

Gold Horn said, "This must be Zhu Bajie, for he looks like a pig. It means that the Sage is not far. Why don't you go have a look around?"

The rest of the team was waiting for Bajie to return. When he did not, they began to suspect that he was sleeping again. Silver Horn turned himself into an old Taoist priest who had injured his leg, and approached the pilgrims.

Sanzang asked, "Friend, where do you come from? We are

from Tang China, on our way to the Western Heaven to obtain the Buddhist sutras. You are hurt. Let me lend you my horse to carry you, and let us go to your temple." Silver Horn said: "That is very kind of you. But I am unable to ride a horse because my leg is broken."

Sanzang took pity on him and asked Sun to carry him on his back. Sun knew this was a monster, so he agreed to carry him, and was going to throw him hard on the ground to crush him. Silver Horn called for a mountain to come and crush Sun, but Sun was powerful enough to fend off the attack. He carried the mountain on his right shoulder and kept going, still looking for a chance to throw the monster.

The monster then called on another mountain which Sun hoisted on his left shoulder. Finally, the monster called the largest mountain. This time, Sun could not hold up so much weight and was pinned down. Silver Horn then flew into the sky and from there stretched his arm to catch Sanzang, and drew him to the cave.

Gold Horn said, "We have five magic tools. One is a red gourd, another is a jade vase, and then we have a banana-leaf fan, the sword of seven stars, and the golden rope. I know Sun Wukong is very powerful. He will surely escape from the three mountains. So before he does that, why not send one or our elves to go and get him. All he has to do is to put the silver vase upside down, with its mouth facing down, and call his name. The moment he responds to the call, he would be sucked into the vase, and within a few hours, he will turn into a pile of rotten puss." One of the elves was given the vase and told to go get Sun from underneath the mountains.

From below the three mountains, Sun summoned the gods of the mountains. They came hurrying to Sun's presence, saying, "Sir, what is your command?" Sun said, "How dare you pin me down like this." They replied, "The monster's power is so great that when he chants the mantra to pull us, we cannot resist. That's why we moved our mountains here. But we did not know it was you that we were pinning down. We will lift the weight tight away."

The gods removed the mountains, and Sun broke free. Pulling his needle-sized magic stick, shaking it into the usual size, Sun shouted, "Now come and get my stick." The gods pleaded with him, "Sir, we did not know it was you. Please do not punish us for our ignorance." Sun relented, and went to the cave to rescue the Master.

On his way, he saw the elf with the vase coming towards the mountains. Sun changed into a Taoist priest and greeted the elf. He paid compliments on the vase and asked the elf what function it performed. The elf said, "It can capture anyone who responds when his name is called. Once inside, the victim will melt into a rotting jelly of puss."

Sun pulled a hair and changed it into a large gourd. He told the elf, "My gourd is also magical. It can not only contain people, it can contain the universe. Let me show you what it does." He pulled another hair and changed it into himself, and he slipped away and went up the Heavenly Gate looking for the gods of the sun and the moon and the stars.

Sun asked them to help by hiding these celestial luminary bodies. They were reluctant, but the Jade Emperor said, "For the sake of helping in the cause of getting the sutra, I will permit this exceptional act this once." So, as Sun threw the gourd in the air, they pulled a black screen over the sky, and suddenly there was complete darkness. The elf was frightened and said, "I see nothing. Where are you?" Sun said, "I am right in front of you, but in this complete darkness you cannot see."

After a while, Sun thanked the gods and asked them to lift the screen, and suddenly the midday light was back. Sun offered to exchange the gourd with the vase and, impressed, the elf agreed to the exchange. Sun flew up to the sky, leaving the elf wondering what happened. He tried to repeat Sun's performance, but the gourd just dropped like a piece of stone.

In a panic, the elf kept throing the gourd in the air, but nothing happened. Sun was laughing in the air, and collected the hair back to his body, leaving the elf with nothing. He then killed the elf and, changing into a fly, went into the cave. There he heard the two monsters discussing how to deal with Sun. They decided to invite their mother who was the custodian of the golden rope, to come and share in the feast of the Sage's flesh.

Sun flew out of the cave, waited for the messenger bearing the invitation. He changed once again into a Taoist priest and greeted the messenger. "It looks as though you have an important assignment. What is it?" he enquired. The messenger told Sun that he was going to the mother of the two monsters to invite her for dinner. Sun asked where she lived, and the messenger told him. Sun now had no use for the messenger, so he killed him, assumed his form, and went to the cave where the mother lived.

As he met the mother, Sun told her about the capture of Sanzang, Bajie and Sandy, invited her to go to the Lotus Flower Cave for dinner. He requested that she bring the golden rope with her. The mother took out the rope, and got into a palanquin carried by eight people, and proceeded on her way to the cave. Sun took out his needle from his ear and changing it into the usual magic stick, killed the mother and her retinue and took the golden rope. The mother, it turned out, was a huge fox. Sun took eight hairs and changed them into the eight sedan bearers, and he himself changed into the shape of the mother. They were received by the two monsters who told of the benefits of eating Sanzang's flesh. Bajie, who was bound to a stick in the room, said, "Aha, this is Wukong in disguise. I can tell from the tail that sticks out." Sun, in the guise of the mother, said, "The monk is the ultimate treat, but the big ear of the pig must also be very tasty."

Bajie panicked when he heard this. He cursed under his breath, "This damned monkey, he never stops playing tricks on me." Soon afterwards, a guard came in, greatly agitated, and announced, "Master, bad news. Your mother was killed by Sun Wukong. The mother in front of you is none other than Sun himself." The two monsters pulled out their weapons to attack Sun, who now reverted to his original form and flew out of the cave. They fought for a while, and Sun decided to use the golden rope. What he did not realize was that there were two sets of mantras for the rope. One was to tighten, and the other to loosen.

When Sun took it out, Silver Horn immediately chanted the tightening mantra, which resulted in Sun being bound tight. The monster captured Sun, searched him and found the vase that he had taken from the elf. He dragged Sun into the cave. Bajie saw him coming bound and said, "Now you are not going to enjoy eating my ears, are you?" Sun said, "Don't worry; I know how to get out. I will rescue you."

He pulled one of his hairs, turned it into himself, and slipped out of the rope. Once outside, Sun shouted, "I am Wu Sunkong. Release the pilgrims and I will forgive you, or else." Silver Horn said, "I will find out who this Wu Sunkong is." Taking the vase with him, he went out of the cave.

There was Sun Wukong, claiming to be Wu Sunkong. Silver Horn asked, "Who are you. What is your business? Get lost or you will be in trouble."

Sun said, "You are the one in trouble. I am the Heavenly Grand Fairy. Release the pilgrims and you can save your skin." They fought for several hours, and Silver Horn was beginning to feel weak. He jumped off, and said "I have a magic vase that will swallow you. Do you dare respond to me when your name is called?"

Sun thought that Wu Sunkong was not his real name. He would therefore be immune to the vase's magic. So he said, "I will respond." Silver Horn called out, "Wu Sunkong!" and Sun said, "Yes!" Unfortunately, the vase would swallow anyone responding to a call, even if the name was false. So, Sun was sucked into the vase.

Silver Horn was triumphant. He took the vase and went back to the cave, and said, "I have Wu Sunkong here. Let's wait for a few hours for him to melt. Sun, inside, tried to break out, but it was too sturdy. He was not worried about melting: after all he had survived the forty nine days in Laotse's oven. But he wanted to get out, and only way to get out was when the vase was open. So he took one of his hairs and changed it to look like himself with legs melted and only the torso remaining.

Then Sun changed himself into a mosquito and waited near the mouth of the vase. He cried out in pitiful tones, "Ah, ah, now my legs have melted. I am soon going to die." Silver Horn heard it and decided to inspect. The moment he opened the cover, Sun flew out. Silver Horn looked into the vase and found Sun with only torso remaining, and said, "He will be finished soon."

Sun, now out, changed into one of the servants and stood near the vase. As soon as everyone's attention had shifted to other things, he took the vase, pulled one of his hair to change into the vase, collected his other hair from inside the vase, and sneaked out of the cave. Now he shouted, "Silver Horn and Gold Horn! Release the pilgrims or Kong Wusun will finish all of you."

The two monsters were puzzled. "Sun Wukong, Wu Sunkong, and now Kong Wusun. What is going on?"

Bajie heard this and cried out, "These three characters are all the one and the same. It's Sun Wukong in various disguises, you better know how powerful he is." Silver Horn went out to see, and Sun attacked him with his magic stick. Soon Silver Horn was feeling not up to it, and jumping off, took out his vase, which was Sun's hair, and said, "Now I have a magic vase that will swallow you, if you dare to answer my call."

Sun, knowing that the vase in Silver Horn's hand was really his hair, said, "Go ahead and call. I will answer." Silver Horn called out, "Kong Wusun!" Sun answered, "Yes!" But nothing happened. Silver Horn was confused and afraid. So he started to run away. Sun called out, "Silver Horn!" Silver Horn, out of habit, answered. "Yes." And he was swallowed into the vase.

The brother's defeat was reported to Gold Horn, and he felt compelled to come out and fight. Sun quickly defeated him. Gold Horn used the banana leaf fan to fan a huge fire that threatened to burn Sun and Bajie. In the confusion, he ran away to another cave, where his mother's brother lived. Sun went into the Lotus Flower Cave to release the Master, Bajie, Sandy and the horse, and pursued Gold Horn to his uncle's cave.

They came out, but were no match for Sun and Bajie. The uncle was struck by Bajie's rake, dying from the nine holes from the rake and turning out to be an old fox. Gold Horn tried to run, but when he answered Sun's call, he too was sucked into the vase.

Sun and Bajie went back to the Master and told him that all was well now, with the two monsters trapped in the vase.

Suddenly there was a brilliant light in the sky, and a voice called out, "Now that you have won, you can give back my two servants and five instruments." They looked up, and saw Laotse standing in the sky, on his cloud. The Master kowtowed, but Sun said, "You mean old man. Why did you send these two to harass us?"

"I had no intention to do any mischief but Kuanyin asked me to send someone down to test your resolve. So I sent the two servants, one looking after my Golden Oven and the other looking after my Silver Oven, down to earth, carrying the vase which I use to put water, the gourd which I use to store my longevity pills, the banana leaf fan that I use to fan my fire in the oven, and the gold rope that was my waist band. Now their job is done, so let me collect them." He opened the vase, and the two monsters turned into two breaths of fragrant wind and blew out.

The Master thanked Sun for his feats, and the pilgrims continued on their journey to the west.

The Master thanked Sun Wukong for his feats, and the pilgrims
continued on their journey to the west.

PART TWO

◎ CHAPTER 1 ◎
The Dead King in the Well

The pilgrims travelled through the summer and autumn. It was now winter, with snow flying. The temperature kept dipping.

After weeks of their hard journey, they saw a large temple complex. Sanzang said, "Let us ask for a night's lodging here."

Afraid that the faces of his disciples would frighten the people, Sanzang decided to go in by himself and ask for the accommodation. So he went to the gate and knocked on the door.

Sanzang introduced himself and asked for lodging, but the monks refused him. Disappointed, he went back to his disciples and said he had not been successful.

Sun Wukong asked, "What is this temple anyway?" Sanzang replied, "The sign on top of the gate says 'Precious Forest Temple, Under the Imperial Charter', so I presume it is a Buddhist temple."

Sun Wukong was annoyed. "Then they should demonstrate more charity and generosity," he said. "This attitude is not acceptable. Let me go and fix them."

Sun Wukong went to the gate, and shouted, "We are pilgrims who are going to the West to obtain the true teaching of the Buddha. You are Buddhist monks. Why do you not have the courtesy of opening your door to us?" The gate keepers reported this to the chief monk, who hurried out to see.

Sun Wukong said, "We are no ordinary monks. We are under the Imperial Order to travel to the Western Heaven. Nobody has ever refused us lodging. And we will not stay too long – only a night or two to rest up, and then we will be on our way. Now clean up enough rooms for us, or else -" Sun smashed a stone lion at the gate with his magic stick.

The monks were truly scared, and invited the pilgrims in and offered them food and lodging.

That night, after the disciples had gone to sleep, Sanzang decided to renew his studies of the sutras. But after reviewing two volumes, he was tired, and went to the courtyard for a walk. Suddenly he heard someone calling him, "Master, Master!" There was a man standing under the moonbeam.

At first Sanzang could not see very well, and said, "I am a monk, and I have nothing of value for you to desire. Besides, my three disciples are super powerful fairies who can kill monsters and demons. I suggest that you go away and not bother me."

The man replied, "I am not a demon. Have a good look at me." Sanzang peered into the dark and took a better look. He found that the man was wearing a king's attire, dripping wet with water. Startled, he asked, "Are you a king? Where have you come from? And why are you wet all over?"

The man said, "I am the king of the Black Rooster Kingdom a few miles from here. Five years ago my kingdom was suffering from a severe drought and people were dying of starvation.

"I prayed and tried everything for some rainfall, but without success. The situation lasted two years, and just as I was afraid the country was going to break down, a Taoist magic worker came to me and offered to bring about the needed rainfall which helped revive the country.

"I was very grateful, and adopted him as my brother. This was three years ago. One day, when he and I were walking in the imperial garden, he pushed me into the well and covered it with a slab of stone, and planted a banana tree on top. He then took my form and has since taken over my throne, my country, and my wives. No one knows about all this.

"The Dragon King of the Well gave me a pill that would prevent my body from decaying, and I have been in the well for three years. I was told that I could be rescued in three years, and that you have a disciple Sun Wukong who is capable of defeating demons, and may be able to save me. That's why I have appeared in front of you."

Amazed, Sanzang said, "Yes, Sun Wukong is one of my disciples. But how can we help when no one knows that the false king is really the Taoist magic worker?"

The king replied, "I have a white jade staff here which, if you showed to my son the prince heir apparent, he would believe you. He will come out hunting, and will come to this temple for rest. That's when you may be able to reveal my story."

Sanzang agreed that he would tell this to Sun Wukong. The king thanked him, disappearing into the moonlit bush.

◎ CHAPTER 2 ◎
REVIVING THE DEAD KING

The next morning, Sanzang told Sun Wukong about his encounter from the night before and explained what the King wanted them to do.

Sun Wukong said thoughtfully, "That would be difficult. When everyone thinks the king is alive and is ruling the country well, why should anyone believe in what we say? But let me go and see if the prince will be hunting and, if so, I can entice him to come to this temple."

Sun Wukong took one of his hairs and turned it into an exquisite small box. He gave it to Sanzang and said, "Put the jade staff from the king of Black Rooster Kingdom in this. When the prince comes here, tell him that you have three treasures. One is the robe you are wearing.

"At this time, I will turn myself into a small elf and jump inside the box, and you could say that the elf is the second treasure. The third is, of course, the jade staff."

Sun Wukong then flew over to the capital of the Black Rooster Kingdom where he saw a team of hunters leaving the gate. It was led by a prince.

Sun Wukong decided to tease the prince. He changed into a white rabbit and started to run in front of the prince. Chasing the rabbit, the prince shot an arrow at him. Sun Wukong caught it, and pretending to have been hit, he ran towards the temple.

As the hunting team approached the temple, Sun Wukong took the arrow, and planted it on the gate, and returned to his own form. The prince was puzzled to see the rabbit disappear and the arrow planted on the gate. He exclaimed, "What is this, is someone playing a trick on me?"

Sun Wukong, now in his own form, asked the prince, "Who are you?" The prince said, "I am the Crown Prince. And who are you?" Sun Wukong replied that he was a disciple of the Sage who is going to the Western Heaven to get the true teaching of the Buddha.

As the prince entered the temple, all the monks knelt to him, but Sanzang and his pilgrims just sat there and greeted the prince. The prince was annoyed. "Who are you? How dare you be so insolent? Why don't you kneel?" he asked.

Sanzang said, "I do not know who you are." When the prince introduced himself, Sanzang said, "My apologies. I have been waiting for you to show you the three treasures I have."

By this time Sun Wukong had changed into a small elf measuring three inches tall, while pulling another hair to change it into his form. The prince was intrigued, and asked to see the treasures.

Sanzang first showed the prince the robe he was wearing, which did not impress the prince at all.

Then Sun Wukong opened the box and said, "The second treasure is this elf. He can see events five hundred years past and five hundred years into the future. Just ask him anything."

The prince was not impressed by the elf, either. "This ridiculous little creature measuring barely three inches, what does he know?" he asked.

At this, Sun Wukong jumped out and stretched his body and all of a sudden he was ten feet tall. He said to the prince, "Is this tall enough for you?"

This time the prince was impressed.

Sun Wukong then said, "You are the Crown Prince of Black Rooster Kingdom, but your father the king has been dead for three years, and the Taoist magic worker has taken his place."

The Prince grew angry and said, "How can you say that, when my father is alive and well and is ruling with wisdom and benevolence?"

Sun Wukong asked the prince to tell his retinue and the monks to leave the room. When they were alone with the prince, Sanzang said, "I saw your father, the dead king, last night, and he told me that three years ago the Taoist magic maker pushed him into the well in the imperial garden, then covered it with a slab of stone and planted a banana tree on top of it. The magic maker then assumed your father's form and took over the kingdom. And he sealed the garden, so no one is allowed into it."

The prince refused to believe it, saying, "How can a dead man come to you?"

Sun Wukong then said, "Look at the third treasure," and showed the white jade staff. The prince remembered the staff, and said, "I recognize this, it was lost and no one could find it. How did you get it?"

Sanzang said he had received it from the dead king, who was lying at the bottom of the well. But the Dragon King of the Well had given him a pill to preserve his body so he could be rescued after three years. This convinced the prince somewhat, but he wanted further proof.

Sun Wukong said, "You could ask your mother, the Queen, how her married life has been for the last three years." The prince agreed. Before he took leave, the Prince said, "I came out here to hunt, and I cannot very well go back without catching some animals."

Sun Wukong chanted the mantra to summon the gods of the mountains and fields, who rushed to him and knelt before him, asking, "Sir, what is your command?"

Sun Wukong said, "This prince needs some animals to take home. Provide him with some deer, wild boar, pheasants, and rabbits." The gods obeyed Sun Wukong, and as the prince took their leave, he found hundreds of wild animals on his way, and he and his retinue could easily catch them and take them home.

The prince went straight to the Queen's room, and after the usual chat, asked how 'father' had been treating her for the last three years.

Tearfully, the Queen said, "Since you ask, he has never touched me, always claiming that he was too old and weak for love."

The prince told her what he had found out, and they shared their sorrow. To console his mother, the prince told her that the king would be rescued after three years by fairies.

After the prince had gone, it was evening, and Sun Wukong decided to go and get the king's body out of the well. He decided to make Bajie work a little. Sun Wukong said to Sanzang, "I would like to go with Bajie to do some treasure hunting."

When he heard about treasure, Bajie was happy to come along. The two of them flew over to the capital and went directly into the garden, where there was a banana tree.

Sun Wukong pushed the tree down and opened the slab. He told Bajie, "The treasure is in this well. You are the swimmer, so you should go in."

Bajie saw how deep the well was, and was reluctant to jump in. Sun Wukong took out his magic stick and turned it into a rope, and told Bajie to use it to lower himself.

Bajie went down, and down below he saw the bottom widen into a palace of the Dragon King of the Well, where there was the body of a man clad in the outfit of a king. He climbed back some distance up and said to Sun Wukong, "There is no treasure down there, only a dead body." Sun Wukong said, "But that dead body is the treasure. Bring it out."

Bajie was not amused. "Now you are teasing me. How is a dead body a treasure?" he asked. "I am not going to carry a dead body on my back."

Sun Wukong said, "In that case you are not going to come out of this well." He collected the rope, and turning it into a needle, put it back into his ear.

Bajie panicked, and said, "All right. I will get the body. But I think you are really trying to make a fool of me."

Later, Bajie went back to the temple with the dead body. Intent on getting even with Sun Wukong, he told Sanzang, "Now here is the dead king, and Wukong is able to bring him back to life." Sanzang, believing Bajie, said, "Wukong, bring him back alive."

Sun Wukong said he did not know how, but Bajie said, "He is lying. If you chanted the ring-tightening mantra, he will bring the dead king back to life all right."

Sanzang chanted the mantra. Crying in pain, Sun Wukong said, "Don't chant! I will bring him back to life." In reality, Sun Wukong did not know how, so he flew up to the Heavenly Palace and went to Laotse's temple.

Laotse asked, "What are you doing here, you pill-stealing monkey?" Sun Wukong said he had come to ask for help to bring a dead king back to life, explaining what had transpired. Laotse told him bluntly, "I cannot help."

"You are the only hope I have," Sun Wukong pleaded. "You say you cannot help. Will you let me check out your ovens?"

Laotse was alarmed, for he knew how Sun Wukong could cause mischief. So Laotse agreed to give Sun Wukong one pill which could be put into the mouth of the dead king.

Sun Wukong took the pill and returned to the temple where Sanzang and others were waiting. Sanzang put the pill into the king's mouth. Right away, there came a gurgling sound. The king's mouth and eyes started to move, but he was not breathing.

Bajie was going to give him a mouth-to-mouth resuscitation, but Sanzang stopped him. "Your breath is contaminated by your eating of meat and fish. You should not give your breath. It should be Wukong who eats only fruits and vegetables."

Sun Wukong administered the mouth-to-mouth resuscitation, and the king started to breathe. The king rose up, then knelt to the pilgrims, saying, "I owe my life to you. I am grateful. Let us return to the palace."

They left the temple and traveled to the capital, with the king disguised as one of the pilgrims. They went to the palace to have their passports stamped. When they went to the throne room, the magic maker said, "Who is the fourth escort? He is the only one that does not look extraordinary."

Sun Wukong explained, "This is the real king whom you killed three years ago. You are a pretender. We are here to expose your sordid crimes."

The magic maker ordered the palace guards to come attack the pilgrims, but Sun Wukong pointed his finger at them and commanded, "Freeze." And all of them froze into icicles.

Sun Wukong then took out his stick from his ear, made it into the usual size and attacked the magic maker. The magic maker was no match for him. So he flew away, chased by Sun Wukong. But the magic maker then wheeled around, flew down, and turned himself into Sanzang.

When Sun Wukong came down after him, he saw two Sanzangs, both shouting, "Wukong, do not hit me." Sun Wukong was confused, and did not know which Sanzang was the real one. Bajie suggested that the real Sanzang would know the ring-tightening mantra. Sun Wukong asked for the mantra to be chanted.

The first Sanzang mumbled something, and it did not cause any pain. Sun Wukong knew that this was the fake one, and lifted his stick to hit him. At this, the fake Sanzang reverted to his original shape and flew into the sky, again followed by Sun Wukong. Sun Wukong was about to finish him off, when there was a voice in the sky, "Wukong, that's enough. Give back my ride."

Sun Wukong looked up, and saw the Bodhisattva Manjushree. The Bodhisattva said, "You see, when I was passing by this place some years ago, the king did not like my lecture, and soaked me in water for three days. So I punished him by having my elephant come down and have him soaked in the well for three years."

Sun Wukong said, "That is very nice, but your elephant usurped the throne, took over as king, and generally fooled the people."

Manjushree said, "No. He ruled with wisdom and the country was well governed for the three years."

Sun Wukong said, "Yes, but how about the imperial wives he abused?"

Manjushree said, "No. You see, the elephant was spayed."

Sun Wukong said, "I believe you, but now I am going to restore the king to his throne."

At this, Manjushree had nothing left to say, and returned to his abode.

The king now reclaimed his throne and rejoined his family. Grateful, he knelt to them and said, "I owe everything to you. Please accept my offer to give you half of my kingdom and stay to rule the land with me."

Sanzang said, "Our mission to obtain the sutras is paramount. We cannot accept your generous offer."

They returned to the palace, and the king happily rejoined his family. After a few days, the pilgrims took leave of the king and went their way.

◎ CHAPTER 3 ◎
Sun Wukong Gets Burned by the Red Infant

The pilgrims journeyed for a few weeks in peace. When they came to a large mountain, Sanzang said, "This mountain looks ominous. Perhaps there is a demon there?" Sun Wukong wondered too, and then quickly added, "Don't be so nervous. I will protect you."

Sanzang was still worried, so Sun Wukong decided to go and find out. Well, it turned out that there was a cave named 'Fire Cloud Cave' occupied by a demon in the mountain, one who had also heard about the benefits of eating Sanzang's flesh. However, the demon was wary of the abilities of Sun Wukong, so he decided to resort to a ruse.

Wukong returned from his investigations and said, "There

seems to be a demon, but maybe we could just pass this mountain quietly without provoking him." Just then, they heard a child calling, "Help, help!"

Sanzang said, "This sounds like a child calling for help. We must help."

Sun Wukong said, "No, this is the demon's trick. Do not be misled. Let's go."

Sanzang was not sure, but decided to trust Sun Wukong this time. Sun Wukong used 'land-shrinking mantra' to make the distance shrink by a hundred times, and they passed through the mountain in no time. The demon was annoyed. "This Sun Wukong is something else," he thought. "But I am not going to give up so easily."

The demon again turned into a child, bound and hanging from a branch of a tree by the roadside. Again, he called out for help. Sun Wukong again saw through the ruse, and tried to persuade Sanzang to keep moving.

This time Sanzang did not listen to Sun Wukong. He approached the child, and asked what the problem was.

The child said, "I am from the nearby village, and my family is very well to do. Yesterday some bandits robbed my house and killed my father. My mother escaped with me, but the bandits caught up. My mother pleaded with them to spare me. They bound me up and left me here to die, and took my mother somewhere."

Sanzang asked Bajie to untie the child, and asked Sun Wukong to carry him on his back. Sun Wukong was preparing to throw the child on the ground, when the child's spirit slipped away into thin air, leaving only the body of a child sitting on Sun Wukong's back but weighing a thousand tons.

Sun Wukong laughed. "This cheap trick is nothing. Let me throw this baggage on the ground." He threw the child down, turning it into a meatball, and flew up to chase the demon. The demon quickly hid in the Fire Cloud Cave.

Sun Wukong summoned the gods of the mountain and lands who came to him and said, "Sir, what is your command?"

Sun Wu Kong went down to challenge the [Red Infant] demon, which again blew fire at him.

Sun Wukong asked them who this demon was. They said, "His name is Red Infant. He is the son of the Buffalo King, and he has learned to master the magic fire."

Sun Wukong said, "The Buffalo King had sworn to be a brother to me while I was running the monkey kingdom. So this demon is really my nephew. Maybe I can try to persuade him to return my Master to me."

Sun Wukong dismissed the gods, and went to the cave.

Meanwhile, the Red Infant arranged five vehicles in accordance with the five elements of the universe – metal, wood, water, fire and earth. Sun Wukong approached the cave, the demon emerged, and as they fought, the demon inhaled a strong wind and then exhaled fire from where he was standing, next to the vehicle of fire. This was so strong that, even Sun Wukong could not stand the heat.

While Sun Wukong was busy trying escape the fire, the demon flew down to Sanzang, who was also being blinded by the fire, along with Bajie and Sandy. The demon snatched Sanzang and took him back into the cave. Sun Wukong came back to where Bajie and Sandy were to discover that the Master was gone.

To counter the Red infant's fire, Sun Wukong decided to go ask for the Dragon King's help. He went to the palace of the Dragon King of the Eastern Ocean and asked the Dragon King to send the rain-making troops to help. The Dragon King was reluctant to help without sanction from the Jade Emperor, but Sun Wukong said this was for a good cause and that they were not really making rain but helping quench a fire.

Reluctantly, the Dragon King agreed and sent his rain-making troops, holding millions of gallons of water.

Sun Wukong went down to challenge the demon, which again blew fire at him. Sun Wukong gave the signal to the rain-making troops who released torrents of water to quench the fire, but it turned out that the demon's fire was a fire of the Taiji, and could be quenched by ordinary water.

Burning hot, Sun Wukong tried to cool himself by jumping into a stream, and the resulting change in temperature caused him to asphyxiate. Bajie saw Sun Wukong faint, and he quickly massaged his chest, hoping to revive him.

◉ CHAPTER 4 ◉
KUANYIN TAMES THE RED INFANT

When he came to, Sun Wukong said, "This demon is strong. I think we should ask Kuanyin to help us."

Bajie asked, "But why would she come to our rescue?"

Sun Wukong said, "She promised us that if we had any trouble, our call for help would be heard in heaven and earth, and help would come. Now we are in trouble, and I have mobilized the Dragon King to no avail. It is time to ask for Kuanyin to come. But I am burnt and tired, and cannot do my somersault. Bajie, you must go to the South Sea Kuanyin Mountain to ask her."

Bajie said, "I have never been there. And I don't know the protocol there. What should I do once I get there?"

Sun Wukong told him just to explain what happened. As Bajie left, the demon saw him flying south, and knew he was going to seek Kuanyin's help. The clever demon then flew ahead of Bajie and turned himself into the shape of Kuanyin.

When Bajie came upon the demon, he thought he was seeing Kuanyin, so he knelt and explained the trouble the pilgrims were in.

The demon said, "Very well, let me help you." And they returned towards the Fire Cloud Cave.

As they approached the cave, the demon took out a magic bag, and put Bajie into it, and took him into the cave. Sun Wukong and Sandy were waiting for Bajie's return, when there was a wind that blew over them.

Sun Wukong said, "This is a bad wind. I smell it. I think Bajie has been captured." So he went to the cave where the small elves reported to the demon that Sun Wukong had returned.

This time, Sun Wukong was feeling sick, so he gave the fight a slip, and turned himself into a fly and flew into the cave.

There he found Bajie, grumbling, "What a sly demon! Changing himself into Kuanyin and capturing me. Wait till the real Kuanyin comes."

Sun Wukong now understood what had happened. The demon came back in, and told his elves, "I want to invite my father to come and enjoy the flesh of Sanzang with me. You take this note to him and ask him to come."

When Sun Wukong heard this, he flew out of the cave, went in the direction of the Buffalo King's cave, and turned himself into the Buffalo King. Soon the elf came by and, when he saw the Buffalo King, presented the note to him.

Sun Wukong, in the form of the Buffalo King, expressed pleasure in accepting the invitation, and came to the cave with the elf. The demon knelt and welcomed his father in, and said he had Sanzang in captivity and would like to share the flesh with his father.

Sun Wukong said, "But my son, is this not the Sage who is protected by Sun Wukong?"

The demon said yes, and Sun Wukong said, "Be careful. This Sun Wukong is extremely resourceful and strong. I know him because I was one of the twelve that swore to be blood brothers with him. Some five hundred years ago."

The demon said, "Father, do not over praise my enemy and downplay my own strength. By now that Sun Wukong is either dead of wounded, and will not be able to fight me."

The demon then proposed they start cooking Sanzang and eat his flesh.

Sun Wukong said, "My son, I would be delighted to enjoy the meal, but today happens to be my day of abstinence. I cannot eat meat."

This aroused the suspicion of the demon and, excusing himself, he went to ask the messenger elf whether he had indeed gone to the Buffalo King's cave.

The elf said that he met the Buffalo King half way, and the demon was convinced that the man sitting in his guestroom was not his father.

The demon went back to Sun Wukong, and said, "It's all right, but we can also celebrate my birthday. Do you remember my birthday?"

Thinking quickly, Sun Wukong said, "I ordinarily remember it, but today I am a bit dazed and tired."

This didn't work. The demon shouted at him, "You are a fake!" and took a sword and slashed at Sun Wukong.

Sun Wukong also reverted to himself and they fought on, but he was tired and weak, so he again gave the fight a slip, and hurriedly flew over to the South Sea Kuanyin Mountain. When Sun Wukong explained what happened, Kuanyin said, "You should have come to me earlier."

Sun Wukong said, "But I wanted to deal with our own troubles myself, before bothering you. This time, the demon's fire was really difficult to deal with. I sent Bajie to come for you, but the demon took your form and deceived Bajie, and captured him."

Kuanyin was annoyed that the demon had the temerity to assume her form. She took her vase and threw it into the sea. The vase sank in the water and then floated up again.

She said, "Wukong, go get it for me." Sun Wukong went down, but he could not lift it. He said, "I don't know what's in it, but I cannot lift it."

Kuanyin said, "It contains the essence of the four seas. This is powerful enough to extinguish the demon's fire. But it may be too heavy for you." She then took thirty-six swords and implanted them into her lotus flower stool. Sitting on it, she and Sun Wukong flew together to the Fire Cloud Cave, and Sun Wukong went ahead to challenge the demon.

The demon came out and blew his fire at Sun Wukong. This time, Kuanyin dipped the willow branch into the vase and sprayed it on the fire, extinguishing it.

The demon asked Kuanyin, "Who are you? Did you come to help the monkey?" Kuanyin did not answer. The demon asked again, "Did the monkey ask you to come?" And again Kuanyin did not answer.

The demon then took his spear and jabbed at Kuanyin, but she turned into a brilliant light and disappeared, leaving behind her lotus flower stool.

Sun Wukong said, "Ma'am, that looks bad, running away and leaving your own seat behind."

Kuanyin said, "Let's see what he does with it."

The demon found the beautiful stool, and sat on it as if it was his booty. The thirty-six swords stabbed into the demon's body, causing him to bleed and be in pain. He tried pulling them out but the swords turned into hooks and would not come off.

Kuanyin said, "Now, if you will surrender and accept the teaching of the Buddha, I will forgive you."

The demon cried, "Yes, yes. I will obey." Kuanyin made the swords to fall off the demon's body and Hui-an collected them all.

No longer in pain, the crafty demon took up his spear again and made a rush at Kuanyin. Kuanyin then took out a golden ring, and threw it at the demon, saying, "Change!" and "Stick!" The ring changed into five rings and attached themselves on the demon's head, two arms and two legs. Then Kuanyin chanted the ring-tightening mantra, and the demon rolled on the ground, screaming with pain.

Kuanyin said to the demon, "Now will you accept the discipline of our teaching?"

The demon, writhing in pain, said, "Yes, yes, I obey."

Kuanyin turned to Sun Wukong, "Now go and release your Master. I am taking this new disciple home."

Sun Wukong went into the cave, released Sanzang and Bajie, and they kowtowed to Kuanyin in gratitude.

◙ CHAPTER 5 ◙
The Black Water Demon Captures Sanzang

The pilgrims traveled on. They came to a river where the water was pitch black and the waves were very rough. Sanzang said with a sigh, "Now what? It seems that the road to the Western Heaven is still full of obstacles. I wonder whether we are going to run into another demon."

Sun Wukong laughed, "You should not worry. Leave the demons and monsters to me. Just keep up your spiritual serenity and sense of piety."

Sun Wukong next turned to Bajie and asked, "How about you, Bajie? Why don't you carry the Master across?"

Bajie said, "No, I can fly over but the Master has a human body. I cannot carry him."

Suddenly, a small boat came from upstream. Sanzang called out, "Ahoy there! Please come and give us passage."

The boatman said, "My boat is too small for all of you. But I can take two at a time."

Sun Wukong thought about it, and decided that Bajie should accompany Sanzang in the first crossing. So Bajie and Sanzang went on board, and the boat started to cross.

Halfway through, the boat capsized and disappeared into a wave. Sun Wukong knew right away this was the doing of a demon.

Sandy offered, "I can go in there to find out."

Sun Wukong warned, "This water looks ominous. Are you sure you can go in?"

Sandy said, "It is no worse than the quicksand river where I lived. Sure I can go."

Sandy took his stick and went into the water. At the bottom of the river he found a building with a sign saying 'Residence of Water God, the Black Water River'.

Sandy shouted, "Open the door."

A demon came out, yelling, "Who are you, making trouble here?"

Sandy said, "You have captured my Master and brother. Release them and you will be forgiven."

The demon said sneeringly, "So I took your Master. And if you don't get lost, you will be the next."

The two started to fight. Sandy pretended to be losing

and gradually withdrew towards the surface of the river so Sun Wukong could finish him off. But the demon did not pursue him. Sandy returned to the river bank, and told Sun Wukong what happened.

◎ CHAPTER 6 ◎
The Dragon King Tames the Black Water Demon

Sun Wukong and Sandy were wondering about the next move when an old man appeared from the waves and said, "The Grand Fairy, please help me."

Sun Wukong asked him who he was, and he said, "I am the god of this river. A few years ago this demon came and occupied my palace and chased me away. He is now ruling this river and causing a great deal of harm to the fish and people. I cannot fulfill my duty of looking after my subjects."

Sun Wukong asked who this demon was, and the god said, "He is the son of the Dragon King of the River Jing. Remember? The dragon, who was beheaded by Minister Wei Zeng for mixing up the amount of rain and the timing of the rain? He is the nephew of the Dragon King of the Western Ocean."

Sun Wukong said, "Then I shall go and see his uncle." He flew over to the western ocean and went into the palace of the Dragon King, where he was received by the Dragon King himself.

Sun Wukong said, "Your nephew has turned into a demon in the Black Water River, and is causing a lot of harm. He even chased away the god of the river. Now he has captured my Master. You should do something about it."

The Dragon King was mortified. He was afraid of Sun Wukong's anger. He said, "This young fellow was the son of my sister, who was married to the Dragon King of the River Jing. After his father was beheaded for his disobedience, my widowed sister came to live with me. But he was unruly, so I banished him there and told him to behave himself and learn more about Buddhism. Obviously he has not done so. I will send my son, the

Crown Prince, to capture him and bring him back here."

The Crown Prince led an army of sea creatures and came with Sun Wukong to the Black Water River. The demon came out and saw the Crown Prince.

"Cousin," shouted the demon, "what brings you here?"

The Crown Prince answered, "You idiot! You don't know how much trouble you are in. Do you realize that you have just captured the Sage who has the blessings of the Buddha, and his first disciple is the famous hero, the Heavenly Grand Fairy? Release the Sage quickly and go with me back to our palace. Otherwise you will be punished."

The demon said, "I am not about to give up what I have got."

So the Crown Prince ordered his army to attack. They quickly defeated the demon and captured him.

Turning to Sun Wukong, the Crown Prince said, "Sir, I have done what my father sent me to do. I take your leave."

Sun Wukong thanked him, went into the palace to relieve the Master, and came out to the river bank. The god of the river came to them, kowtowing, and offered to stop the river from flowing. So the pilgrims walked the river bed across to the other side.

◙ CHAPTER 7 ◙
THE MONKS OF CHECHI KINGDOM
ENSLAVED BY DEMONS

The pilgrims left the river, and the travel was easy and the landscape pleasant and agreeable, with majestic mountains, bubbling rivers, beautiful trees, flowers, and birds.

One day they saw some light in a distance. Sanzang said, "This does look quite nice. I believe it is not like a place of demons."

Sun Wukong, careful as always, said, "Let me go and find out."

Sun Wukong flew over, and came upon a large number of monks working in hard labour. He changed himself into an itinerant Taoist and went up to the Taoist acolyte who was supervising the work.

Sun Wukong introduced himself as an itinerant Taoist and asked what was going on. The acolyte said, "I am responsible for seeing the monks do not slack off or run away. We have painted images shots of all of them so if they should run away, they will surely be captured."

The acolyte told Sun Wukong that, twenty years ago, there was a serious drought and the monk's prayers were not effective in bringing the rain. At the time, three Taoist priests came and immediately called the rain to help the farmers.

The three were named Tiger-power Fairy, Deer-power Fairy, and Goat-power Fairy. The king was grateful, and accorded the three the highest position in the country, and banished the monks and made them the slaves of the three.

Sun Wukong said, "The purpose of my journey is to find enlightenment, and to find my relatives. My relatives may be amongst the monks. If I find them, will you let me take them with me?"

The acolyte agreed. "You have come from far away. As a brother monk, the least we can do is to accommodate your need."

Sun Wukong then approached the monks. He asked one of them what they were doing, and the monk said, "We are monks from this country. A few years ago there was a serious drought, and all of us prayed for rain without success. Three Taoist priests came and managed to produce the rain. The king, who had been disappointed by our inability to produce rain, decided to ban Buddhism. He destroyed all temples, and gave us to these three as slaves. That is why we are labouring here on their construction project."

Sun Wukong suggested, "Why don't you run away?"

"No. They have our pictures. No one can escape."

"Then what?" asked Sun Wukong. "Do you just work and die here?"

"Oh, many have died," answered the monk, "some died of disease, and others have killed themselves. But some of us, we are keeping ourselves alive because we have been told in our dreams by the God of the Northstar that one day the Heavenly Grand Fairy Sun Wukong will come to our rescue."

Sun Wukong was surprised, and said, "I am Sun Wukong."

The monks were skeptical, and said, "No, you do not look like him. The God of the Northstar said that he has a monkey's face, fiery eyes with golden pupils, his mouth like that of Garuda (large mythical bird), and he uses a magic stick. He can fly one hundred and eight thousand miles in an instant, and has mastered seventy-two supernatural tricks."

Sun Wukong was flattered by this and said, "Your saviour is here."

The monks, only seeing Sun Wukong in his form of an itinerant Taoist, still did not believe him.

Sun Wukong then revealed his original form, and the monks knelt and cried out, "O saviour, help us."

Sun Wukong said, "Now I want you all to just leave this place. I will deal with the Taoists."

Sun Wukong pulled a handful of hair, chewed them into smaller pieces, and spitting out, called, "Guard." He handed one piece of hair to each of the monks, and said, "If you are in danger, just say 'Grand Heavenly Fairy' and I will come to protect you. At the end, when you are no longer in danger, just say 'End' and the hair will come back to me."

The monks, throwing away their sickles, hoes, picks and other implements, dispersed. Sun Wukong then went to the two acolytes there and told them, "You know, all five hundred monks are my relatives. So I want you to let them all go."

The acolytes said, "Don't be silly. How can you have so many relatives?"

"Well," Sun Wukong replied, "one hundred are my neighbours on the right, one hundred are neighbours on the left, one hundred are on my mother's side, and one hundred on my father's side, and another one hundred are my adopted sworn blood brothers."

The acolytes, annoyed by this frivolity, refused. Sun Wukong then took out his magic stick and beat them into meat balls.

Meanwhile, Sanzang was becoming a bit worried that Sun

Wukong had not returned from looking around. He and the others continued on their way west, when they saw Sun Wukong with a few of the monks. Sun Wukong explained what happened, and proposed to go into the capital. There they found a Buddhist temple that had survived the earlier destruction because it had been built by the current king's father. The monks received them and gave them food and lodging.

◎ CHAPTER 8 ◎
SUN WUKONG, BAJIE AND SANDY ENJOY THE FEAST DISGUISED AS DEITIES

Near midnight, Sun Wukong decided not to sleep because he wanted to find out some more about the three Taoist priests. He changed into a small bird and flew to the Taoist temple.

There was a lot of commotion. The priests were performing ceremonies to offer food and incense to Taoist deities - Laotse, God of the Origin of the Universe, and the God of Supernatural Jade.

Sun Wukong flew back to the temple, and woke up Bajie and Sandy. "Wake up, there is a feast going on. Let's go and enjoy the food."

Bajie complained, "This is near midnight. Where is the feast?"

Sandy added, "Moreover, we are not invited."

Sun Wukong reassured them. "Don't worry. I will handle it. Let's go, but don't awaken the Master."

They went to the Taoist shrine where the ceremony was still going on.

Bajie said, "They are still at it. How long are we going to have to wait?"

Sun Wukong said, "Watch!" He sucked the air from the direction of north, and blew towards the shrine.

Soon there was a fierce wind blowing over the shrine, with tree and rocks flying all around. Tiger-power Fairy said, "Well, this wind is too much. Let's call it a night." And they left the shrine to go to their home next door.

Sun Wukong, Bajie and Sandy went into the shrine, and Bajie immediately proceeded to eat. Sun Wukong said, "Wait. We have to assume the form of their deities before we eat. We have also to remove the three statues and dispose of them."

Bajie asked, "Where do you propose we take these statues?"

Sun Wukong said, "I see there is a place to recycle the food. Let's put them in there."

The three statues of the deities were thrown into the septic tank. Then the three started to eat the offerings, laughing and talking.

One of the acolytes had forgotten his pot, and he returned to the shrine. When he entered the altar room, he heard Sun Wukong and his friends laughing and chatting. He became frightened, and rushed back and reported to the three priests.

"I went back to the shrine and heard the three deities laughing and talking while they were eating the offerings."

Intrigued, the priests said, "Perhaps the deities have heard our prayers and decided to grace our shrine and accept our offerings. Let's go and have a look."

The priests went to the shrine where Sun Wukong and his friends were still eating. The priests saw them in the form of the deities and said, "O venerable Gods, you have deigned to accept our humble offerings. Now bless us further by giving us some magic pills or magic potions which we could offer to our king."

Sun Wukong said, "We have just come from the Jade Emperor's Peach Party, and do not have any pills with us. Perhaps next time."

The three priests were very persistent. "O venerable deities, hear our appeal and grant us something, anything."

Sun Wukong decided to play a dirty trick, so he said, "Leave thee vessels and we will give you some magic potions. But you must leave this altar room, as the Heavenly Secret must be protected."

When they left the room, Sun Wukong said to Bajie and Sandy, "Take the pots, and pee in them." So they relieved themselves and Sun Wukong called the priests to come back in the room.

The priests took the pots, and took a sip from them. Tiger-power Fairy said, "This tastes funny." Deer-power fairy said, "It smells funny." And Goat-power fairy said, "It tastes like pee."

Sun Wukong decided to tell them who he was.

"You perverse demons!" he shouted, "we are pilgrims on our way to the Western Heaven to obtain the true teachings of the Buddha. I am the Grand Heavenly Fairy Sun Wukong. If you have heard of me, you should tremble in fear. Now we are leaving, having eaten your food and having given you our piss." And the three revealed their original form and flew away.

◙ CHAPTER 9 ◙

ENCOUNTER WITH TIGER, DEER AND GOAT DEMONS

The next day the pilgrims went to the palace and asked for their passports to be stamped. The king was about to stamp the documents when the three Taoist priests came in, and seeing the pilgrims, they cried, "Here! These are the villains who played a trick on us. Your majesty, they are evil monks. They killed my two acolytes, stole our offerings at the shrine, and then peed into our pot. Do not let them go."

Sun Wukong said, "There is neither proof that we killed your acolytes nor that we stole your food. As for peeing into your pots, why, that was done in your shrine. If you say that we did all that you say we did, why did you not arrest us on the spot? Besides, your majesty, these three are demons. I can show you what they really are."

As they were arguing, there came sounds of a commotion. The guards came in to report that some very loud farmers had arrived demanding that the Taoist priests bring rain.

Sun Wukong said, "Here is the opportunity to show who the real god is. Your majesty, why don't you get these three to call for rain? If they cannot do it, you will know that they are fakes. Then we will bring you rain."

The king thought this a good idea and agreed.

Tiger-power Fairy went up the altar and chanted the mantra for rain, and the sky was covered with clouds.

Sun Wukong pulled his hair and said, "Change," and it changed into Sun Wukong himself. The real Sun Wukong then went up to the sky, shouting, "Who is in charge of the clouds?"

The Cloud Roller hurriedly came and reported to him. Sun Wukong said, "These are demons down below. You should not bring the clouds for them. Wait here and I will give you a signal. You can then roll the clouds." The Cloud Roller agreed.

The sky suddenly cleared, and the Tiger-power Fairy was helpless. Then he chanted the mantra for thunder, and there was thunder and lightning. Sun Wukong, still in the sky, shouted, "Where is the Thunder God?"

When the thunder God came to him, Sun Wukong said, "Do not help the demons. Wait for my signal." Suddenly, all the lightning and thunder stopped.

Tiger-power fairy chanted the mantra for rain, but Sun Wukong again stopped the rain from falling.

So the Tiger-power Fairy was revealed as incapable of bringing rain. Sun Wukong, coming down and retrieving the hair, said to the King, "You see your priest is useless. Now let me show you what I can do."

Sun Wukong raised his magic stick once, and the cloud rolled in, twice, and there was thunder and lightning. The third time the rain came down.

◎ CHAPTER 10 ◎

THE CONTESTS AGAINST THE THREE DEMONS

Unwilling to accept defeat, Deer-power Fairy said, "Let them compete with us another way. They are monks. Let us compete to see who can sit in the lotus position and meditate longer."

Sun Wukong said, "Well, I am not too good with that, but

Master, this is right up your alley. Why don't you accept the challenge?"

Sanzang said, "I can sit for hours without any problem. I'm willing to volunteer for this."

Tiger-power Fairy then set up a platform consisting of one hundred tables piled on top of one another, going up three hundred feet. He then went up by riding cloud, and sat there in lotus position.

Sanzang could not fly, but Sun Wukong held him and raised him to his platform. A few hours into the contest, Tiger-power Fairy released a flea, which flew to Sanzang and bit his neck. Sanzang felt the itch, but could not scratch, as the rules did not allow any movement of arms and other limbs.

Sun Wukong saw the Master's agonized face and knew something was wrong. He flew to Sanzang without being seen, found the flea, crushed it, and scratched the Master's itchy spots. Sanzang felt perfectly composed once more, and ready to go on for many more hours.

Knowing this to be the Tiger-power Fairy's dirty trick, Sun Wukong decided to repay him. He flew over to Tiger-power Fairy, turned into a huge centipede, crawled to his face, and bit him hard on the nose.

Tiger-power Fairy could not maintain his composure, and he fell to the ground. Sun Wukong declared victory and asked, "Will you now stamp our documents and let us go?"

Tiger-power Fairy said, "Not so fast. There are other ways to compete. We can guess the contents of a box without seeing it. Can you do the same?"

Tiger-power Fairy asked the king to put something into the box, and the king placed a new robe inside the box. Sun Wukong changed into a termite and ate his way into the box, then tore up the robe and put dirt on it. He then flew to Sanzang's ear and told him to guess the contents to be a dirty rag.

Deer-power Fairy said, "Inside the box is a new robe."

Sanzang waited for his turn and said, "It is a dirty rag."

The king said to Sanzang, "You lost. I myself placed a new

robe inside the box."

Sun Wukong said, "Open it up and see."

The king opened the box, and they found a dirty rag. Everyone was dumbfounded, but Deer-power Fairy said, "Try another time."

The King put a peach inside, and Sun Wukong went into the box and ate up the peach, leaving only the stone behind. He flew over to Sanzang and said, "It is the seed of a peach."

Bajie laughed and commented, "You're certainly an expert at eating a peach!"

When the box was presented, Deer-power Fairy said, "It's a peach."

Sanzang said, "No, it's just a seed."

The king was dubious, and Sun Wukong urged him, "Open it and see."

When the box was opened, they were astounded to find the seed. Deer-power Fairy shouted in desperation, "One more time!"

The king put an acolyte into a big box. Sun Wukong went into the box in the form of a senior Taoist priest and told the acolyte to shave his head. He also gave him a sutra to chant, then flew to Sanzang and told him that inside the box there was a monk.

The box was brought to them and Deer-power Fairy said, "It's a Taoist acolyte."

Again Sanzang disagreed. "No," he said, "it's a child monk." When the box was opened, they found a small monk with shaved head, chanting a sutra.

Sun Wukong said, "See, these priests are useless. Now please stamp our documents and let us go west."

The three priests told the king that they should be given another chance to compete. The king, being weak, urged the pilgrims to compete further.

Sun Wukong said, "We are not afraid. What would you like us to compete for?" The priests said, "We can survive beheading, we can be disemboweled, and you may throw us into a vat of boiling oil."

Sun Wukong said, "Great! That is perfectly up my alley. Let's do it."

The king asked who would go first. Sun Wukong said, "If you don't mind, let me go first."

An executioner came and chopped off Sun Wukong's head and kicked the head away. But there wasn't even a single drop of blood. Sun Wukong said, "Head, come back."

But the Tiger-power Fairy summoned the god of the land to hold the head, and Sun Wukong could not retrieve the head. So he grew another head from inside his torso.

Sandy was amazed. "I wonder how many heads he has?" he asked.

Bajie answered calmly, "At least seventy-two, since he knows seventy-two supernatural tricks."

Now it was the turn of Tiger-power Fairy. As the executioner chopped off his head and kicked it away, Sun Wukong changed into a dog and, grabbing the head in his mouth, ran way.

Tiger-power Fairy could not retrieve his head, but he could not grow another one like Sun Wukong. After a short struggle, he died, and his corpse turned into that of a dead tiger.

Now Deer-power Fairy asked, "Do you dare have your belly cut open and the entrails taken out?"

Sun Wukong said coolly, "Fine. Let me go first," and he cut open his belly and pulled out the entrails, saying, "Ah! It feels good to take these entrails out to have some fresh air." He then put them back in and closed the wound, without a single drop of blood anywhere.

When Deer-power Fairy cut his stomach open, Sun Wukong changed into an eagle and grabbed the intestines, livers and kidneys and flew away. Deer-power Fairy struggled for a while, and finally succumbed, turning into a dead deer.

It was Goat-power's turn. A huge vat filled with boiling oil was prepared. This time, Sun Wukong said, "I have not had a warm bath for some time. Let me go in first."

Sun Wukong took off his robe and jumped into the vat, and appeared to be having a good time in it, scrubbing his body and

Sun Wukong took off his robe and jumped into the vat, and was having a good time in it, rubbing his body and humming songs.

humming songs. Of course, he was unaffected by the hot boiling oil. After all, he had survived the heavenly fire inside the oven of Laotse.

After a while, Sun Wukong jumped out, and said to Goat-power Fairy, "Your turn, sir." Goat-power Fairy did not hesitate. He also jumped into the vat, and was unaffected. Surprised, Sun Wukong peered inside the vat and saw a creature, an Icy Dragon, embracing Goat-power Fairy.

Sun Wukong immediately flew up to the sky and called out, "Hey, Dragon King of the Northern Ocean, where are you?" The Dragon King came crawling to Sun Wukong, saying, "Sir, what is your command?"

Sun Wukong commanded, "Withdraw the Icy Dragon right away; you are helping the evil demon." The Dragon King ordered the Icy Dragon to leave the vat right away.

At this, Goat-power Fairy started screaming in agony, and in no time he was dead, fried into a dead goat.

The king was now in shock. Sanzang said, "Now you see that these were nothing but the demons of three beasts. What you should do is to adopt the teachings of the Buddha. Then your kingdom will prosper and be at peace for ever."

The king issued an edict pardoning the monks and releasing them from slavery. The monks came out of the woodwork, and approached Sun Wukong, kowtowing.

Sun Wukong retrieved his hair, and told them that they were free. Finally, after having their documents stamped, the pilgrims left for the west.

◙ CHAPTER 11 ◙
Crossing the Trans-Heaven River

The journey was pleasant, with spring flowers blooming, the air balmy, and birds singing. Then the pilgrims came upon a big river. Sanzang said, "This is a very big river. I wonder how deep it is."

Bajie said, "You can tell by throwing a stone into it. If it splashes, then it is not deep. But if it sinks without a splash, then it is deep."

Bajie picked a stone and threw it, and the stone sank. Bajie cried out, "It's deep, it's deep."

Sun Wukong said, "Let me size up how wide it is." He rose to the sky and cast his eyes around. "It is at least a hundred miles wide. I can barely see the other side."

Sanzang saw something at the riverbank and wondered if it was someone standing there. Sun Wukong went over and saw that it was a stone stele, bearing the sign 'Trans Heaven River: One Hundred Miles Wide. Few Have Crossed It Successfully'.

This had Sanzang worried since it would be difficult to cross.

Sun Wukong assured him, "Don't worry too much. It's getting late. Let's find a lodging and tomorrow morning we will figure out how to cross."

There was a village near the river, so Sanzang went there to ask for lodging. When he knocked on the door, the servant who opened the door was scared out of his wits to see the three disciples' faces.

"O my goodness, these are monsters. Have mercy on me!" shrieked the servant, and started to run away. Sanzang tugged on his sleeve and said, "Please do not be alarmed. These are not monsters; they are my disciples. We are pilgrims on our way to the west to get the sutra of the Buddha's true teachings. We just want to ask for a night's lodging."

The servant said, "You look like a decent human, but your disciples look like monsters."

Sun Wukong said, "Don't be fooled by appearances. We may not be very handsome, but we are good monks, and we know how to kill monsters and demons."

The servant, somewhat calmed, let them in. They were introduced to the head of the household, who said, "My surname is Chen."

Sanzang replied, "My name was also Chen before I became a

monk. So we share the same ancestry."

As they were talking, there was a sudden gust of wind shaking the tiles on the roof. Sanzang wondered, "This is unusual. Do you get this often?"

Old Chen said, "This is the King of Divine Sense flying over us."

Sun Wukong asked, "And who is this King of Divine Perception? Why is he flying over us now?"

Old Chen burst into tears and said, "He is here to make sure that I will offer my son and my brother will offer his daughter for him to eat. The sacrificial ceremony is supposed to take place tonight."

"What? Why? Who is this monster?" Sun Wukong exclaimed.

Old Chen said, "He calls himself the King of Divine Sense, and he has been living in the river for the last twenty years. He told us that he would guarantee good weather for harvest and safety from bandits and thieves, but every year the village must offer one boy and one girl to him. We do not know what he does with the children, but from the blood-stained clothing that are left behind, we fear they are eaten by the King."

Sun Wukong was outraged. He said, "This is utterly criminal. Don't worry, my brothers and I will fix it for you."

Old Chen was still frightened and asked, "But what if you are not successful and then he decides to extract revenge?"

Sun Wukong explained, "So you don't know our abilities, and I don't blame you. But killing monsters is our specialty. Bring your son and daughter here. We will help you."

The two children were brought to them. Sun Wukong shook his head and changed into the boy.   The whole Chen clan was amazed.

"This is incredible, now we cannot distinguish the real boy and the transfigured one," said Old Chen.

Sun Wukong then told Bajie to change into the girl. Bajie shook his head and changed, but he only managed to change the face, leaving his body unchanged.

The Chen clan laughed, "This 'girl' has a fat body. The transformation is not complete."

Sun Wukong also laughed, and blew a wisp of supernatural breath at Bajie and the body was changed into the exact replica of the girl.

Sun Wukong then said, "Old Chen, keep your children here, and take us to the King's shrine. We will fix this monster for you."

◎ CHAPTER 12 ◎
BAJIE BEATS UP THE KING OF DIVINE SENSE

Sun Wukong and Bajie were taken to the shrine near midnight. Bajie complained, "It's getting late. When is the King of Divine Sense coming?"

"Shhh, quiet. He should be here by midnight," whispered Sun Wukong.

At midnight, there was a gust of wind, and a tall monster entered the shrine. He asked, "What is your name, boy?"

Sun Wukong answered, "I am Chen Wukong, and I am six years old."

The King of Divine Sense was surprised. "Usually the children are scared out of their minds and cannot speak," he declared. This one is a little different. Maybe I should start by eating the girl."

Bajie cried, "No, no, no. Please follow the usual routine."

Ignoring Bajie's plea, the monster grabbed his arm. Bajie, frenzied, decided to reveal himself, and hit the monster with his rake.

The monster fled in a panic, turning into a wind, but leaving behind a curious object.

"Bajie, you should have been more patient," Sun Wukong admonished. "I was about to capture him when you hit him. Now you let him get away."

They examined the object the King of Divine Sense had left

behind. Sun Wukong exclaimed, "This looks like the scale of a fish. The monster must be a fish."

They flew out of the shrine and found the monster in the air, smarting from his wounds. The King of Divine Sense complained, "Who are you and why are you interfering in my affairs?"

Sun Wukong replied, "You fishy monster! How dare you eat children! I will tell you who we are. We are pilgrims from Tang and we are on our way to the Western Heaven to collect the true teaching of the Buddha. And I am your master. My name is Sun Wukong, and if you know me you would kowtow to me."

Sun Wukong and Bajie attacked the King of Divine Sense, but he escaped in a swirl of wind. So they returned to the Chen household and explained what happened. The Chens were happy, and Sun Wukong and Bajie promised to finish off the monster the next day.

◙ CHAPTER 13 ◙
The King of Divine Sense Freezes the River and Captures Sanzang

The next day, the three disciples went to the river. Sun Wukong said, "Bajie and Sandy, you are much better off in the water than I, so the two of you go in to fight the monster. I will wait out here. When you lure him out, I will finish him off."

The three went back to the Chen's to discuss their strategy, while the King of Divine Sense stayed inside his fortress, moping. One of the monster's henchmen, a lobster spirit, asked him why he looked so downcast, when he was usually so happy every year after receiving the village offerings.

The King of Divine Sense told him, "This year was different. When I went to the shrine, there were two children all right, one boy and one girl, except that they were not scared at all. They even talked back when I asked them questions. When I grabbed the girl, she suddenly turned into a pig-headed monster and hit me with a rake. The two of them turned out to be pilgrims. The other fellow's name was Sun Wukong."

The lobster asked, "You mean Sun Wukong the monkey king? That is bad news. He is very powerful and tricky. Better not to confront him."

The King of Divine Sense said, "But I've heard that their Master is a holy man and anyone who eats his flesh would live a long time. How can I catch him when he is protected by so many strong and powerful disciples?"

"Master," said the lobster, "do you think you could use your power to freeze up the river?"

"Yes, I can."

"Then I believe you can capture the Sage. Just freeze the river, and when they try to walk across, crack the ice open and let them fall into the crevice, and you can capture the Sage."

The King of Divine Sense thought that was a smart idea, so he proceeded to create extremely cold weather. The river started to freeze. It took a few days before the freezing was sufficient to allow crossing the river by walking.

Meanwhile, at the Chen's the pilgrims were being treated as honoured guests. The Chens said that this freezing was unusual since it was only September. They suggested that the pilgrims wait till the ice melted, and that the Chens would provide a boat for them to cross.

They were offered feasts to enjoy the snowy scene, and it was very agreeable. But Sanzang was growing restless, and asked to leave by walking across.

Bajie said, "Let me test whether the ice is solid enough. If I hit with my rake and the ice cracks, then it is dangerous, but if not, we can cross safely."

Bajie took his rake and hit the surface of the river, and there were nine holes, without any cracks. "It's thick enough. We can walk across," he declared.

The pilgrims prepared to leave. The Chens wished the pilgrims would stay longer, but seemed resigned to let them go.

As they started to walk across the river, the King of Divine Sense saw them coming. He waited till they were half way across, and then used his power to crack the ice.

Everyone fell into the water except Sun Wukong who flew up in time. Sanzang, Bajie and Sandy fell, as did the horse. But Bajie, Sandy and the horse were used to water, and were able to deal with the situation. Only Sanzang was not used to water, and he was captured by the King of Divine Sense.

Bajie, Sandy and the horse collected their bags and came up to the surface of the ice, where Sun Wukong pulled them out. Now they made plans to go into the fortress to attack the King of Divine Sense and release the Master.

Sun Wukong said to Bajie, "I'm not very good in the water. So why don't you carry me to the underwater fortress?"

Bajie agreed, and they went down to the fortress. Sun Wukong, knowing Bajie's nature, pulled a hair and turned it into himself, and he turned into a fly and perched just behind Bajie's ear.

Sure enough, Bajie pretended to trip on a rock and threw Sun Wukong down, but since it was only Sun Wukong's hair, it just floated slowly downstream, instead of dropping to the floor of the river.

Sandy said, "Now look what you've done! You tried your dirty trick on Sun Wukong and now where is he?"

Bajie was frightened. "Where is he indeed," he asked, "don't tell me he just disappeared?"

As Bajie and Sandy were growing nervous, Sun Wukong could not resist revealing himself. He shouted into Bajie's ear, "Here I am. Now Bajie, behave yourself."

Bajie felt chastised. He kowtowed - although he could not see Sun Wukong since Sun Wukong was still perched behind his ear - and said, "Sorry, brother, I will behave myself and not play funny games with you."

Sun Wukong said, "All right. I will now go inside to find out about the Master. You wait here." He went in as an old lobster. Inside, he looked for Sanzang and found him locked inside a stone case. He went close to the case and heard Sanzang lamenting, "Woe is me. My dream of going to the West is so difficult to realize. Where is Sun Wukong? Why is he not coming to rescue me?"

Sun Wukong whispered to Sanzang, "Master, I am here. We will rescue you soon. Just wait and be patient."

Sun Wukong went out and told Bajie and Sandy that the Master was alive. He said, "I will go back out of the river, and you should challenge the King of Divine Sense to a fight. Then pretend to lose and lure him out of the water and I will then finish him off."

The two called out to the monster. The King of Divine Sense came out and the two fought him long and hard. Pretending to lose, they gradually withdrew to the surface of the river.

Sun Wukong was going to finish him, but the monster quickly escaped again, and hid inside his fortress. His lobster adviser suggested that he should not respond to any more challenges; just lock the door and wait till the pilgrims lose their patience and leave.

The King of Divine Sense agreed, and refused to accept any further challenges. Bajie and Sandy threw all kids of abuses and insults at him but he did not respond. After a while, Bajie and Sandy went back out of the river and told Sun Wukong that the monster was turning a deaf ear to their challenges.

Sun Wukong said, "In that case I can think of only one person who can help. Let me fly over to the Kuanyin Mountain."

◎ CHAPTER 14 ◎
KUANYIN RETRIEVES THE GOLD FISH IN
A BAMBOO BASKET

So Sun Wukong went, flying one hundred and eight thousand miles south to the Kuanyin Mountain where divine lights and auspicious clouds surround the magnificent mountain and the serene temple which is Kuanyin's abode. He was received by the Red Infant, who had caused Sanzang and him a lot of trouble and almost burned him to death, but now had converted and became a gentle, mature acolyte known as the Namaste Boy because he always had his palms put together in namaste (traditional South Asian greeting).

The Namaste Boy welcomed Sun Wukong and thanked him for bringing him under Kuanyin's benevolent influence. Sun Wukong asked to see Kuanyin immediately, but the Namaste Boy told him that she was bathing and not ready to see him.

Sun Wukong decided to at least tell her the problem from outside the bathroom, so he went in to the residential quarter.

He was dazzled to see Kuanyin undressed. Her supreme elegance and beauty was divine and held Sun Wukong in awe.

Kuanyin said, "I was expecting you to come. A few days ago, I noticed that a gold fish was missing and knew he had gone to Trans Heaven River. This river is in your path, so I knew he would harass you. This gold fish was kept in a pond just outside the room where I give my sermons. He used to stick his head out to listen to my sermons. After centuries of this, he acquired knowledge and wisdom and became capable of supernatural tricks. Let me go with you to collect him."

She took a bamboo basket with her, and flew off without dressing up.

When they arrived in the Trans Heaven River, Bajie and Sandy kowtowed to Kuanyin and said, "O Goddess of Mercy, please help our Master."

Sun Wukong went down to the underwater fortress and destroyed the gate. The King of Divine Sense saw he could no longer hide. As he came out to fight, Kuanyin called out, "Come back to me!" The monster obeyed, jumping into the bamboo basket and turning into a big gold fish.

All this happened so fast that Sun Wukong did not even see it. He asked Kuanyin, "Now please tame the monster."

Kuanyin was amused. She said, "Look at my bamboo basket." Sure enough, there was a big gold fish in it.

Sun Wukong then went into the underwater fortress to rescue Sanzang, who came out and kowtowed to Kuanyin in gratitude.

Sun Wukong then suggested to Kuanyin, "The family of Chen is a devout family. I believe it would help strengthen their faith if you reveal yourself to them. Will you do that for us?"

Kuanyin agreed, and Sun Wukong went to the Chen family to tell them to come out and worship Kuanyin.

As they came out, Kuanyin revealed herself, standing in the cloud above the river. Everyone was awe struck and deeply moved. There was a painter amongst them, who painted this amazing revelation. That's why the world is blessed today with a picture of Undressed Kuanyin.

Then Kuanyin returned, leaving a trace of divine cloud and more brilliant light.

◎ CHAPTER 15 ◎
Old Tortoise Ferries the Pilgrims
Across the River

The Chens were going to prepare a boat for the pilgrims to cross the river, when a voice called out from the river, "Master Sanzang! Master Sanzang!"

It was an old tortoise, with huge white carapace. Sanzang was surprised, and Sun Wukong said, "For an animal to be able to talk like humans, this tortoise must have received some divine uplifting. Let's hear what he has to say."

Sanzang asked, "How did you know me? And what do you want?"

The old tortoise said, "I am the original owner of the underwater fortress. Then the gold fish monster came and forced me out of it. He has killed many of my fish and eels, and then went on to terrorize the population on both sides of the river.

"For a long time, I had to hide and did not dare show my face. Now I heard the fighting and saw the arrival of the Goddess of Mercy. I knew that my salvation had arrived. What you have achieved not only helps the people on the river banks, but me. For that, I would like to offer to ferry you across on my back."

The pilgrims were delighted, and they got on the back of the tortoise to cross. They waved goodbye to the Chens and embarked on the crossing.

When the pilgrims arrived at the other bank, they thanked the tortoise. The tortoise said, "This is the least I can do. But I understand that you are going to see the Buddha. I understand that his mercy is limitless, and he is capable of granting higher status of being to every human and animals.

"I have meditated and studied the Buddhist teachings and tried to achieve nirvana. I have also done many good deeds. I hope I qualify for the status of a fairy. When you see the Buddha, could you inquire on my behalf whether he would be prepared to grant me the status of a fairy?"

Sanzang happily agreed to do so, and the tortoise nodded contentedly and went back into the water.

◙ CHAPTER 16 ◙
THE ONE-HORNED MONSTER WITH A
PLATINUM BRACELET

The pilgrims now journeyed in a wintry landscape, stomping over the snow and walking across icy paths. It was a wearying journey.

One day with darkness approaching and no human trace in sight, they suddenly saw a temple complex in the distance. Sanzang said, "This has been a long day. I am tired and hungry. Wukong, please go and seek a donation of some food for us. See if you can also find a place for our lodging."

Sun Wukong used his vision to examine the nature of the temple complex, and said, "I don't think that place is very good because I see some malevolent qi (flow of energy, life force). I can go elsewhere and get some food, but you should not enter that complex. I will draw a circle around you. It will protect you from any assault as long as you stay inside of it. Do not get out of it till I come back."

After Sun Wukong left, Sanzang stayed in the circle for a while, then he grew bored and said, "I am not going to stay in this prison."

Sanzang walked out of the circle, followed by Bajie and Sandy, and started towards the temple complex.

Bajie went ahead to find out about the place. He discovered a large complex with many rooms, but nobody was there.

Bajie then found a pile of skeletons on a table. Afraid, he went to other rooms, and found three vests of very warm wool. He took the vests and came back to Sanzang and Sandy, saying, "The temple looks ominous, but I found these vests. They will help keep us warm."

Sanzang said, "No. You must not take what is not yours. Take these vests back."

Bajie did not heed him, and put the vest on himself. Sandy saw how cozy and warm the vest looked, and he also put one on.

These vests quickly turned into ropes that bound the two tightly. They were panic-stricken, and started screaming.

The commotion attracted the attention of a one-horned monster who came to take them back to his temple complex.

Sanzang pleaded with him, "Please, we are pilgrims going to the west to bring back the Buddha's true teachings. We are not thieves. Do forgive the two disciples of mine, who did not know that the vests belonged to you."

The one-horned monster said, "Ah! So you are the Sage whose flesh is precious! Well, you've come to me of your own free will. That's my luck, isn't it?"

◎ CHAPTER 17 ◎
FIGHTING THE ONE-HORNED MONSTER

As Sun Wukong went to get some food donation, he ran into two old men who told him that the complex was occupied by a monster with one horn. The old men gave him some food, and then they confided, "Sir, we are the gods of the land and the mountain. We just wanted to warn you about the monster."

Sun Wukong sounded annoyed. "Why did you appear in a disguise?" he asked. "Now tell me, what kind of a monster is he?"

The gods told him the one-horned monster was very strong and full of supernatural tricks, and he ate humans.

Hearing this, Sun Wukong took the food and immediately returned to the spot where he had left the rest of his company, but by now, there was no trace of them.

Sun Wukong used his vision to look around, and saw the temple complex with dazzling demonic lights. He went there, and informed the guarding elves that he had come to rescue Sanzang.

The elves went inside to tell the one-horned monster of Sun Wukong's demand. The one-horned monster came out and asked, "Are you Sun Wukong? I did take your friends because they stole my vests. You cannot have them back unless you can defeat me."

Sun Wukong scoffed at this, "Ha! Have you any idea about my strength? Here is my stick!" and he hit him.

They fought for quite a while, without either side prevailing. The one-horned monster was impressed by Sun Wukong's prowess. "Good technique with the stick! No wonder they had problems with you at the Heavenly Palace."

The one-horned monster then ordered his troops to attack. Sun Wukong turned into a three-headed, six-armed being to continue the fight. He threw his stick in the air and commanded, "Change!" and the stick turned into thousands of sticks that rained down on the enemy troops like deadly spears.

The one-horned monster took out a platinum bracelet and shouted, "Collect!" and all the sticks got sucked into the bracelet.

Then the one-horned monster took the bracelet and went back to his cave behind the temple complex. Having lost the stick, Sun Wukong did not know what to do next. Then he recalled the one-horned monster's comment on his fighting prowess and reference to the fight he had with the Heavenly Horde. He surmised that the one-horned monster must have come from the Heavenly Palace, and decided to go up there to find out who this monster was.

The one-horned monster ordered his troops to attack, and Sun Wukong turned into a three-headed, six-armed entity to continue the fight.

Sun Wukong was received politely at the gate, and went to the throne room to ask the Jade Emperor to check on who might be absent. A thorough check was made on the gods, fairies, spirits, stars, and other heavenly officials, and no one appeared missing.

Sun Wukong then requested for a heavenly army to help. It was agreed that an army, under the command of the Tower King and his crown prince.

Sun Wukong said, "Great! This is the same army sent to fight me five hundred years ago. I hope they will have some success this time around."

They came down to the one-horned monster's cave, and the monster came out taunting, "Hey, monkey! You have lost your weapon. What are you coming to fight with?"

Sun Wukong said, "Here is my fist," and the two fought with bare fists for several hours, with the heavenly army watching entranced.

Then the heavenly army attacked, led by the crown prince, who turned into another three-headed and six-armed entity. The one-horned monster again took out his platinum bracelet and captured all the weapons.

Sun Wukong decided to go back to heaven and ask for the God of Fire to help. Together, they came down and let loose a host of fire-making instruments. Again, the one-horned monster captured all the instruments of battle with his platinum bracelet.

Sun Wukong thought, if the monster is not afraid of fire, then maybe he could be afraid of water. So he summoned the Heavenly Water God to come down. The same fate befell them as the one-horned monster used his bracelet once more.

Everyone was at a loss. Sun Wukong proposed that he should go into the cave to steal the platinum bracelet. Everybody thought that would be a good idea. "You are an expert in stealing things – the divine peaches, longevity pills and so on," they said. "This job is cut out for you."

Sun Wukong turned into a fly and went inside the cave. The one-horned monster, after celebrating his victory, was lying down to rest. He was wearing the bracelet on his upper arm.

Sun Wukong changed into a flea and bit him in the arm, hoping to make him remove the bracelet. The one-horned monster murmured, "What is this? Some insect!" and he tried to keep on sleeping, without removing the bracelet.

Sun Wukong went around and found Sanzang, Bajie, and Sandy all bound up. He assured them that they would be rescued soon. Then he found all the captured weapons and instruments. He pulled some hair and turned them into hundreds of monkeys and moved all the captured items out of the cave.

Armed with their weapons, the army renewed their attack. But they failed to prevail and again all their weapons were captured by the monster using the bracelet.

Sun Wukong said, "I believe the only one who would know who this one-horned monster is would be the Buddha himself. Only he has unlimited knowledge and wisdom. Let me go and seek his help."

The Heavenly Horde agreed to stay behind while Sun Wukong went to the Western Heaven.

When Sun Wukong flew over the one hundred and eight thousand miles to the western Heaven, the Buddha was preaching a sermon, and the acolytes asked Sun Wukong to wait.

Sun Wukong said the matter was urgent, and simply rushed to the Buddha's platform and kowtowed.

The Buddha said, "Wukong, you should have come earlier without having to bother the Heavenly Horde. I will give you eighteen tablets of golden pills which should turn into a desert and engulf the one-horned monster. I will also send one of the sannyasis (Hindu ascetic, holy man) to go with you and administer the golden pills."

Sun Wukong was most grateful. He thanked the Buddha and went back the monster's cave with the Sannyasi.

Another attack was launched and the monster came out to fight. The Sannyasi poured the golden pills, which turned into torrents of golden sand filling the valleys and rivers. The sand buried the one-horned monster up to his waist, and he was taken aback, but soon he took out the bracelet and the golden pills were sucked into it.

Now Sun Wukong was desperate, as he realized the Buddha's help was not effective. The Sannyasi told Sun Wukong, "His Holiness the Buddha told me if the golden sand does not work, to go and ask Laotse."

Sun Wukong was annoyed. "Why did the Buddha not tell me to go to Laotse in the first place?"

Sun Wukong then flew up to the ashram of Laotse, which was located in the thirty-third level of Heaven. As he arrived, he saw Laotse taking a stroll outside of the ashram.

Sun Wukong asked Laotse to check if anyone was missing from his entourage. One of the disciples reported that the ox was missing. This was the ox that Laotse rode when he left the human world and entered Heaven two thousand years ago.

Laotse said, "I had not ridden the animal for some time, and he has gone missing. I also find that he disappeared with the platinum ring on his nose. Fortunately, he did not take the banana-leaf fan, because if he did, I don't think even I could control him. But let us go now."

Sun Wukong asked, "That platinum ring, is it the one you threw down to hit me in the head five hundred years ago?" Laotse laughed and said yes.

So they went down to the one-horned monster's cave. The monster, now more confident about his strength, came out laughing. "Hey, monkey, you have been defeated so many times. When are you going to give up?"

Laotse, still standing in the sky, called out, "My ox! It's time for you to come home." And he fanned a magic wind with the banana-leaf fan. The one-horned monster said, "This Sun Wukong really knows his stuff. How did he find out about my Master?"

He shrunk and knelt, turning himself into a blue ox. Laotse chanted a mantra and put the platinum bracelet through his nose.

Sun Wukong immediately went into the cave to rescue Sanzang, Bajie and Sandy. They all came out and thanked Laotse for his help.

The Heavenly Horde swarmed into the cave to retrieve their respective weapons.

◙ CHAPTER 18 ◙
SANZANG AND BAJIE GET PREGNANT

It was spring again after crossing the Trans-Heaven River and the Single Horn Cave in winter. The pilgrims were enjoying the pleasant season and the agreeable scenery, chatting happily.

They came upon a small river. Bajie shouted, "Ahoy, is there someone here to ferry us across?"

A boat, rowed by an old woman, drew close them and offered them a ride.

Bajie said, "How come we have a boat-woman instead of a boatman?"

The woman did not say anything. She just rowed the boat and soon they were on the other side of the river. They paid the old woman, and got off the boat.

Sanzang said, "I am thirsty. Bajie, bring me a bowl of water."

Bajie went to the river to get some water and, feeling thirsty too, took a sip. After a few minutes, both Sanzang and Bajie started to complain of stomach pain.

They went to the nearest house to ask for some stomach pain medicine. When they got there they found only women in the house. They told the women their problem.

The women said, "Stomach pain medicine will not help you. You see, you are in the West-Beam Women's Kingdom. Here we only have women; no man exists. To perpetuate our tribe, we take a sip out of the river that you just crossed. We call it Child-making River. When you drink from the river, it forms a fetus and you become pregnant. We only give birth to female babies, and this is how our line is sustained."

Now Sanzang and Bajie were in a panic. Bajie asked, "How can I give birth? I do not have the outlet to let the baby out."

Sun Wukong, laughing, said, "Maybe your side will open

up?"

The old woman said, "There is a mountain about one thousand miles south of here. Here, there is a spring called 'Fetus Dropping Spring' that produces the water that would terminate the fetus of a pregnant woman who drinks of it. The problem is that it is guarded by a Taoist priest who will not part with the water without a heavy bribe."

Sun Wukong said, "That's no problem. I will get the water."

Sun Wukong flew over to the spring which was protected by a pavilion. He greeted the guard and asked him to tell the priest he wanted some water. The priest asked who he was and Sun Wukong told him.

The priest said, "You have defeated my nephew, the Red Infant. I was going to find you and kill you, never mind giving you the water."

Sun Wukong pointed out, "But, sir, you are mistaken. Red Infant is now a disciple of Kuanyin and has the opportunity of becoming an enlightened spirit. I did him a favour, and you have no reason to want to kill me."

The priest said, "Your clever logic will not work with me. My nephew was independent and his own boss. Now he is a disciple confined to a small area. That's no favour. No. No water."

Sun Wukong realized that no amount of cajoling would persuade him, so he took out his stick and attacked him. The priest was no match, and he ran away in defeat.

Sun Wukong was not interested in chasing after him. He went to the spring to get some water. The priest, from his hiding place, took out a hook and threw it at Sun Wukong's feet. Then he pulled it in. Sun Wukong was caught by surprise and fell. But he got up and went back to the spring, and he was hooked again.

After a few times, Sun Wukong decided to get some help. He flew back and asked Sandy to come with him.

Bajie said, "You are leaving the two of us sick men behind. We feel helpless."

Sun Wukong said, "Don't complain. We will get you the relief." He then turned to Sandy, "I will go and fight off the priest;

you just go and get the water and bring it back to the Master and Bajie."

Sandy agreed, and they proceeded to the spring.

Sun Wukong asked the priest, "Now will you give me the water?" The priest was surprised to see Sun Wukong back, and asked, "How much bribe money have you brought?"

"None!"

"Then there will be no water!"

Sun Wukong took on the priest and pinned him down with his stick, while Sandy went to the well to get water. There was also a junior priest guarding the well. Sandy hit him with his weapon, wounding him, and said, "I could kill you, but I take pity on you. I will let you live."

When he got the water, Sandy shouted, "Brother, I got the water!" When he heard this, Sun Wukong said to the priest, "I could have killed you. But for the sake of the Red Infant, I will let you live."

The two flew back and gave the water to Sanzang and Bajie. Sanzang took one sip and immediately felt his stomach roaring. Bajie said, "I am in so much pain that I could swallow a whole pail of water."

The old woman warned, "No. If you drink too much your entrails would all melt away. Be careful."

This alarmed Bajie, and he only took one sip of water. Soon both Sanzang and Bajie were overcome with an attack of diarrhea. They let out large amounts of blood and pus, and the lumps in their stomach were soon gone.

Sun Wukong joked, "Now that you have delivered your fetus, would you like to have sesame-oil chicken?"[1]

After a day or two, the two recovered enough to resume their journey.

---

1   In Chinese custom, women who give birth are given sesame-oil chicken to restore their loss of blood.

CHAPTER 19

The Amazon Queen Wants to Marry Sanzang

On their way ahead, the pilgrims had to enter the Kingdom of Women. In the capital, they saw no men in the streets. Everything was being done by women. They went to the passport office to have their documents stamped.

When the officials noticed that they were male, they reported it to the palace. The Queen asked to see them.

When the Queen saw Sanzang, she was attracted to him and decided to keep him as a consort.

Sanzang said, "I am a celibate person and I will not break my vow of celibacy. Nor will I break my vow of never killing and never eating any meat or fish." But the queen was adamant and decided to go ahead and marry Sanzang. She ordered them to be given accommodation in the official state guest house.

Sun Wukong advised, "Master, do not worry. You just agree to everything and play along. I could kill them all and take us out of this place, but I know you do not like me to kill. So you just play along and leave the three of us the task of getting our documents stamped. When the time comes for us to take leave, you just say you must see us off. Then come to the border and I will freeze them so they cannot move. After we are gone for a day or two, I will unfreeze them. This way, no one will be hurt."

Sanzang happily agreed to this plan.

When the palace summoned Sanzang, he went with the envoys to the palace. The Queen received him joyfully, calling him "My dear husband." This made Sanzang cringe but he tried not to appear upset.

The preparations for the wedding started and a date was fixed. Sun Wukong and the rest decided to take leave the day before the wedding. Sanzang said to the queen, "I must see them off. They have escorted me for many years and helped rescue me from many demons and monsters. The least I can do is to see them off at the border. Let me go."

The queen, unsuspecting, agreed and offered to come along.

As they neared the border, Sun Wukong said, "Well we are now about to leave this kingdom. Goodbye. Good luck."

Taking the cue from Sun Wukong, Sanzang said, "My dear queen, I also must take your leave here. I join my disciples on my journey to the west."

The queen was surprised and shocked, but Sanzang had already leapt down from the carriage. But before Sun Wukong could cast his freezing spell, someone in the crowd of women spectators shouted, "Sanzang, come with me and you will marry me."

She grabbed Sanzang and flew away in a whiff of wind. Sun Wukong rose up to the sky and used his vision to look around. He saw the demon's wind going in a northerly direction.

Sun Wukong came down and told Bajie and Sandy to follow him. The three then flew into the air and then proceeded to the north. The Queen and her retinue stood in awe. They said, "We did not realize they were fairies. Now we know how foolish it was to think of marrying Sanzang."

◙ CHAPTER 20 ◙
THE TROUBLE IN PEEPAH[2] CAVE

Sun Wukong, Bajie and Sandy followed the demon to a mountain, where they saw a cave with the stele bearing the sign 'Peepah Cave'. Bajie was about to smash the gate, but Sun Wukong cautioned him, "Wait, we are not sure this is the demon's place. Let me go in to find out."

Sun Wukong turned into a bee and flew into the cave where he found Sanzang sitting stiff as a log, while the female demon was trying to seduce him. He was afraid that Sanzang would refuse too angrily and annoy the demon who might harm him. So he revealed himself and smashed the furniture and attacked the demon.

The demon took out her weapon, and the two of them fought

---

their way out of the cave. Bajie and Sandy joined in the attack. The demon was no match for them, but she suddenly took out a needle and stung Sun Wukong in the head. He felt excruciating pain, and they all retreated.

The demon was triumphant and proceeded to try and seduce Sanzang. But Sanzang remained adamant. He would rather die than give up his celibacy.

After a few hours of trying, the demon lost her patience, and had Sanzang bound up and thrown in one corner of the room.

Following their retreat, Sun Wukong remained weak and suffering. Bajie said, "I thought your head was impervious to everything, having been burned in Laotse's oven and hardened by divine peaches and longevity pills. What's going on?"

Sun Wukong also wondered, but the next day his headache was gone. Only a slight itch remained. He said, "If it was anyone else, I suspect he would have died by now."

Then they made their way back to the cave. Sun Wukong said, "When I was in there last I saw the demon trying to seduce the Master. So far he was resisting. But who knows what happened through last night? Let me go in and see if he remains chaste. If so, we will spare no effort to rescue him, but if not, it's all over and we can go home."

Again, Sun Wukong flew in as a bee, and saw Sanzang bound up and dumped in one corner of the room. Sun Wukong went to him and whispered, "Master, I am here, how are you? Have you succumbed to the charms of the demon?"

Although he could not see him, Sanzang knew it was Sun Wukong. He said, "Wukong! Rescue me quick. I have resisted every charm. I would rather die than give in. Rescue me and we go on to the west."

The demon overheard "go on to the west" and came over to Sanzang. Fearing what she might do, Sun Wukong revealed himself again and they fought, all the way to the outside of the cave.

Bajie and Sandy joined in too, but this time she stung Bajie on his snout, again causing terrible pain and forcing the three to retreat.

Bajie was moaning with pain, and Sun Wukong consoled him, "All you need to do is to suffer through the night and you'll be all right."

As they were trying to figure out what to do next, they saw a woman walking towards them. Sun Wukong recognized the divine cloud and light and knelt down and cried, "Goddess of Mercy! You have come to help us."

It was Kuanyin. She said, "The demon here is a scorpion. The only one that can deal with her is the God of Dawn. Go and ask him for help." Then she left.

Sun Wukong flew up to the Heavenly Palace and asked to see the God of Dawn, who was away introducing a new day to the world, crowing. He found the god and asked him to help. The god agreed and came down to the cave.

When the demon came out, Sun Wukong shouted, "God of Dawn, come and help!" The God revealed himself to be a huge rooster, like one that crows in the morning to start the day, and pecked at the demon, who turned herself into a big scorpion.

Seeing this, Bajie went up to the scorpion and smashed it with his rake. They thanked the God of Dawn, and went into the cave to rescue Sanzang.

◎ CHAPTER 21 ◎
Sun Wukong is Banished for Killing Bandits

As the pilgrims proceeded, they were discussing everything under the sun. One day they were talking about the speed with which they were traveling, and commenting on the fact that their speed seemed to be set by the speed at which their horse marched.

Sun Wukong said he could speed up the pace, but maybe the Master's body might not stand it. The others asked, "But how can you make the horse go faster?"

Sun Wukong said, "You watch!" and he patted the horse on

its hip. The horse dashed out at great speed, carrying Sanzang and leaving the three of them behind.

Sun Wukong was in charge of the Heavenly Stable where he had learned his way with horses, and he could make horses do what he wanted them to.

The horse carried Sanzang and went ahead of the three disciples. After a while, it was stopped by a band of bandits who demanded that Sanzang stand and deliver.

Sanzang pleaded with them that he was a poor monk on his way the west, that he had nothing of value, that he had three disciples following behind who were very powerful and ill-tempered.

The bandits laughed at him and said, "We will wait for your disciples to get here and rob them too. Meanwhile, we will bind and hang you up."

Before long, the three disciples arrived on the scene and the bandits demanded their loot.

Sun Wukong said, "First let my Master free." As soon as the Master was freed, he rode the horse fast and furious to get away from the bandits. Bajie and Sandy followed, but Sun Wukong remained behind with the bandits.

Sun Wukong said to the bandits, "Now come and get it. But if you do, you will have to get a taste of my stick." The bandits surrounded Sun Wukong and slashed and chopped at him, leaving him totally unscathed. They were in shock, wondering how their swords and spears meant nothing to Sun Wukong.

Sun Wukong slowly pulled out his stick and hit the two chief bandits, turning them into meatballs, leaving the rest running for their lives.

Bajie and Sandy caught up with Sanzang and told him that Sun Wukong had remained behind to deal with the bandits.

Sanzang said, "Go and tell Wukong to be merciful and spare the lives of the bandits. Evil as they are, they are god's creatures."

When Sanzang found out that Sun Wukong had already killed two of them, he said, "You need not have killed these two. I am upset with you."

In punishment, Sanzang chanted the ring-tightening mantra, causing Sun Wukong to reel in pain, shouting, "Don't chant, please don't chant. I won't do it again."

Sanzang stopped chanting, and said, "Let us now find a night's lodging."

There was a village ahead of them, and Sanzang went to the largest house and knocked on the door. They were warmly received and offered supper by their host.

As they were chatting with the host, they found out that his surname was Yang, and that he had only one son who had turned out to be a thug, drinking, gambling, womanizing and aiding bandits in their robbery. Sanzang sighed, "It is sad that a good man like you is not rewarded with a good son. I hope he will one day see the light."

Sun Wukong said, "Mountains and rivers can change, human temperament does not change. I see no hope for your son. You may as well be prepared to write off that son of yours. I suspect he might be one of the bandits we encountered this evening."

They went to bed, but before they rose the next day, Yang's son came home along with a number of his friends. It turned out that young Yang was indeed one of the bandits.

When Yang's son found out that the pilgrims were staying at his father's house he said, "Great, we can kill them to avenge our friends."

The bandits ambushed the pilgrims as they took leave of the old Yang, but they were crushed by Sun Wukong who asked, "Which one is Yang?"

One of the bandits pointed to the one wearing a yellow vest, and Sun Wukong went up to him and chopped off his head.

Sanzang was furious at this, and chanted the mantra again. Sun Wukong was in excruciating pain as the golden crown squeezed his head, eating into his skull by almost an inch.

In extreme agony, SunWukong cried, "Don't chant, don't chant! It is killing me."

Sanzang said sternly, "It seems to me you are not willing to change your ways. I do not want you to go with me to the west.

Go home and do not bother me. If you leave, I will not chant the mantra again."

Sun Wukong said, "You would have a lot of trouble and, without my help, you would not be able to get out of them. I am willing to help fight off demons and monsters. Forgive me this time and let me serve you."

But Sanzang was adamant. "I do not want to see your face. Be gone or else I will chant the mantra." Sun Wukong had no choice. He made a somersault and flew away.

Sun Wukong was flying towards his old home, the Water Screen Cave, but he thought to himself, "If I go home, my monkey subjects will say I was kicked out again a second time. That would be most embarrassing. But where should I go?"

He finally decided to go to the Kuanyin Mountain to appeal to the Goddess of Mercy. He arrived at the mountain, was received by the Namaste Boy, and taken to Kuanyin's presence.

Sun Wukong knelt and, weeping, said, "I saved my Master from the swords of bandits but he banished me for killing some of them. I have helped him so much and saved his life on so many occasions, and now he says he does not even want to see my face. Have I not earned some merits? Do I not deserve some of his gratitude? It's unfair. If I am to be relieved of this duty, can you please chant a ring-loosening mantra to remove this crown from my head?"

Kuanyin replied, "I have no mantra to loosen the crown. I was given the three rings by the Buddha who only gave me the three mantras to tighten the three rings. Besides, you know you could have overcome the bandits without killing them. So you are at fault. You stay here with me for a while. Sanzang will be in serious trouble soon and I will use the occasion to get you back your job. Just be patient."

Sun Wukong obeyed, and remained by the side of Kuanyin's Lotus Flower Stool.

◎ CHAPTER 22 ◎
THE FAKE SUN WUKONG HARASSES THE PILGRIMS

Now the three remaining pilgrims continued on their journey. One evening Sanzang was hungry and asked Bajie to go get some food. Bajie went up to the sky, looked around, and found a manor in the distance. He thought his face would frighten people, so he changed into a human monk and proceeded to knock at the door.

When the door opened Bajie said, "I am a monk on my way to the west. I would like to ask for a donation of food and lodging." The man gave him some food and told him the pilgrims would be welcome to stay with him.

All this took quite a long time, and Sanzang was getting a bit impatient. He asked Sandy to go and find out what Bajie was doing. He was waiting alone, feeling lonely, when he saw Sun Wukong coming back. He cried, "You brazen monkey! I don't want you around. Get lost."

Sun Wukong said, "Look, I am sorry I killed those bandits. Forgive me and let me rejoin your journey. Otherwise, I don't think Bajie and Sandy will be able to deal with the monsters and demons that infest your path to the west."

Sanzang was adamant. He said, "Get lost, or I will chant the mantra."

Sun Wukong became very angry. He hit Sanzang with his stick and took away his luggage, leaving Sanzang lying on the ground, wounded. After a while Sandy and Bajie came back to find Sanzang lying on the ground. They asked what had happened, and Sanzang told them, "Wukong came back and asked to rejoin. When I refused, he got mad and hit me with his stick."

Bajie said, "That's curious, his stick is so heavy that anyone hit by it would turn into a meatball. How did you survive that?"

Noticing that the luggage was missing, Bajie said, "It is not like Wukong to steal our luggage. I will go to his home at the

Water Screen Cave to ask for it back."

Sanzang said, "No, that is not a good idea. There is some tension between you and Wukong and, if you go, he might refuse to give it back to you. I think Sandy should go."

Sandy agreed, and flew away. It took him a few hours to get to the Water Screen Cave where he saw Sun Wukong sitting on a rock with his monkey subjects.

Noticing Sandy, Sun Wukong called out to him, "Who are you?" Sandy went up to him and asked, "Brother, you don't recognize me?"

Sun Wukong said, "Yes, you are Sha Wujing, or Sandy. What do you want?"

Sandy said, "Brother, you took the luggage from the Master. I want to ask for it to be returned. Why don't you come with me, give back the luggage, and rejoin the pilgrimage?"

Sun Wukong said, "No, I asked to rejoin and the idiot monk refused me. So I have resolved not to go. Instead, I am going to organize a separate pilgrimage and get the sutra before Sanzang can reach the west."

Sandy tried to reason with him. "Brother, you cannot do that. The Master was the one that was designated by Kuanyin and the Buddha to be the legitimate pilgrim. How can you go west without him and expect the Buddha to give the sutra to you?"

Sun Wukong said, "But I have a complete set of new pilgrims that look exactly like you." He took Sandy to the 'Pilgrims', which consisted of Sanzang, Bajie, and Sandy.

Sandy was so offended to see himself copied that, raising his stick, he smashed it down and killed the false Sandy, which turned out to be a dead monkey.

Sun Wukong was angry and had his monkey army surround Sandy, who escaped by flying out.

Sandy decided to go and ask Kuanyin for help, and went to the Kuanyin Mountain in the South Sea.

At the foot of the mountain, Sandy asked to see Kuanyin, and was brought to her presence. When he came in front of Kuanyin, he was startled to see Sun Wukong standing at her side. Raising his stick, Sandy tried to hit him.

Sun Wukong did not fight back, but dodged the stick instead.

Kuanyin said, "Sandy! Do not be violent. Why do you attack your Brother?"

Sandy said, "This miserable monkey! He hit my Master, robbed his luggage, and when I went to ask for it back, refused it. Not only that, he has the temerity to launch a fake pilgrimage by creating false copies of the four of us and the dragon horse to travel west and get the sutra."

Kuanyin said, "No. You are wrong. Wukong has been here for four days, never leaving my side. You must have run into another monkey pretending to be Wukong. Why don't the two of you go together to deal with this?"

Sun Wukong and Sandy obeyed. They flew over to the Water Screen Cave where the false Sun Wukong was still presiding over the monkeys.

Sun Wukong shouted, "You shameless impostor! Here is my stick." The other Sun Wukong got up and started to fight. They fought furiously, their identities so mixed up that Sandy could not help, for fear that he might hit the wrong Sun Wukong.

The two of them fought for a long time, and moved their fight to the sky, then on to the south, soon reaching the Kuanyin Mountain.

Sandy went to report to Kuanyin, who came out to see them. Both of them shouted together, "O Goddess of Mercy! Kill this impostor."

The real and the fake Sun Wukong were so similar that even Kuanyin was unable to make out who was who. So she decided to chant the ring-tightening mantra in the hope that the real Sun Wukong would respond to it. But when she chanted, both of them were in pain, so it was impossible to tell.

Kuanyin then said, "Wukong, you had worked in the Heavenly Palace and have many colleagues who recognize you. Go up to Heaven and ask them to tell you apart."

They went up, but all of Sun Wukong's former colleagues –

The other Sun Wukong got up and started to fight. They were fighting furiously and were so mixed up that Sandy could not help for fear that he might hit the wrong Sun Wukong.

from the heavenly stable, the peach garden, and those who fought him after he stole the peaches - were stumped.

Kuanyin then said, "Go to the Netherworld and ask the Price of Hades to tell you apart."

So they went to the Netherworld, where they took out the register of all souls, but could not find anything. They had lost every record on Sun Wukong from the time he destroyed the records when he was taken there five hundred years ago.

Finally Kuanyin said, "The only person who can help is the Buddha himself, with his infinite wisdom, knowledge, and inspiration. Go to the Western Heaven."

So they went there. The Buddha saw them coming and, with his all-knowing mind, knew what they had come to him for. The two again said, "Almighty Buddha! Help identify the impostor!"

The Buddha said "Reality and Illusion are one and the same, and yet the Reality and Illusion are also separate."

As the Buddha was saying this, Kuanyin came and paid her homage. The Buddha asked her, "Do you know which is Wukong and which is not?"

Kuanyin bowed and said, "I do not have the wisdom to distinguish between these two."

The Buddha said, "The monkey that is taking the form of Wukong belongs to a species called the Six-Eared Ape, because it has six transcendental senses. It has great ability, but this time it has overstepped its limitations."

When the false Sun Wukong heard that he became afraid of being captured. So he turned into a bee to fly away. The Buddha threw the cup he had in his hand, and the bee was captured in it.

Kuanyin opened it and Sun Wukong, seeing the bee there, hit it, killing it and turning it into a dead monkey.

The Buddha, in his infinite mercy, said "Requiem, requiem."

Then he told Sun Wukong, "Now go back to Sanzang and escort him and bring him here for the sutras."

Sun Wukong said, "O merciful Buddha! My Master has banished me and says he does not want to see my face again. Please relieve me of this duty by removing the ring from my head."

The Buddha said, "Don't be silly. He has to accept you because I wanted you to be his disciple. Go to him, and I will send Kuanyin with you to ask him to accept you."

Sun Wukong knelt and kowtowed, and went back to the Master with Kuanyin and Sandy.

As they arrived, Sanzang knelt and kowtowed to Kuanyin.

She said, "Sanzang, you must accept Wukong as your disciple. You may punish him appropriately. But you cannot banish him."

Sanzang said, "I obey."

So Sun Wukong rejoined the pilgrims.

◉ CHAPTER 23 ◉
The Flaming Mountain Obstructs the Journey

The pilgrims' journey continued all summer, until it became cooler as the seasons entered autumn. Bur all of a sudden they felt hot, and were puzzled why it should be so hot in the fall.

They came to a village and found a place to stay the night, and asked why it was so hot. Their host, an old man, told them there was a mountain nearby in flames, and that was making the area so hot throughout the year. What was worse, the mountain was smack on the path to the west and there was no way around it.

Asked how the people around there sustained themselves since the heat was such and the air so dry that surely no crops could grow, the old man told the pilgrims that there was a 'Banana Fan Cave' in which lived a woman called Iron Fan Princess who owned a magic banana leaf fan.

The fan caused the fire to stop with one fanning, caused cool wind to prevail with two sweeps of the fan, and brought enough rain to grow crops for a season. The people of the village paid the Iron Fan Princess considerable money to borrow the fan, and this practice continued year to year.

Next day the pilgrims approached a mountain spewing flames into the air. Sun Wukong summoned the god of the mountain and asked him about the fire and the mountain.

The god said, "Forgive me, but this mountain was caused by you!"

Surprised, Sun Wukong said, "Nonsense! How could I have formed this mountain?"

The god said, "When you escaped from the oven of Laotse after you caused the commotion in Heaven, the oven collapsed and fell on the earth and this mountain was formed."

"I see," said Sun Wukong, nodding his head. "Now tell me about the Iron Fan Princess."

The god told Sun Wukong that the Iron Fan Princess was really the wife of the Buffalo King, and mother to the Red Infant, now the Namaste Boy.

Sun Wukong was taken aback. If the experience of the encounter with the uncle of Red Infant at the Fetus-Dropping Spring was any indication, the encounter with the mother would probably not be very pleasant.

◎ CHAPTER 24 ◎
Sun Wukong Tries to Borrow the Banana-Leaf Fan

Still, Sun Wukong had to go and ask to borrow the fan. He went to the Banana Fan Cave and asked for the princess, introducing himself and explaining that he was escorting the Sage on his journey to the west to get sutras.

When the princess heard the name Sun Wukong, she grabbed her weapon and came out.

Sun Wukong bowed, and said, "Dear sister-in-law, my greetings."

The Princess scowled, "How dare you call me sister-in-law? And how dare you come to me after doing so much harm to my son? Here is my sword!"

Sun Wukong quickly avoided the blow and said, "Sister-in-law, I have sworn brotherhood with your husband. As for your son, he was once a demon, but now he has found acceptance by the Goddess of Mercy as a disciple and is on his way to achieving sainthood.

"You should thank me, rather than blame me for what happened."

She said, "I don't believe your sweet talk. Get lost."

Sun Wukong said, "I have a request. Could I borrow your magic fan to stop the fire so we could cross the mountain on our way to the west?"

The princess was angry. "You will not get the fan. Go away!" and again she attacked Sun Wukong with her sword.

Sun Wukong fought back, and she was really no match for him. She took out the magic fan and fanned at Sun Wukong, who was blown into the sky and landed five thousand miles away at the foot of the Bodhisattva of Auspicious Inspiration.

Upon landing there, Sun Wukong said, "That was one powerful fan! Luckily I had the power to ride the wind; otherwise I would have been blown much further."

Recognizing the place to be the residence of the Bodhisattva of Auspicious Inspiration, he went to the residence to pay his respect. The Bodhisattva said, "Hello. It has been some time since I helped you tame the Yellow Robe Demon. What brings you here this time?"

Sun Wukong explained what happened. The Bodhisattva said, "You are in luck. I have a Pill To Calm Wind that the Buddha gave me. You can keep it in your pocket and it will help you overcome the wind from the fan."

Sun Wukong was very happy. He thanked the Bodhisattva and returned to the Banana Fan Cave.

When he arrived, he smashed and destroyed the gate. The princess came out with the fan and fanned at Sun Wukong, but this time, no matter how hard she fanned, Sun Wukong did not budge.

The Princess retreated into her cave and closed her inner gate. Sun Wukong turned into a mosquito and flew inside.

Seeing the princess was taking a frothy drink, he jumped

into the foam, and was sipped into the princess's stomach along with the foam. Once inside, he kicked the wall of the stomach and poked it with his stick, causing the princess to writhe in pain.

Sun Wukong then came to her mouth and shouted, "I am inside you, and I can kill you by tearing your organs to pieces!"

The princess pleaded in desperation, "Please save me, dear brother-in-law!"

Sun Wukong laughed. "So now all of a sudden I am your dear brother-in-law, eh? All right. Let me have the fan. After I've passed the mountain, I will give it back to you."

The princess said, "Yes, yes. Just come out and I will give you the fan."

As she was uttering the words, Sun Wukong flew out of her mouth and, revealing himself, took the fan and left.

Sun Wukong arrived at the mountain, waved the magical fan, but the flame got stronger rather than weaker. Puzzled, Sun Wukong called out the god of the mountain and asked him about the fan. The god told him that the fan was a fake, as there were red threads on the real one while the one Sun Wukong had did not have any red thread. The god also informed Sun Wukong that the husband, the Buffalo King, would be able to persuade the princess to give the fan. But he was not in the cave because he had a new lover called Jade Princess, and was living some five hundred miles away.

Sun Wukong decided he needed to see the Buffalo King. When he arrived there, he saw a woman walking outside of the cave. He went up to her and said, "I am a brother of your husband. My name is Sun Wukong and I am on my way to the west, escorting a Sage to obtain the teaching of the Buddha. I want to see the Buffalo King. Take me to him."

The woman was frightened by Sun Wukong's appearance and ran inside in panic, telling the Buffalo King that there was a monster named Sun Wukong asking for him.

The Buffalo King was angry when he heard Sun Wukong's name, and came out ready to fight, shouting, "You miserable monkey! How dare you frighten my second wife?"

Sun Wukong politely greeted him, "Brother, I did not know she was your second wife. I am sorry to have frightened her."

The Buffalo King continued, "And what are you doing here? You have hurt my son, and have no business coming to me."

Sun Wukong said, "But, brother, your son is now a disciple of the Goddess of Mercy and on his way to sainthood. You really should thank me rather than remain angry with me."

"I don't believe in your lies!" said the Buffalo King.

Sun Wukong said, "I am facing problems passing through the Flaming Mountain. I would be grateful if you could lend me the Banana Leaf Fan to stop the fire. Of course, I will return it as soon as I pass the mountain."

The Buffalo King said, "You brazen monkey! Even if you brought me a lavish offering, I would not lend you the fan. Get lost. Unless you can win in a fight with me, don't even dream of borrowing the fan."

So they fought for hours without either side showing any weakness. After a few hours, the Buffalo King jumped back and said, "Take a break. I am going to a dinner at the Dragon King of Wansheng's."

Sun Wukong used his vision to look around, and saw the Buffalo King riding his Golden-pupil Lion over to a cave.

He followed the Buffalo King to the cave, and saw him sitting down to his dinner. Sun Wukong decided to take the Lion and ride it off to the Banana Fan Cave, in the form of the Buffalo King.

When Sun Wukong arrived at the cave, the guards went in to report to the Iron Fan Princess, "Ma'am, your husband has returned."

The princess came out to receive him, and told him about her encounter with Sun Wukong.

Sun Wukong, disguised, said, "This fellow Sun Wukong is very resourceful. Be careful with the fan. Where do you keep it?"

The princess said, "I have it securely hidden inside my mouth." She took it out to show Sun Wukong, thinking that she was showing it to her husband.

Sun Wukong took it in his hand, and asked, "How do you make this small fan large?"

She said, "You have forgotten. Just press the third red thread and say 'ohm mani peimei hou' and it will grow large."

Sun Wukong rubbed his nose, revealing himself, and said, "Thanks, my dear. Now I go and fix the Flaming Mountain." He left the Banana Fan Cave, leaving the princess angry and frustrated.

Sun Wukong took the fan and was soon on his way to the mountain. Along the way he tried the mantra, and the fan grew to be ten feet long. He was delighted but then he did not know how to shrink it back to the small size. So he just carried the huge fan with him.

◉ CHAPTER 25 ◉
THE FIGHT WITH THE BUFFALO KING

Meanwhile, the Buffalo King finished his dinner and took leave of his host. When he came out, he noticed that the golden-pupil Lion was missing. He immediately suspected Sun Wukong's dirty tricks and, remembering Sun Wukong was asking for the fan, he flew over to his first wife. He found her weeping inconsolably.

When she saw the Buffalo King, she grabbed him and complained, "You rascal! Look what you have done. Sun Wukong came in here pretending to be you and stole my fan."

The Buffalo King said, "Calm down, I will go and recover the fan for you."

He went looking for Sun Wukong and soon found him walking with the fan on his shoulder. The Buffalo King thought to himself, "I better not challenge him head on, for he might fan me and send me flying thousands of miles." So he changed himself into Bajie and called out to Sun Wukong, "Hey, brother, the Master was wondering why you are taking so long, so he sent me to come looking for you."

Sun Wukong told him what happened, and the two of them walked together to the mountain. The Buffalo King said, "Let me carry the fan for you. You have been carrying it a long time." Sun Wukong, unsuspecting, handed over the fan.

The Buffalo King then revealed himself, saying, "You stupid monkey! Now I have the fan back. Get lost!"

Sun Wukong cried out, "My mistake! I should not have given the fan to you. Give it back to me. The fan has to help in our endeavour to obtain the sutras."

The Buffalo King was not about to give the fan back. Instead, he took out his weapon to attack Sun Wukong, who took out his stick. And so the two started to fight again.

The commotion they created was heard by the pilgrims, and Bajie said, "I had better go and help brother Wukong."

As Bajie went to the fight, Sun Wukong said, "I had the fan, but this treacherous monster came disguised as you, and I foolishly gave the fan to him."

Bajie was annoyed. "How dare you assume my appearance?" he asked as he attacked the Buffalo King with his rake. The Buffalo King was unable to resist the two of them, so he retreated towards the cave of his second wife.

When they came near the cave, the Jade Faced Princess came out with her troops to help the Buffalo King. Sun Wukong and Bajie were undaunted, and they fought even more fiercely.

The Buffalo King tried to escape by turning himself into a partridge and perched on a branch of a tree. Bajie lost him, but not Sun Wukong who turned into a hawk and went after the partridge.

The Buffalo King quickly changed into a mouse deer, and Sun Wukong changed into a tiger and jumped towards the mouse deer.

Finally, the Buffalo King reverted to his original form, a huge white bull, with a head the size of a mountain, mouth the size of a volcanic crater, and horns the size of a tower.

By this time, the fight had attracted the notice of the Heavenly Horde, and they all came too help Sun Wukong. The King of Tower wielded his sword and chopped of the head of the bull, but a new head immediately sprang forth. After a few times of chopping and growing, the King of Tower's Crown Prince put his flaming-ring on the horns of the bull.

The Buffalo King was burning and in pain. He tried to shake off the ring, only to have the flame burn even more fiercely. He tried to change his form, but the King of Tower trained his 'counter-demon mirror' on him, preventing him from using his supernatural tricks.

Finally, the bull cried, "Please spare my life. I will convert to Buddhism."

Sun Wukong told him firmly, "And give us the fan."

The bull said, "It is with my first wife." The Heavenly Horde and Sun Wukong took the bull to the Banana Fan Cave and called out to the Iron-Fan Princess to surrender the fan. She saw the bull and broke down weeping. Taking the fan out of her mouth, she surrendered it to Sun Wukong.

Sun Wukong took the fan, and reported to Sanzang what happened. As they were celebrating the victory, there blew a gust of wind and with it Bajie arrived.

Bajie said he had gone to attack the second wife's cave and had killed her. She turned out to be the demon of a fox.

The pilgrims then went to the Flaming Mountain, and fanned it once, and the fire stopped. They fanned a second time, and a cool wind started to blow over the mountain. At the third fanning, rain started to fall on the mountain and the surrounding land, cooling the area sufficiently to allow their passage.

With the bull and the Iron-Fan Princess in captivity, the Heavenly Horde came to take leave of Sun Wukong and Sanzang. The Iron-Fan Princess begged of Sun Wukong, "Please give the fan back to me."

Sun Wukong said, "No. This fan is needed by the people here, because every year the mountain needs to be fanned three times." The Iron-Fan Princess said, "All you need to do is to fan forty-nine times and the mountain will cool off permanently."

Sun Wukong then fanned the mountain forty-nine times, and there was a torrent of rain which completely put out sizzling fire. He then gave the fan back to the Iron-Fan Princess.

The pilgrims then went to the Flaming Mountain and fanned it once,
and the fire stopped.

The Heavenly Horde then took the bull and left, and Iron-Fan Princess pledged to follow the teachings of Buddhism. The pilgrims continued on their journey.

◙ CHAPTER 26 ◙
THE TREASURE THIEF: A NINE-HEADED DEMON

The pilgrims continued their journey west, and found the season turning cold again. They saw a town ahead, and Sun Wukong said it was a capital city where a king resided.

As they approached the town, they met a group of monks dressed in rags and with chains on their feet. Sanzang asked them what was wrong, and they replied, "You must be the Sage on your way to the west, and there must be a Sun Wukong amongst you. We are a group of monks being punished unjustly, but we have been told in our dreams that the powerful fairy Sun Wukong would come our way to save us."

Sanzang asked what the cause of their punishment was. They said, "We are the monks of the Golden Light Temple. The temple has a thirteen-story high tower that housed a treasure – a bone of the Buddha – at the very top of the tower. The treasure gave out beautiful light and its magic power caused the kingdom to prosper and led its neighboring kingdoms to pay tribute. Three years ago there was a rain of blood, and the treasure disappeared. The king accused us of stealing the treasure. Now we are all in chains."

Sanzang said, "I have promised myself that I will worship at all the temples and sweep all the towers on my way west. Let me sweep that treasure tower of yours."

Sun Wukong said, "I should accompany you, in case something happens." Sanzang was pleased. As they swept from the ground up, they heard someone talking on the top floor.

Sun Wukong went up to see and found two little monsters eating and chatting. He shouted, "You must be the treasure thief. Come with me."

They tried to escape, but Sun Wukong froze them and put a

needle through their collar bone to prevent them from changing into something else. He brought them down for questioning.

The two little monsters said, "We did not steal the treasure. It was the Dragon King of Wansheng. Three years ago he married his daughter to the Nine-Headed Consort, and he caused the blood rain to fall and stole the treasure."

Sun Wukong laughed. "Ah! This is the Dragon King who invited the Buffalo King to dinner when I was fighting him to get the banana-leaf fan. Now he is up to no good here as well. Let me go and fix him."

The pilgrims took the two little monsters to the court, and explained that the treasure was not stolen by the monks but by a monster. The king questioned the two little monsters and they confessed that it was indeed the Nine-headed Consort who had stolen the treasure.

The king wanted to retrieve the treasure and was about to dispatch an army, when Bajie said, "You don't need to send an army. The army will be useless before the supernatural power of the monsters. My brother and I can fix this."

Sun Wukong and Bajie then flew to the sky and went to the cave of the Wansheng in Random Rock Mountain. The king was awe-struck to see them fly away and said, "O my goodness, I did not realize that you were fairies. Let me treat you to a state dinner."

Sun Wukong and Bajie took the little monsters with them, and when they arrived at the cave, cut the ear off one and the nose off the other, and told them to go into the cave to report that Sun Wukong and Bajie were there to reclaim the treasure.

The Dragon King and the Nine-Headed Consort were startled to see the little monsters and went out of the cave to see who had cut them up.

Sun Wukong said, "You treasure thief, return the treasure!"

The Nine-Headed Consort took out his weapon to fight, but was no match for Sun Wukong. The Consort then revealed his original form, which was a nine-headed snake, and started attacking Sun Wukong.

Bajie raised his rake, and went to the back of the Consort and hit him with the rake, causing a wound. But the Consort then turned one of his heads to bite Bajie's robe, and dragged him back into the cave.

Sun Wukong turned into a fly and went into the cave, only to find Bajie all bound up. He went to Bajie and said, "Bajie, I am here."

Bajie asked, "Brother, what are you waiting for? Help get me out of this."

Sun Wukong said, "I will let you loose. You start fighting them and slowly get out of the cave. I will wait for you to come out and finish them off."

Sun Wukong then took a hair and turned it into a razor, cutting Bajie loose. Bajie took his rake, and started attacking the Consort and the Dragon King.

As they fought, Bajie slowly retreated towards the exit and, once out of the cave, Sun Wukong wielded his stick and attacked. Bajie succeeded in killing the Dragon King, and the Consort withdrew into the cave.

As Sun Wukong and Bajie prepared to attack the cave, they saw the Second Prince approaching them in the sky. This was the very same god who had defeated Sun Wukong five hundred years ago. He was returning from a hunting trip when they had last met.

The Second Prince greeted Sun Wukong, now that Sun Wukong was a disciple of the Buddha, and offered to help.

Now Bajie went ahead and destroyed the gate, provoking the Consort to come out and fight. This time the Nine-Headed Consort was out of luck. One of his heads was bitten off by the Second Prince's dogs, and he had to escape into the distant sky.

Bajie wanted to pursue him, but the Second Prince said, "Now he is missing one head. He will not survive long. Don't bother chasing him." So Bajie went into the cave and retrieved the treasure.

Sun Wukong and Bajie thanked the Second Prince, and they went back to the palace to return the treasure.

CHAPTER 27

Thorns Block the Path to the West

As the pilgrims journeyed west, they saw a mountain path covered with thick thorns. The thorns were so thick and so sharp, the path looked impassable. Bajie said, "My rake has supernatural powers. Let me clear these thorns and open a path for us."

He raised his rake, and started to clear the path. The rake cut through the thorns so quickly and so easily that it looked as if the thorns were like soft cotton. They were able to proceed as though there was nothing in their way.

At the end of the day, they came to a small pavilion, and Sanzang wanted to rest there. But Bajie said, "I am doing great. We may as well continue going." So they went ahead.

Before sunset, an old man showed up and offered the pilgrims food. Sanzang thanked him and proceeded to accept the food, but Sun Wukong saw through the disguise and shouted, "Master, don't touch that food. This is a demon."

At this, the old man suddenly grabbed Sanzang and disappeared. Sanzang was very frightened that something terrible was going to happen to him, but when they arrived at a cave, the old man held Sanzang's hand and led him into the cave.

There Sanzang saw three more old men. They said to Sanzang, "We have heard about you and your great learning. So we would like you to join us in tonight's poetry-chanting party."

Sanzang was relieved to see that they were not going to eat him, and he joined them in composing poems on various themes. Sanzang was enjoying this but, as the night progressed, he felt that he should take his leave.

At this time, a young woman came accompanied by a young man, and the young man said to Sanzang, "We know you by your reputation. I offer my sister as your wife. She will make an excellent wife for you."

Sanzang was shocked. He said, "I have made a vow of celibacy and I cannot break this vow. I cannot marry your sister."

The young man and the four old men insisted that Sanzang marry the woman, but Sanzang was adamant. He tried to get away, and was walking out of the cave when he heard Sun Wukong calling, "Master, where are you?"

Overjoyed, Sanzang shouted, "I am here!"

Sun Wukong, Bajie and Sandy came down from the sky, and the four old men, the woman and the young man disappeared.

Sanzang said, "Wukong, I am sorry I did not heed your advice. But who are these people? To be fair, they did not do any harm to me except this young man and young woman."

Sun Wukong said, "These are the spirits of the trees. The four old men are the spirits of a pine tree, a maple tree, an oak tree, and a willow tree. The woman is the spirit of an almond tree, and the young man is the spirit of a mulberry tree."

He pointed to the trees standing just outside of the cave. "Here they stand."

Bajie, raising his rake, uprooted the trees. As he did so, blood streamed out of the roots. After this, Bajie continued raking the thorns all night, and they were able at last to get through the mountain path by dawn.

PART THREE

◙ CHAPTER 1 ◙
Fake Buddha Captures Sanzang

A few weeks after they had traveled the thorn-filled path, the pilgrims approached a mountain so high that they could not see the top of it. It was the dragon horse that enabled Sanzang to climb the mountain and get to the other side.

When the pilgrims were finally descending from the mountain, they saw a large temple ahead of them, from which divine lights were shining forth.

Sanzang asked, "Is that the Buddha's abode? Why is it so divine-looking?"

Sun Wukong laughed and replied, "No. The Buddha temple is still far away. This is not it." Moments later, Sun Wukong decided to use his vision to take a look. He saw something odd.

"I see that there is divine light," he said, "but behind the divine light there is something ominous. We had better be careful."

Sanzang replied, "Still, as long as there is a temple, we must pay our respects."

Then Sandy said, "We are going by that place anyway, as it is on our way. Why not go and observe, then decide what to do?" Everyone agreed, and they proceeded to the temple.

As they approached the temple, it looked truly magnificent, and it bore a sign that said 'Junior Thundering Temple'.

Sanzang said to Sun Wukong, "This is the Thundering Temple, Wukong. We have to go in and pay our respects."

"Look, the sign says 'Junior Thundering Temple' and not 'Thundering Temple'," replied Sun Wukong. "Clearly this is not the real residence of the Buddha. Be careful."

Sanzang ignored him, and walked into the temple complex. The others followed. As they entered, they were in the midst of all the saints, bodhisattvas, bhikkhus[3], as well as all the other disciples of the Buddha.

When they approached the main temple, one of the disciples called out, "Sanzang, you are in the presence of the Buddha. Why are you hesitating?"

Sanzang knelt and kowtowed, as did Bajie and Sandy, but Sun Wukong stayed aloof, as he had recognized the Buddha to be a fake.

Sun Wukong rose to the sky, but the fake Buddha threw a golden bowl in the sky, capturing Sun Wukong inside it, and the bowl came falling back to the ground. Sun Wukong was sealed inside, and could not get out.

He tried to make himself tall, but the golden bowl grew tall with him. He tried hitting it with his stick, but could not even make a dent. He tried using his stick as a drill, but could not pierce the golden bowl.

Finally, in frustration, he summoned the gods that were on duty to protect Sanzang.

One of them, Rhino God, suggested, "I could try to penetrate the bowl with my horn. You could then try and escape through the gap." Rhino God pushed his horn forward, and it did pierce the bowl, but the bowl grew around the horn, leaving no gap.

Sun Wukong had an idea. "I am going to drill a hole into your horn," he said, "and hide in the hole as a small insect. Then when you pull out of the bowl, I will come out with your horn." This did the trick.

After he got out, Sun Wukong raised his stick and hit the bowl, breaking it into pieces. He then released Sanzang, Bajie, and Sandy and they all escaped from the temple.

Once outside, Sun Wukong summoned all the gods assigned to protect Sanzang. He then went back to attack the demon.

The demon came out and they fought for half a day. Bajie went behind the demon to hit him with a rake. But the demon

---

3   A fully ordained male Buddhist monastic (females are Bhikkhunis)

took out a white cloth bag and opened it. Everyone - Sun Wukong, Bajie, Sanzang, Sandy, and the gods – was sucked into the bag.

The demon returned to the temple with the bag, and emptied it, binding up each of his captives as they fell out of the bag.

That evening, Sun Wukong heard Sanzang lamenting, "Woe is me for not listening to Wukong. Now who is going to save my life?"

Sun Wukong shrunk his body and got out of his bonds. He went to Sanzang and released him, and then he released the others – Bajie, Sandy, and the gods.

Sun Wukong then decided to seek some help. He flew over to the temple of 'Demon-Beater Buddha', and asked for assistance. The Demon-Beater Buddha said, "I will send my best demon fighter to go with you to tame the fake Buddha."

Sun Wukong thanked him and flew back to the demon's temple. As they attacked the demon, the demon again took out the bag. As soon as Sun Wukong saw it, he quickly flew away from the fight, shouting, "Watch out! That bag will capture you!"

The others did not understand what Sun Wukong was talking about, and they all got sucked into the bag.

Sun Wukong was again left alone. This time he made up his mind to go to the Heavenly Palace to ask for aid. The Jade Emperor decided to send the King of Tower to help.

Unfortunately, when they came down to the demon's temple, they met the same fate.

Sun Wukong did not know what to do. Just as he was wondering where else he could go ask for help, he heard a voice in the sky calling him. "Wukong, do you recognize me?" cried the voice.

It was Meytleya Buddha. Sun Wukong knelt to him and told him of the trouble with the demon.

The Meytleya said, "I have come just to help you. That demon is a servant of mine, the Yellow Eyebrow Boy. He ran away with the golden bowl, a stick that I use to stir my potions, and the bag which I used to store food and to carry sundry things."

Sun Wukong asked, "You sent this demon to harass us?"

The Metleya responded serenely, "All because your pilgrimage is destined to come up against obstacles. Now I will change into an old man tending a watermelon field. You go and lure the demon to the field, and turn yourself into a melon. I will offer the demon a melon, which will be you in disguise. You can make him suffer by poking around inside of him."

Sun Wukong was happy to oblige. He went and challenged the demon. The demon saw that Sun Wukong was all alone, and laughed, "Now that you have exhausted all of your various allies, here, feel my stick on your head."

Sun Wukong pretended to lose, and lured the demon to the watermelon patch where he turned himself into a watermelon. The demon chased Sun Wukong to the patch, and suddenly lost him.

But then the demon saw an old man tending the patch and asked him if had seen Sun Wukong. The old man said no, and offered the demon a watermelon. When the demon swallowed the first mouthful, Sun Wukong leapt inside, and started to dance around, poking his stick on the demon's stomach wall. The demon was writhing ithat of – n pain, when the old man revealed his true form, that of the Metleya Buddha.

"Yellow-Eyebrow Boy!" thundered the Metleya Buddha, "Do you recognize me?"

The demon, still writhing in pain, said, "Master, I repent. I shall never do this again."

Metleya Buddha took the white bag and the weapon from the demon, and asked him where the golden bowl was. The demon told him that it had been smashed by Sun Wukong.

Metleya ordered the demon, "Go bring me the pieces." The demon returned with the pieces and Metleva blew a divine breath at them. The pieces flew together into one intact bowl again.

Metleya then said to Sun Wukong, "You can now come out."

Sun Wukong jumped out of the demon's nostril, and was about to hit him with the magic stick, when Metleya said, "Spare him. I can use his services. Now I leave you the task of rescuing your Master and everyone else. I am going home."

Sun Wukong thanked him, and went into the temple to release everyone.

◙ CHAPTER 2 ◙
The Killing of the Boa Constrictor

The pilgrims came upon a village and asked for night's lodging. Their host, Li, was cordial and generous. He asked how Sanzang collected the three disciples, and Sanzang told him that they were given to him by Kuanyin, the Goddess of Mercy, and that they were very capable of conquering demons and killing monsters.

Upon hearing this, Li said, "About thirty miles from here there is a demon who eats our cattle, our domestic animals such as chickens and pigs, even dogs. We have tried everything we could think off, from priests to witch doctors, but nothing has worked. The people we hired to deal with the demon were all eaten up."

Sun Wukong replied, "Don't worry, we will take care of him for you."

"If you can do that," replied Li, "how much of a reward would you like?"

"Nothing," replied Sun Wukong. "We are monks. Besides, we are going to the west, and cannot carry too many things."

As they were talking, there was a strong wind with a fishy smell to it.

"Speak of the devil!" cried Li. "This is the demon."

Sun Wukong and Bajie went out to see. They saw two huge lights in the sky.

Bajie said, "This is a demon that travels in style, eh? He carries two lanterns."

"Bajie, you are blind," replied Sun Wukong, "these are not lanterns. These are the two eyes of the demon."

Sun Wukong flew up to the sky and confronted the demon. He asked, "Hey, who are you?"

The demon did not answer, so Sun Wukong asked again, "Where are you from?"

Still the demon did not respond. "If you do not acknowledge who you are, get my stick!" Sun Wukong said as he attacked the demon.

The demon was no match for Sun Wukong, and fled to his nest.

Sun Wukong and Bajie followed him This time Bajie hit him with the rake. Now the demon reverted to his true form, which was that of a huge boa constrictor, and slithered his way into a hole.

There was about ten feet of his tail left outside of the hole, and Bajie tried to pull it out without success.

"This snake was not able to talk," observed Sun Wukong. "I think he has not achieved the level of spirituality that enables him to change into human and other forms. Seeing as he is so big and awkward, I bet you he cannot turn around in that hole. There must be an exit on the other side. Let's go there and wait for him to come out."

Bajie went to the other side of the mountain, and sure enough there was a hole. Sun Wukong used his stick to poke at the boa constrictor, forcing him to come out from the other side. But the snake managed to come out of the hole when Bajie was not looking, and escaped.

Sun Wukong joined Bajie on the other side and when he arrived, Bajie asked, "When is the snake coming out?"

Sun Wukong laughed and replied, "He is out already. He got out when you were not looking."

So they gave chase after the snake which opened his mouth, trying to swallow Bajie and Sun Wukong. Bajie ran away to avoid being swallowed, but Sun Wukong leapt into the mouth instead so he would be swallowed. Not knowing that one of Sun Wukong's favourite tricks was to get inside the enemy's body to cause the enemy great pain, Bajie panicked, shouting, "Ai-yah! Brother! You are going to be the snake's excrement!"

Sun Wukong laughed from inside the snake, and said, "Here, I will turn him into a bridge!" He pushed his stick into the snake's innards and the snake bent himself upwards like a bridge.

Bajie shouted, "That's fine, but this bridge is useless because no one dares to cross it."

Then Sun Wukong said, "Now watch him turn into a gondola!" He pushed the stick downwards, and the snake bent himself like a gondola, with his head and tail turned up.

This time Bajie said, "Yes, but this boat has no mast." So Sun Wukong made his stick long, piercing the back of the snake. "Here, is your mast," he said.

After teasing the snake for a while, Sun Wukong decided to come out. He poked another huge hole in the snake's belly and flew out through it.

As soon as Sun Wukong was out, Bajie hit the snake over the head, killing it and leaving nine holes. They took the dead snake with them back to the Li residence, where everyone celebrated the elimination of the scourge.

Around the snake's pit, there was a mountain of rotten persimmons that stunk horribly, and it covered the entire west side of the mountain. Sun Wukong estimated that the distance covered by the rotten persimmons was about a hundred miles, and said that this was the sort of thing that a pig could help with by pushing the rot with its snout to make a path.

Bajie said "You are having me on again. Still, I do see your point. All right, I will clear it."

Bajie then turned into a monster pig, the size of a small mountain, with a snout the size of a tower. He pushed the rot away the way pigs burrow through mud, and blew a strong wind out of his snout to clean up the path. The pilgrims covered their nose and passed by the mountain in a hurry, and then they thanked Bajie. Sun Wukong said, "This time the merit is entirely yours."

CHAPTER 3

RESCUING A KIDNAPPED QUEEN

The pilgrims next came upon a city, prosperous and crowded. It was the capital of the kingdom that they were in and they proceeded to have their documents stamped.

Sanzang went to the palace, and was welcomed by the king. He noticed that the king looked sick, with his complexion pale and wan.

Meanwhile, Sun Wukong, Bajie and Sandy who were waiting in the state guest house, decided to go out and find food.

In the street, they noticed a poster issued by the king seeking medicine to cure his illness. Sun Wukong pulled down the poster and put it into Bajie's pocket while he was not looking. The palace guards noticed this and came to Bajie. They asked him what he proposed as the cure for the king.

Bajie knew this was a result of Sun Wukong's mischief, so he asked Sun Wukong to help.

Sun Wukong said, "I can fix the King's illness. But I have to examine him first."

Bajie and Sun Wukong were taken to the palace where Sanzang was still in the king's audience.

"I can diagnose your majesty's illness by taking your pulse," Sun Wukong told the king.

He pulled out three hairs and blew a magic breath on them. They turned into three golden threads, each ten feet long.

Sun Wukong then said to the king, "Put these threads on your wrist, elbow and neck, and I will diagnose your illness and propose a solution."

The king put the threads where Sun Wukong told him to and Sun Wukong said, "Your illness is caused by fright, worry about your loved one, and loneliness because you miss your loved one. The symptoms include nervous breakdown, lack of appetite, insomnia, and paranoia. These can be fixed, but the cause of the illness needs to be removed."

The king was impressed. "You are exactly right. Three years ago, a demon from the Lion King Cave, some three hundred miles west of here, came to take my queen away. His appearance was so scary that I was frightened out of my mind.

"He had a face of a lion, with huge fangs, and he came and went with storms of wind and flying sand. After he took my queen, he came every year to demand two ladies in waiting to serve my queen in captivity. Now is about the time that he will be returning."

Sun Wukong said, "Let me fix your illness first, then I will go and kill the demon."

Sun Wukong went with Bajie and Sandy back to the state guest house to make a medicine for the king. He asked Sandy to bring some soot from the bottom of a wok. He also collected some herbs to mix with the soot. Then he asked Bajie to go and collect the urine from the horse.

Bajie asked, "How can a horse's urine be useful for any illness?"

Sun Wukong replied impatiently, "You forget that the horse is really a dragon, and a dragon's urine has magic power. Go and collect it."

When Bajie approached the horse, the horse said, "My pee is not to be casually given. When I pee in the field, the grass will turn into magical herb. You cannot just collect my pee."

Bajie explained the reason why he wanted to collect the urine, and the horse relented. "All right," said the horse, "I will donate my urine."

Sun Wukong concocted three pills and took them to the palace, where the king took them, and after a dramatic spell of diarrhoea, expelled a piece of meat.

The king said, "This is the meat I ate three years ago, just as my queen was abducted. Since then I felt something was stuck in my stomach. Now you have helped me expel it."

As they were talking, there was a wind that smelled strangely.

The king and his retinue went into an underground hiding place, and Sanzang followed them.

Bajie and Sandy were going to follow suit, but Sun Wukong stopped them, saying, "No. You will come with me to deal with the demon."

The three of them flew up to the sky and facede the demon who said, "I am the vanguard of the Lion King. I have come to collect two ladies in waiting to serve the queen. Who are you to dare to obstruct me?"

Sun Wukong said, "You ignorant demon! Here is my stick!"

The demon was hit by Sun Wukong's magic stick and collapsed into minced meat. Sun Wukong picked up the body, and went down to the palace, calling to the king and Sanzang to come out of hiding. He showed them the body of the demon.

The king was very happy, but Sun Wukong said, "This is not the chief demon. He was just the vanguard. Let me go to get the chief demon."

Sun Wukong and Bajie flew over to the Lion King's Cave. When they were close to the cave, they saw a small demon carrying a letter. Sun Wukong, in the form of a fly, perched on the demon's hair and listened.

The demon was murmuring to himself, "The Master wants to challenge the king into fighting; I know the king's army cannot resist the Master's. It doesn't seem right not to overwhelm the kingdom after kidnapping the queen. But what can I do? I am just an errand boy."

Sun Wukong reverted to his original form, took the stick out of his ear, killed the demon, and took the letter.

Sun Wukong and Bajie then went to the cave, and told the small demons guarding the entrance to tell the chief demon to come out and face their challenge.

The Lion King came out and said, "Who are you, and why are you disturbing my peace?"

Sun Wukong replied, "I am the great Grand Heavenly Fairy Sun Wukong. I am escorting the Sage to go west to get the sutras of the Buddha's true teaching. We have been treated with hospitality and respect by the king, and heard that you had kidnapped his queen. This is outrageous. Release the queen at once or face punishment."

Unconcerned, the demon laughed, "I've heard of you but did not realize that you were such a small, skinny and ugly monkey. If you do not get lost, you will die!"

Sun Wukong and Bajie raised their weapons to attack him. The demon fought back but was soon feeling weak and withdrew. When Sun Wukong and Bajie pursued him, he took out three bells and shook them at Sun Wukong and Bajie.

The bells produced a fire storm with flying sand, causing Sun Wukong and Bajie to retreat.

Bajie said, "I thought you are immune to fire and sand. What happened?"

Sun Wukong answered with some irritation, "I was not expecting this, and did not have time to use my anti-fire mantra." After thinking for a while, Sun Wukong said, "Let me get inside the cave to see how the queen is doing."

Sun Wukong left Bajie waiting outside and flew into the cave in the form of a fly. He soon found where the queen was, and whispered in her ear, "Queen, I am a fairy. I will help reunite you with the king. But tell me how you were treated by the demon this past three years?"

The Queen answered, "The demon has not been able to touch me because whenever he touches me he is stung by poisoned thorns. I do not know how this works, but I have remained unharmed during these three years. But please rescue me now."

Sun Wukong said, "I have a request. Can you overcome your disgust and flatter the demon, then convince him to give you the three bells? I would then steal them, so that he can't use them against us."

The queen agreed, and Sun Wukong then changed into a lady-in-waiting standing near the queen.

When the demon came to her, the Queen pretended to change her attitude, and became solicitous and seductive. The demon said, "I am happy that you are now friendlier to me. What can I do for you?"

The queen said, "I heard that you have three magic bells. Can you show them to me?"

The demon took the three bells from his arm and showed them to the queen. She took it in her hand to admire them, and then put them down on a side table, while chatting amiably with the demon.

The demon was distracted by this, and Sun Wukong quickly stole the bells, replacing them with fake bells that he created by using his hair. Sun Wukong then snuck out of the cave and showed Bajie the bells.

Armed with the real bells, they challenged the demon again, Bajie hit the gate with his rake and broke it open. The demon came out to fight, shouting, "You have not learned your lesson! You have been defeated by me. How dare you come back? I will burn you again!"

Sun Wukong laughed and said, "You are not the only one with the bells. We also have them. Now shake your bells at us." The demon did, and nothing happened.

Sun Wukong then took out the bells which he had taken from the demon and shook them at him. A firestorm with flying sand burned the Lion King's mane.

Sun Wukong and Bajie were going to finish him off, when they heard a voice in the sky saying, "Wukong! Wuneng! Spare the life of the lion!"

It was Kuanyin, and Sun Wukong and Bajie knelt in front of her. Kuanyin said, "This demon is the lion that I used to ride. When the king you wish to help was a crown prince, he went hunting and accidentally hurt the wife of the Peacock God. For that he was punished with separation from his wife for three years.

"This lion was listening when I was discussing this incident and decided to come and take the queen, thinking he might be able to take advantage of her. But steps were taken to make sure that he could do her no harm.

"Now that three years are up, I have come to collect him."

Sun Wukong said, "Yes, but he took the queen and hurt her. That is inexcusable."

Kuanyin said, "No. The queen is unharmed, because she was given a magic vest that protected her. The vest would sting anyone with such pain that no one could touch her."

Kuanyin turned to the demon and said, "Now, come back to me," He rolled down, and turned himself into the lion on which Kuanyin once rode.

Kuanyin then asked Sun Wukong, "Where are my bells?"

Sun Wukong replied, "I don't know, Ma'am."

"You mischievous monkey!" exclaimed Kuanyin. "Your nature has not changed. You are still a thief! If you don't surrender the bells, I will chant the ring-tightening mantra!"

This frightened Sun Wukong, so he took the three bells out of his pocket and returned them to Kuanyin. Kuanyin tied the bells on the neck of the lion, and flew away.

Sun Wukong and Bajie went into the cave and said to the queen, "Now all is clear. We are going to take you back to your loving husband."

Sun Wukong took a piece of brass and gave it a blow of his divine breath, turning it into a dragon. He then told the queen, "Ride on it, and close your eyes. Do not be afraid. We are flying back to the palace." Sun Wukong then chanted a mantra and they flew into the sky.

Before long, they were back in the king's palace. The king was overjoyed to see the queen, and he went up to embrace her, but he then fell to the ground crying, "My arms hurt, and my whole body hurts."

As everyone was wondering what had happened, there was a voice in the sky which said, "Master Sun Wukong, I have come to help."

It was the God of Purple Sun. The God said, "Three years ago, when the queen was kidnapped, I came and gave her a vest to wear. As soon as she put it on, anyone trying to touch her would be stung by poisonous thorns. This preserved the virtue of the Queen. Now that the three year's punishment is over, I have come

Kuanyin tied the bells on the neck of the lion and flew away..

to remove the vest."

The God pointed his finger at the queen, and the vest came off. Sun Wukong thanked him and he left.

Everyone was grateful and happy, and after much celebration, the pilgrims left too.

◙ CHAPTER 4 ◙
ADVENTURE IN THE COBWEB CAVE

Having endured a cold winter, the pilgrims were enjoying the nice climate of the spring. One evening, Sanzang decided that he would go and obtain donated food for everyone.

Sun Wukong said, "Master, you need not do that. Let us do it for you."

"No," replied Sanzang, "as a monk, it is important for everyone to go and ask for a good deed. This helps the monk, and also the giver who would be given a chance to feed a monk, thereby doing a good deed. Let me go." So he went. He approached a gate to a mansion and knocked at it.

A woman opened the gate, and let Sanzang in.

"I am a Tang monk on my way to the west to obtain the sutras of the true teaching of the Buddha. I would like to ask for a donation of some food, so I and my three disciples could sustain ourselves," said Sanzang.

As he entered, Sanzang noticed that there were seven women. They offered some dumplings to Sanzang, but they smelled like meat, so Sanzang said, "I cannot eat any meat. Do you have vegetarian food?"

"Beggars are no choosers. Take this meat dumpling, or else," threatened the women.

Sanzang could not accept that, so he said, "Please, if you have no vegetarian food, then let me leave."

The women refused to let him leave. They bound him and hung him from a beam of the room.

Sun Wukong, Bajie and Sandy were waiting for their Master

to return, and when he did not, Sun Wukong used his vision to look around. He saw an ominous light rising from the middle of the mountain, and said, "I think the Master is in trouble. Let me summon the gods of this place."

The local god came rushing. "Sir, what is your command?"

"Tell me. What is that which gives out the strange light there?" asked Sun Wukong.

"Sir, that is the Cobweb Cave," the local god hastily replied. "It is occupied by seven spider demons. They have been there for some twenty years, and they also took over a hot spring nearby called Dirt Cleansing Spring which used to be the place where heavenly fairies came to take their bath.

"Since the seven spiders took over the place, the fairies do not come any more. The spiders go there very often, about three times a day. If I am not mistaken, this is about time they would be going to the hot spring."

Sun Wukong dismissed the god, and flew over to the Cobweb Cave, where he saw seven women leaving and going to the hot spring.

Sun Wukong was surprised as to how splendid the hot spring was, surrounded by beautiful pavilions and a manicured garden. He changed into a fly and perched on the hair of one of the women, and saw them undress and get into the hot spring.

Once the women were in the hot water, he thought to himself, "I can kill them off here and now, but it would do me no credit for killing naked women in their most vulnerable condition." So he flew off the woman's hair, and changing into a falcon, he grabbed all their clothing and flew off back to Bajie and Sandy.

Sun Wukong told his companions what happened, and Bajie said, "You should have killed them there and then."

Sun Wukong disagreed. "No I will not. If you want to, why don't you go?"

Bajie said, "I have no scruples about killing demons. I will go." And so he went to the hot spring where he found the women cursing the falcon that had grabbed their clothing.

Bajie went up to the women and said, "You seem to be

enjoying your bath, and there seems to be enough room in the hot spring for another person. So why don't I join you?"

The women cursed at him, "You impertinent pig! Stay out!"

Bajie jumped into the bath pool, changing into a trout and swam quickly amongst the women, pecking at them.

After a while, he changed back to his own form, and got out of the pool. Picking up his rake, Bajie attacked the women. They jumped out of the pool, naked, covering themselves with one hand and using the other hand to pull white thread out of their belly buttons, creating and casting a net over Bajie.

Bajie did not expect this, so he was caught by the threads and fell down, helpless. The women, still naked, covered themselves with their threads, and went back to their cave. They went to their rooms, running by Sanzang who was still hung from the beam, semi-naked and giggling.

The women put on their clothing, and left for the Yellow Wind Cave where their elder lived.

Gradually and with great effort, Bajie cut through the threads that were entangling him, freed himself, and went back to Sun Wukong and Sandy. When told what happened, Sun Wukong and Sandy decided to go to the Cobweb Cave to rescue Sanzang.

As they arrived, Sun Wukong and Sandy saw that the cave was covered with silky-white threads, with small demons guarding the entrance.

Sun Wukong and Bajie cut the threads with their weapons and Sun Wukong used his hair, which he turned into thousands of little duplicate Sun Wukongs. Each duplicate was armed with a pair of scissors to cut the threads.

Soon the threads were chopped up and put in a pile. The thousands then killed the guarding demons and went into the cave to rescue Sanzang. Since the seven female demons had left the Cobweb Cave, the pilgrims took over the cave, preparing their meal, and stayed there overnight.

The next day the pilgrims continued their journey and came upon a Taoist temple with a sign saying 'Yellow Wind Cave'. As it was late in the day, the pilgrims decided to ask for lodging there.

They had no idea that this place was the home of the Yellow Wind demon, who was in fact the elder to the seven female demons.

The demon, in the form of a Taoist priest, received them, and was asking them who they were and what they were doing, when a servant came to the priest and whispered something in his ears. The priest excused himself and went inside.

There, the Yellow Wind demon was told by the seven female demons about their encounter with Sanzang and Bajie. He was annoyed by what Bajie and Sun Wukong had done, and he also was excited by the prospect of eating Sanzang's flesh. He opened a red box, in which there were several small envelopes containing poison.

The female demons said, "These monks seem to have supernatural powers, so it may not be easy to kill them with the poison."

The priest replied, "This poison was concocted from magic plants. If ordinary people took a spoonful of it, they'd die in three seconds. If a fairy takes it, he dies within three days."

The priest then went back to the pilgrims and offered them some soup to drink. Sun Wukong, with his quick penetrating glance, saw the difference between the soup the priest was having and the soup that was offered to him and his colleagues, and said, "Why don't I exchange my soup with yours? Your soup looks more delicious than mine."

Before the priest had responded, Sanzang, Bajie and Sandy started to drink the soup. They immediately started to complain about stomach aches. Sun Wukong knew the soup was poisoned, and threw the soup bowl at the priest, who ducked and avoided it, but the bowl was smashed into pieces.

Sun Wukong took out his stick and started to hit at the priest. Soon the two were engaged in a fight. Then the seven female demons came out, shouting, "Brother, let us help capture this monkey." They opened their blouse, exposing their belly buttons, and started to pull silver-white threads and casting them above Sun Wukong.

Sun Wukong was quick to react. He jumped out of the cave

to escape capture. When he looked back, the entire Yellow Wind Cave had become covered by the silver-white threads.

Sun Wukong took out his hair, turned them into hundreds of small Sun Wukongs, and destroyed the cobweb. When the cobweb was broken, he discovered that there were seven spiders, each the size of a horse, squirming, begging to be spared. Sun Wukong killed them all.

The priest, wielding his sword, then took on Sun Wukong. After a while, the priest found himself unable to carry on the fight, so he took off his gown and exposed his upper torso.

Sun Wukong said, "So you want to save us the trouble of corpse-washing?"

The priest raised his arms, and under his arm there were a thousand pairs of eyes, shooting golden rays at Sun Wukong. Sun Wukong managed to escape by turning himself into an armadillo, and burrowing underground for some twenty miles to the other side of the hill.

For the time being, Sun Wukong had escaped unharmed, but he had no idea what had become of his colleagues, who had swallowed poisoned soup. Outside the cave, he saw an old woman. She told him, "This Yellow Wind Cave is occupied by a demon. The only person who can tame him is Bodhisattva Binayaka who lives three thousand miles to the south. She may also be able to help your friends with pills to save their lives." Then she disappeared, leaving only a trail of divine light and clouds.

Sun Wukong asked, "Madam, may I know your name?"

She replied, "I am the Matron of Pear Mountain."

Sun Wukong thanked her, and flew over to the mountain where Bodhisattva Binayaka lived.

After hearing Sun Wukong explain the situation, Bodhisattva Binayaka agreed to come with him to the Yellow Wind Cave.

Once there, Sun Wukong went to challenge the demon, and as he emerged from his cave, the Bodhisattva Binayaka took out a sewing needle and pointed it at the demon. The demon shrivelled, and reverted to his original form, which was that of a seven-foot long centipede.

Sun Wukong was going to kill him, but the Bodhisattva picked up the centipede, saying, "Spare his life. I can use his service."

Sun Wukong obeyed, and asked her to come with him into the cave to save Sanzang, Bajie and Sandy.

The Bodhisattva said, "You are in luck. I have brought with me some recovery pills."

Sun Wukong then placed a pill each in the mouths of Sanzang, Bajie and Sandy. After a few seconds, they started to vomit the poison out, and soon recovered.

The Pilgrims thanked the Bodhisattva as she took the centipede and left.

◎ CHAPTER 5 ◎
The Three Demon Masters

The pilgrims passed through fields and hills, crossed rivers and marshes, and they came to a high mountain. They saw an old man who asked them who they were and what they were up to.

Sanzang told him about their mission, and the old man said, "There is a cave called 'Lion-Camel Cave' which is occupied by three very powerful demons. Unless you have supernatural abilities, you have no chance to pass by these demons. In addition, these demons command fifty thousand smaller demons, all of whom more powerful than ordinary humans."

Sun Wukong scoffed at him. "You seem to be singing their praises. You make them sound more formidable than they actually are. Are you their friend or relative? I tell you, I can take on these three demons and crush them like jelly. As for their army of small demons, they can be crushed by my magic stick rolling over them, like kneading flour."

"If you have supernatural ability, good for you," replied the old man. "I just wanted to warn you." With that, he left.

There was a divine light in the wake of the old man, and Sun Wukong realized that this was no ordinary mortal. So he flew up and eventually caught up with the old man, who turned out to be the God of North Star.

"Hey, old fellow!" called Sun Wukong, "if you wanted to warn us, why didn't you come to us straight out, instead of playing this game with us?"

The God of North Star replied, "Sorry, I thought you might be more likely to listen this way."

Sun Wukong returned to Sanzang and told him that he would do some checking around, and flew over to the Lion-Camel Cave.

As he approached the cave, Sun Wukong turned into a fly and perched on a tree. The small demons were talking.

One, named Wind Rider, said, "I wonder when this fellow Sun Wukong will show up. The Master said he could turn into a fly and come into the cave to investigate."

Sun Wukong was surprised. "So they know me, do they?" he thought. "And they know I can come in as a fly? I wonder how they learned that about me."

So he decided to take on the form of one of the small demons, and struck up a conversation with the Wind Rider.

"I do not know you. Are you one of us?" asked the Wind Rider.

Sun Wukong replied, "Of course I am one of us. But I am new. I am not too familiar with the Masters. Do you mind telling me who they are and their abilities?"

"There are three of them," the Wind Rider told him. "The first demon Master can swallow one hundred thousand troops in one gulp.

"The second demon Master can crush his enemy by catching him with his trunk and squeezing the blood out of the body.

"The third demon Master has two vases, which can melt any person thrown into them."

Sun Wukong felt this information was enough to go by, so he took out his stick and hit the Wind Rider, turning him into minced meat. He then took on the form of the Wind Rider.

Sun Wukong then went into the cave and approached the

three demon Masters. They asked him what he had found out about Sun Wukong.

Sun Wukong said, "Yes, I saw this Sun Wukong. He said he would chop the first demon Master into pieces, skin alive the second demon Master, and pull the sinews of our third demon Master. He also said he would come into the cave by changing into a fly."

One of the three demon Masters said, "I knew it. Everybody! Pay attention to any fly that can be found in the cave. It could be Sun Wukong."

Sun Wukong then decided to tease them. He took one of his own hairs and blew a breath on it, changing it into a fly, which buzzed loudly around the cave. Everybody chased after it, and there was chaos.

Sun Wukong couldn't resist, and he laughed out loud. In this momentary lapse, he inadvertently revealed his own face.

The third demon Master saw him laught, and said, "Hey! this is not Wind Rider! This is Sun Wukong."

Thereupon, everybody descended on Sun Wukong and bound him up. It happened so fast that Sun Wukong did not have time to defend himself.

The third demon Master said, "Bring me the magic vase. We'll throw Sun Wukong into it."

They brought the vase, and Sun Wukong was cast into it.

But wait!

◙ CHAPTER 6 ◙
ENCOUNTER WITH THE BLUE LION,
WHITE ELEPHANT, AND THE CONDOR

Inside the vase, with great effort, Sun Wukong managed to free himself from the rope. He next ried to get out by hitting the vase with his stick, but the vase just stretched without breaking. He tried various other ways, but without success.

Then he remembered the three hairs given to him by Kuanyin, which were to be used in case of an emergency. He pulled one of the special hairs out and changed it into a diamond drill. He drilled a hole into the vase, and got out by changing into a small insect.

Sun Wukong then went out of the cave to challenge the demon Masters. The first demon Master came out, and opened his mouth to swallow Sun Wukong.

Sun Wukong jumped into his mouth, went into his stomach, and started to beat around the wall of the stomach with his magic stick. The demon Master was in terrible pain, and pleaded with Sun Wukong to stop.

Sun Wukong said, "I will come out if you agree to give us safe passage."

He agreed, and Sun Wukong came up from the stomach to the demon Master's throat. The demon Master opened his mouth to let him fly out.

Sun Wukong, not trusting the demon Master, stuck out his magic stick ahead of him, and the demon bit down hard on the stick, smashing four of his teeth.

"I knew you were not trustworthy. I am going back in," said Sun Wukong.

The demon Master once again pleaded with Sun Wukong to come out. He swore that this time he would not dare play any tricks with him. Sun Wukong pulled one of his hairs and turned it into a rope, tying it around the demon's heart, then, he climbed to his nostril, causing the demon to sneeze. The sneeze made Sun Wukong fly out of the demon's nose, with his heart hanging on the rope.

As he came out, Sun Wukong revealed his true form and said, "Now I go back to my people. You must prepare your escort to see us across this mountain." So Sun Wukong went back to Sanzang and told him what had happened.

The old demon Master returned to his cave. But while he might have been willing to escort the pilgrims, but his two younger brothers were adamant. One of them said, "Sun Wukong may have tricked you, but we were not defeated by him. We should fight the pilgrims and see if we can capture Sanzang and eat his flesh."

So the second demon Master led an army of ten thousand against the pilgrims.

Sun Wukong said to Bajie, "Well, they are three brothers, and when the eldest was defeated by me, the second demon has come to seek revenge. Bajie, why don't you go and fight the second demon Master, since I fought the oldest?"

Bajie was reluctant, and asked for the rope Sun Wukong used to tie the knot around the oldest demon's heart.

Sun Wukong laughed, "It's nothing but my hair. If you want it, I can make another one for you."

Bajie said, "Tie it around my waist, and if I am being defeated, pull me back. But if I am winning, loosen the knot."

After a few hours of fighting, Bajie started feeling a bit weak, and shouted, "Pull me back! Pull me back!" But Sun Wukong ignored him.

The second demon Master swung his trunk around Bajie, and threw him down. Sun Wukong saw this, and went up to fight.

This time, the second demon Master was defeated by Sun Wukong's superior fighting skills. What happened was this. When the second demon Master swung his trunk around Sun Wukong, Sun Wukong raised his arms so high that the trunk did not catch his arms, leaving them free.

Sun Wukong then used his stick to hit the demon Master's head, and Bajie, seeing this, shouted, "Good! Now what if Wukong shoved his stick through the demon Master's nose?"

This gave Sun Wukong an idea. He did just that, shoved his stick into the trunk and cried, "Lengthen!" It lengthened, making the whole trunk stiff as a rod, releasing Sun Wukong.

Sun Wukong came down, and started to poke the demon Master with his stick, causing him great pain. The demon Master pleaded for mercy and swore to escort the pilgrims across the mountain.

"Your promise is worth nothing," said Sun Wukong to the

demon Master. "Why should I trust you?"

The demon Master replied that both the oldest demon Master and he had now seen the power of Sun Wukong, so he would not dare go back on his word.

Sun Wukong agreed to let the second demon Master go. The second demon Master went back to the third demon Master and told him of his promise to escort the pilgrims.

But the third demon Master said, "I have not fought them and I would really like a chance to capture them. Let us organize an escort party and carry them across, then we should deploy our troops on the way and ambush them."

The two elder demon Masters agreed. So they went to the pilgrims with a large carriage, and carried the four of them on their way across the mountain, with their horse following.

Suddenly, when they were half way through, the ambush was sprung on the pilgrims, capturing them with ropes. They then took the pilgrims into their cave, and prepared a big fire to steam them.

Sanzang cried, "This is the end of me. I am going to die of heat and asphyxiation."

But Sun Wukong was undaunted, for he knew how to get out of this jam. He said to Sanzang, "Do not worry. I can help. Just wait for a while when I get help."

Sun Wukong took one his hairs and turned it into a copy of himself, while the real Sun Wukong left the vat.

Sun Wukong then called the Dragon King of the North Sea, who came immediately, and asked him, "Sir, what is your command?"

Sun Wukong replied, "My Master and brothers are in that vat, and they are about to be steamed. Please help them by keeping them cool."

The Dragon King immediately ordered the Ice Dragon to enter the vat and wrap himself around Sanzang, Bajie, and Sandy.

Soon the fire started, but because of the Ice Dragon's presence, none of the three were touched by the heat. Sun Wukong then pulled out some of his hair and turned them into sleep-causing insects, which then stung the demons looking after the vat. The demons fell asleep and Sun Wukong went up to the vat.

Sun Wukong heard Sanzang crying that he was going to die without fulfilling his mission. Bajie said, "Yes, but as long as they have not closed the lid, we may still be able to breathe."

Sun Wukong took the lid, and covered the vat. Bajie then panicked and cried, "This time, I think we are going to be cooked for sure."

Sun Wukong chuckled, and said, "Master, I am here."

"How come you are out there?" asked Sangzng, "I still see you inside here!"

Sun Wukong replied, "I have been out the entire time, and what you see is just one of my hairs. Now I will help you get out." With that he pulled Sanzang, Bajie, and Sandy out of the vat.

The pilgrims scurried over to get the horse and the luggage. They went to the front gate, only to find that it was sealed. They then went to back door, which was sealed as well.

Sun Wukong then suggested that they climb over the fence. Bajie protested, "I have never climbed over fences. I have always entered and exited through the door. This climbing of fences is what thieves do. I will not do it."

Sun Wukong replied, "Well then, goodbye. We will climb, and you can stay here and be eaten by the demon Masters. You will make them good bacon and ham."

Seeing no choice, Bajie reluctantly followed, but before they could finish climbing, the demon Masters awakened. They went to check the vat, and realized that the pilgrims had escaped.

The demon Masters searched the entire place, and eventually found the pilgrims trying to climb the fence.

All the pilgrims were recaptured, except Sun Wukong. This time, the demon Masters decided not to steam them, and locked Sanzang in a box in Velvet Cloud Pavilion.

Sun Wukong changed into one of the small demons, to find out where Sanzang was. He went to Bajie, who said he had heard the demons had eaten Sanzang without cooking him. Sandy said he too had heard the small demons talk about Sanzang having been eaten.

Sun Wukong felt greatly distressed, and decided to go to the Buddha. He flew one hundred and eight thousand miles to the Thunder Temple, and asked to see the Buddha.

Sun Wukong approached the Buddha's presence, and said to the Buddha, "You have given this assignment which is so arduous and perilous. Now Sanzang has been eaten up. Why don't you release me by chanting the loosening-the-ring mantra?"

The Buddha said, "I tell you, Sanzang has not been eaten. He is alive. I will help you."

The Buddha summoned two Bodhisattvas to join him, and went with Sun Wukong to the Lion-Camel Cave.

As the three demon Masters came out of the cave, the Buddha called out, "Your term is up. Go back to your masters."

The oldest demon Master turned into a blue lion and went to one of the Bodhisattvas, the second demon Master turned into a white elephant and went to the other bodhisattva. The third demon Master did not want to yield, and instead attacked Sun Wukong, who quickly hid behind the brilliant golden light of the Buddha.

The Buddha told the demon Master, "You should yield and follow me, and you might still have a chance to become a saint."

The demon Master saw no chance of escape, and so turned himself into a condor and went to the Buddha.

Sun Wukong knelt to the Buddha. He said, "I'm grateful for your help, but the demon Masters ate my Master."

The third demon Master, now a condor, said, "No, he was not eaten. He is locked up in a box in the Velvet Fragrance Pavilion."

Sun Wukong was very happy to hear this, and rushed into the cave to save everyone.

The oldest demon Monster turned into a blue lion ... the second
demon Master turned into a white elephant ... the third demon
Master turned into a condor.

◙ CHAPTER 7 ◙
RESCUE OF ONE THOUSAND, ONE HUNDRED AND ELEVEN BABIES

The pilgrims came to a city, the capital of the Bhikkhu Kingdom, and were struck by the sight of chicken coops at the door of each house, holding not chicken, but babies. At the guest house, Sanzang asked the workers what the babies in chicken coops were all about, but the workers simply said, "Let's not talk about it."

Sanzang persisted, and one of the workers finally worked up his courage and said, "Three years ago, a Taoist priest came to town, bringing a beautiful young girl with him, and he went to offer this girl to the king. The king immediately fell in love with the girl and started spending all his time with her, ignoring the affairs of the state. As a result, he grew sick, weaker and weaker by the day.

"The priest, who was given the title of Royal Father-in-Law, suggested to him that there was a magic potion that would not only cure the king's illness but would grant him long life. But there was a catch - the potion had to be prepared with the hearts of one thousand, one hundred and eleven babies.

"The babies you saw in the chicken coops are those that the king has commandeered. Their parents do not dare resist the royal order, but everyone is overcome with sorrow and helplessness."

Sanzang was shocked. "How can a king be so selfish as to kill so many babies just because he was foolishly in love with a young woman?" he asked. "This cruelty must stop. Wukong, can you do something?"

Sun Wukong said, "I suggest that we hide these babies for a few days untill I find out what is what. If there is a demon involved in all this, I will take care of it."

Sanzang was happy, and Sun Wukong summoned the gods of the area as well as the gods assigned to protect Sanzang and told them to collect the babies and hide them in a safe place until further notice.

The next morning, Sanzang decided to visit the palace. Sun Wukong said, "I had better accompany you to see whether the Royal Father-in-Law is a demon or not."

Sanzang was afraid that if Sun Wukong came along, people would be frightened by his appearance. Sun Wukong assured him, "Don't be alarmed. I will be invisible."

They went to the palace and Sanzang told the king the purpose of his mission, and his document was duly stamped. After the stamping, they chatted for a while. In the meantime, the Royal Father-in-Law showed up.

Sun Wukong, who had turned himself into a fly and perched on Sanzang's hat, whispered to Sanzang, "That is a demon."

Sanzang took leave of the king and went to the guest house. Sun Wukong stayed behind to observe.

An official came rushing in, panting, "Sire! A strong wind blew through the city, and all one thousand, one hundred and eleven babies have disappeared."

The king was in tears. "I am doomed," he cried. "Now I do not have the most important ingredient for the potion."

The Royal Father-in-Law said, "Well, you are in luck. That monk Sanzang is a highly virtuous monk. If you ate his flesh you can still gain long life. His heart would be far more valuable than all those babies' hearts combined."

Upon hearing this, the king decided to order all the gates sealed to prevent the pilgrims from leaving the city. Next, he sent a number of soldiers to capture the pilgrims.

Upon hearing this, Sun Wukong flew back to Sanzang and told him, "Master! There is trouble brewing!"

Sanzang was in a panic when Sun Wukong explained what had happened.

Sun Wukong said, "If you want to avoid being captured, why not switch with me?" So saying, Sun Wukong took a mud ball and put it on Sanzang's face, crying, "Change!" Immediately, Sanzang changed into Sun Wukong. Next, Sun Wukong himself changed into Sanzang.

When the king's men came for Sanzang, Sun Wukong went along with them to the palace.

The king said, "I have a request, and if you agree, I shall build a big temple in your honor."

Sun Wukong, pretending not to know anything, asked the king what he wanted.

The king said, "I would like to ask for your heart to be used as a part of a potion that the Royal Father-in-Law has concocted."

Sun Wukong asked, "What heart do you want? There is a kind heart, a brave heart, a jealous heart, an angry heart, a glad heart, and many other kinds of hearts."

The Royal Father-in-Law said, "What we want is the black heart."

To this, Sun Wukong said, "Let me see what I have." He took a knife and cut his belly open, taking out his entrails, heart and all, and showing them to the king, who was by that time shocked and horrified.

Finally, Sun Wukong said, "Well, I don't seem to have a black heart. You are out of luck. But that Royal Father-in-Law of yours, he has a black heart. If you do not believe me, let me cut his belly open and you will see."

Sun Wukong then revealed his own face. The Royal Father-in-Law recognized him, and instantly escaped in the form of a cold wind, but not before taking the king's young concubine with him.

Sun Wukong then asked the king where the demon's nest was, and the king said that when the demon first came to him, he said his cave was named Clear Flower Cave, some seventy-nine miles south of the city.

Sun Wukong decided to tell Sanzang. He explained what had happened, and suggested Bajie join him in the chase.

Bajie said, "I would be happy to go, but I am hungry now. Let me eat something before going."

The guest house workers were by now aware of what happened, and they quickly prepared food for Bajie.

Sun Wukong and Bajie flew south, but could not find anything. So Sun Wukong summoned the god of the area, and asked him about the demon.

The God told them, "The demon lives in a cave hidden behind coded magic. The name of the cave is Clear Flower Cave."

Sun Wukong asked the god how powerful the demon was, and the god said, "With my limited powers I cannot really judge his strength. But I know the code. You go there and find a willow tree. You go around it three times clockwise and three times counter-clockwise, then cry 'Open!' That will reveal the gate to the cave."

Sun Wukong and Bajie went over to the tree and did what the god told them to do. The gate was revealed, and the demon came out. Sun Wukong took out his stick to hit him.

They fought for a while, and the demon could not match Sun Wukong, and again he tried escaping in a wind. Sun Wukong was going to kill him, when there was a voice in the sky, "Sun Wukong! Spare his life."

It was the God of Longevity. He said to Sun Wukong, "This demon is a white deer that I ride. I was at a party and when I came out I found him missing. When I cast my eye around, I found him here. This animal is lucky that I came here in time, otherwise he would have been killed by you."

Sun Wukong agreed to let the God of Longevity keep the deer, but demanded that he come along with him to the palace to show the king who his Royal Father-in-Law really was.

Next, Bajie went into the cave and found the concubine. He hit her with his rake, killing her. She turned out to be a fox.

Sun Wukong, Bajie, and the God of Longevity went back to the palace, Bajie holding the dead fox.

The king was really embarrassed, and begged the God of Longevity to cure him of his illness. The god offered the king three prunes that he happened to have.

The king ate them, and immediately felt better. The gods said to Sun Wukong, "Sir, we have been keeping these babies for two days, and now we would like to return them." A cold wind appeared and brought the one thousand, one hundred and eleven babies back to their parents.

◙ CHAPTER 8 ◙
SEDUCTION IN THE BOTTOMLESS CAVE

After leaving the Bhikkhu Kingdom, the pilgrims had a few weeks of uneventful journey. Then they came upon a dark forest, and when it got dark, Sanzang asked Sun Wukong to go and seek some food donation.

Sun Wukong left, and when he looked back, he saw magnificent light. He sighed, "No wonder! The Master is indeed a very virtuous sage to be surrounded by such divine light."

Suddenly, he noticed an ominous light interfering with the master's glow. He was alarmed and thought to himself, "Something bad may be threatening the Master. Food can wait. Let me go back to check."

As he went back, he saw a woman bound and half buried, calling out, "Help me! Have mercy on me."

Sanzang was ready to help, but Sun Wukong said, "Look, that is not a woman, it's a demon. Let us not help her."

Bajie retorted, "I am afraid Wukong is always suspicious. He is allergic to pretty women."

Sanzang replied, "No, Wukong has been right many times when he identified a demon. Let us just proceed."

The woman was indeed a demon, and Sun Wukong's vision saw through her disguise. She muttered to herself, "They say Sun Wukong has extraordinary abilities, and that reputation does not seem to be exaggerated. Let me try another way."

So she went ahead of the pilgrims and this time hung herself on a branch. When the pilgrims came near her, she pleaded for help again. Sanzang was fooled this time, and asked Sun Wukong to unbind her.

Bajie suggested, "Master, why don't you share your ride with her? She is a pretty lady."

Sanzang said, "I cannot share the horseback with her. Why don't we all walk." So they all walked on until they came upon a temple named Sea Calming Temple. The lamas received them, and put up the pilgrims in one room and the woman in another.

The next morning, Sanzang complained of bad cold, and was unable to proceed with the journey so they stayed another day. On the third day, they were still marooned in the temple, and Sanzang heard the lamas weeping.

He asked what their lament was about, and they said that their fellow lamas had been dying everyday, two a day.

Sun Wukong said this must be because the woman was a demon, and decided to go and examine the situation. He said, "I will see if the demon is the culprit, and if it is, I will fix it."

He changed into the form of a young lama, and went to the room that had been given to the woman. She said, "Come, young friend, let us have some fun. You come with me and we can make love."

Sun Wukong replied, "I am still too young, and I don't know how to make love." She said, "That doesn't matter. I will teach you."

She proceeded to embrace him and then she walked towards the bed. Sun Wukong thought to himself, "This demon is both lascivious and unscrupulous." He grabbed her and threw her to the ground.

The demon was surprised. "Hey, young lover, what are you doing?" she cried.

Sun Wukong revealed himself and, wielding the stick, shouted, "Demon, don't run."

The demon took out her sword, and started to fight, but proved no match for Sun Wukong. She turned one of her shoes into a copy of herself, and escaped, grabbing Sanzang and flying back to her cave.

Sun Wukong hit the demon on the head, and the demon fell, turning into a shoe. Realizing that he had been duped, Sun Wukong went back and found Sanzang missing. So he asked Bajie and Sandy to go with him chasing after the demon.

Sun Wukong flew into the sky and cast his magic vision, but could not see anything. So once again he summoned the god of the mountain and asked about the demon.

The god said, "Sir, there is a cave west of this place, named the Bottomless Cave. It is occupied by a female demon that is more powerful than I. I cannot get rid of her even though she is doing harm to the people under my care."

Bajie went to the mountain but could not find the cave. Eventually, he found a slab with the sign saying 'Bottomless Cave'. So he worked with his rake to clear the trees and soil away, revealing a large shaft.

"Bajie, you should go in, as you are better with the water," said Sun Wukong.

Bajie replied, "But I would not know how to change myself so readily. It would be dangerous for me to go. If you go in and then lure the demon to the outside, maybe we can ambush her."

Sun Wukong agreed, and went inside as a small bug. He found the demon trying to seduce Sanzang with her sweet talk, holding Sanzang's hand, kissing his lips, and touching him.

Sanzang was resisting her as best he could. Sun Wukong flew up to Sanzang's ear and said, "Master, it's me. Why don't you pretend to be more agreeable, and ask for something to drink? I will jump into the drink, and hide in the bubbles. When she drinks, I will get inside of her and make her suffer pain from the inside."

Sanzang said to the demon, "Lady, I am thirsty, can you offer me something to drink?"

She was delighted to hear him talk, and offered him some juice. Sun Wukong jumped into the jug of juice and hid himself in a bubble, but she did not drink it right away.

After a while, the bubble burst. She saw the little bug in the juice and picked it up with her fingers, throwing it away.

Sun Wukong was frustrated, and changed into a vulture and grabbed the food, plates and bowls and made a mess. The demon was annoyed. "I have never seen this bird before. I wonder how it got here."

Sun Wukong then changed back to the small bug, and went to Sanzang's ear. "Master, why don't you ask to go to the orchard, where I will change into a red peach, which you can offer to the demon? I can get inside her that way."

Sanzang said to the demon, "I find this place a bit stuffy. Do you think we could go to the orchard?"

The demon was happy to oblige. When they went to the orchard, Sanzang picked two peaches, one red and one green. He offered the red one to the demon, who put it to her mouth.

Sun Wukong was so impatient that, without waiting for to chew the peach, he ran into her stomach, and started to wield his stick.

The demon was in terrible pain, begging for her life.

"I will leave if you send the Master outside of the cave so he may be received by my other brothers," said Sun Wukong to her.

The demon agreed and had Sanzang carried out of the cave. Sun Wukong jumped out of the demon's mouth, and Bajie and Sandy attacked her.

The demon again took one of her shoes and duped them, grabbing Sanzang again and this time she hid him in the deep interior of the cave.

Sun Wukong again went in to find Sanzang, but could not find him. Instead, he found a stone stele dedicated to 'My Revered Father, the Tower King of Heaven',

Sun Wukong thought to himself, "So this demon is the daughter of the Heavenly Tower King? I should go and complain to him."

He wrote a note to the Jade Emperor accusing the Tower King of letting loose a demon to harm people, and then flew up to the Heavenly Gate.

He was received by the guardian gods who asked what his business was. He said, "I want to see the Emperor to lodge a complaint."

The gods asked to see the complaint, and when they saw it, they were alarmed. "You are accusing the senior god of wrong-doing!" They let Sun Wukong through, but at the same time they also notified the Tower King of the complaint.

Sun Wukong respectfully handed over the memo, and the Emperor asked the Tower King what he had to say.

The Tower King said, "I have four children and all are accounted for. I have no other child anywhere."

Sun Wukong said, "But this demon calls you her father. Have you not at least adopted her?"

The Tower King denied adopting anyone. But his third son said, "Father, indeed you have. Remember the Golden-Nosed White Mouse?"

The Tower King remembered, and said, "I never adopted her. I only saved her life, and if she wants to call me her father, it is not with my consent. Let me go and deal with her."

They went down together to the Bottomless Cave and Sun Wukong sent Bajie to go down and challenge the demon. As she came out of the cave, the Tower King called out, "You insolent beast! Revert to your own form and surrender!"

The demon fell to the ground, and turned into a white mouse with golden-coloured nose.

Sun Wukong then went into the cave with the heavenly soldiers, looking for Sanzang. But Sanzang was hidden away in a cave-within-a-cave so deep that it was impossible to find him.

Fortunately, one of the demon's underlings heard the commotion outside and stuck his head out to see, and he was noticed by one of the heavenly soldiers.

The soldier called out, "Here is another cave. Maybe Sanzang is in it!"

He was, and Sanzang was rescued. Sun Wukong ordered the god of the mountain to put a fire to the cave and burned everything in it.

CHAPTER 9

THE BUDDHIST-KILLING KINGDOM

The pilgrims journeyed happily, chatting and laughing and relishing stories of their own adventures. Then they met an old woman who greeted them and told them that it would be impossible for them to cross the next kingdom.

Sanzang asked why and the old woman told him, "The next kingdom is known as the 'Buddhist-Killing Kingdom'. Its king has vowed to kill ten thousand monks. Having so far killed nine thousand, nine hundred and ninety-six, mostly obscure monks, he is hoping to kill four more, possibly of greater reputation."

Sanzang was afraid, and asked if there was any alternative route to the west, but the old woman said there was no such alternative.

As they were talking, Sun Wukong noticed that the old woman had a halo behind her, and he knelt and said, "O Goddess of Mercy, please tell us what we should do." But the old woman simply vanished.

Sanzang was startled, and complained that Sun Wukong had not alerted him early enough. As Sanzang knelt and kowtowed, Sun Wukong said, "Don't bother. She is already back on her mountain. But since she did not leave any instructions, I think she figured we would be capable of dealing with the situation ourselves."

"But if we go in now, we would be arrested and executed. What should we do?" asked Sanzang.

Sun Wukong answered, "Let me go ahead of you and find out the best way."

He flew over to the capital, and changed into a fly and entered an inn to see how best to find a night's lodging. He decided that the best way would be to come disguised as ordinary men rather than dressed as monks. So he waited for everyone to fall asleep and grabbed four sets of clothing for each of the pilgrims.

Sun Wukong went back to Sanzang and said, "We should go in disguised as laymen. It is important that we do not show our shaved heads. We should tell them that we are horse merchants, and change our names. Master, you should be Mr. Tang; Bajie, you will be Mr. Zhu; Sandy, you, Mr. Sha; and I will be Mr. Sun Wukong."

They now put on laymen's clothing, wearing their hats to hide their shaved heads, and went to a roadside inn to stay for the night, telling the proprietor that they were horse merchants.

By way of explanation, Bajie started to tell him that they were owners of thousands of horses, worth a fortune. This was overheard by a thief, who decided to plan a robbery.

The pilgrims were ushered into a room which they were supposed to share with others. Sun Wukong did not want to share a room, for fear that their shaven heads might be discovered. So he asked for a private room, but there was no private room.

Sun Wukong said to the proprietor that one of them was suffering from fear of light. The proprietor told them that there was a large container, which was big enough to accommodate them. They happily accepted the container.

After midnight, the thieves sneaked into the inn and made off with the container. Sanzang, noticing that the container was being moved, said, "I feel we are being moved."

Bajie added, "That may save us the trouble of having to go through the Buddhist-Killing kingdom."

Trying to calm their fears, Sun Wukong said, "Never mind. Whatever happens, I can handle it. Don't worry and just go to sleep."

The proprietor noticed the theft and alerted the garrison, who chased after the thieves. The thieves had no choice but to abandon the container and run away, leaving it for the garrison to collect and return it to their headquarters.

Sun Wukong climbed out of the container and flew over to the royal palace. On his way he saw the palace surrounded by an auspicious light. He thought to himself, "This shows that the king is a decent ruler. I wonder why he kills monks."

He went to the palace and pulled some of his hair from his left arm and turned them into sleep-inducing bugs which proceeded to bite everyone in the palace. Then he pulled some hair from his right arm and turned them into thousands of small copies of himself. He then took out his magic stick and commanded, "Change!" and turned the one stick into thousands of sharp razors.

Each small Sun Wukong took a razor and went to work, shaving the hair off of everyone, including the king, the queen, the royal concubines, princes and princesses, and of course all the ladies in waiting, the ministers, the palace guards and soldiers.

After that, Sun Wukong collected his hair, and went back to the container. The next morning, the queen woke up first, and she was shocked to find that her head was shaved clean. She screamed, waking up the king.

The king was also shocked to find his own head shaved clean. Then everyone else found out their heads were shaved clean, and there was widespread panic.

The king said, "I wonder whether it is because I killed monks. This must be the punishment for my deeds."

When the king started his daily court, the garrison reported the capture of the container that the thieves had abandoned. The container was brought to the king's presence to be opened.

Sanzang asked, "Now what do we do?"

Sun Wukong said, "Don't worry. When the container is opened, you just emerge with your palms together, chanting the sutra. Everything will be all right."

The container was opened, and the pilgrims emerged dressed as monks, chanting sutra. The king trembled with fear, and asked, "Your Reverence, where do you come from?"

Sanzang explained that he was sent by Emperor Taizong of Tang Empire to go west to collect the true teaching of the Buddha.

The king said, "I have killed many monks because of a minor offenses. Now I repent."

The pilgrims were given the best treatment and were fed and accommodated. When they were ready to leave, Sun Wukong said, "The name of your kingdom should be changed to 'Buddhist-Honouring Kingdom.'"

The king agreed. The pilgrims were sent off with great pomp.

◎ CHAPTER 10 ◎
The Demon With a Pestle

Sanzang asked Sun Wukong what exactly happened to change the king's attitude. Sun Wukong explained and they had a good laugh. Then they came to a mountain.

Sanzang said, "We should be on guard. Every time we see a mountain, there's usually a demon."

Sun Wukong replied, "Why don't I go do some reconnaissance." And he flew ahead of the rest.

He felt a wind that he thought was strange, and saw a demon sitting on a rock. Sun Wukong decided to tease Bajie, so he went back and told Sanzang, "I saw a village, where people are devout Buddhists and are generous in offering food and lodging."

Sure enough, Bajie was tempted. "I will go and get us some offerings."

Sun Wukong said, "But you cannot go asking for offerings when you are so ugly. You have to change your form, into someone better looking."

So Bajie changed into a young monk, and taking the begging bowl, went ahead. Before long, he was surrounded by a swarm of little demons who tugged at him, trying to capture him.

Bajie was surprised. "Aren't you going to give me something to eat?" he asked.

The demons laughed and said, "You want us to feed you? We are going to feed on you!"

This was not what Bajie had expected, so he changed back to his own form and started to wield his rake and attacked the head demon.

They put up a stiff resistance, and Bajie did not feel he could prevail. Meanwhile, Sun Wukong decided to see how Bajie was doing, so he took one hair and turned it into a copy of himself, standing beside Sanzang, and then he flew over to the battle site, and shouted, "Bajie, I am here."

This encouraged Bajie, and he fought with redoubled ferocity, defeating the head demon. After that, both went back.

Bajie was panting and foaming in his mouth, saying, "If it were not for Wukong coming to my aid, it would have been difficult."

Sanzang said, "But Wukong never left my side."

Bajie said, "Master, you cannot tell. Wukong knows how to slip away while leaving a decoy behind."

Meanwhile, the demon was very distraught. When one his sidekicks asked him why, he said, "I am told that the Tang monk is a highly moral person who has kept his celibacy all his life, and if one eats his flesh, one will live for ever. But I met this Zhu Bajie, who is the second disciple to this monk, and he was too strong for me. And I heard that there are two others that are just as strong. if not stronger. So I don't know what to do."

The sidekick replied, "We can use the technique of divide and conquer. I say we organize three groups to take them on, except that we send one group at a time. When one group has successfully engaged one of them, the next group could go on attack, engaging the second, and so on."

The demon was delighted at the suggestion. "I will make you a Vanguard if we succeed."

As the pilgrims continued their journey, one group of elves blocked them, and Bajie went ahead and fought them. Then another group showed up to attack, and Sandy started to fight them. Finally, a third group showed up, and Sun Wukong was forced to engage them.

Meanwhile, the demon snatched Sanzang and retreated into his cave.

The three disciples defeated the three groups of elves, only to find out that Sanzang was gone. They realized that they had been fooled by this divide and conquer trick.

The demon bound up Sanzang, and threw him into a room

where another victim was bound up. The other victim asked Sanzang who he was, and explained that he was a wood cutter who had strayed too close to the cave and was captured.

To dupe the three disciples, the demon took a block of wood and turned it into the severed head of a man, and threw it out of the cave.

The three disciples came to the cave, and found this head. Bajie and Sandy were distressed to see it, but Sun Wukong was able to see that it was just a block of wood.

This was observed by the demon's henchmen. The demon marveled, "This Sun Wukong is really something. I have heard about his abilities, and the reputation is well deserved."

This time they used the real severed head of a man, and threw it out of the cave. Even Sun Wukong saw that it was a real head, and the three were persuaded that Sanzang had been killed.

They buried the head, and went to the cave determined to avenge the Master. The demon's Vanguard came out to fight, but he was quickly killed by Bajie, who discovered the dead Vanguard was in fact a dead wolf.

The demon had blocked the gate with rocks, wood and soil, so it was not possible to break it open.

Sun Wukong said, "The demon cannot block himself in. There must be a back door. Let me go find it."

He went to the other side of the mountain, and saw a waterfall. Beyond the fall, he could see a gate, much like his own Water Screen Cave. He thought to himself, "This has to be the back door. Let me go in as a snake; no, a crab; no, how about a mouse."

So he went in as a mouse, and once inside, changed into a fly, and he found Sanzang still bound up there. He went up to Sanzang and called him, "Master!"

Sanzang said: "Wukong! Rescue me!"

"Let me put these demons to sleep before I rescue you," replied Sun Wukong. And so he pulled out some hair from his arms and turned them into sleeping bugs, which soon bit everyone in the cave.

Sun Wukong freed Sanzang and was about to leave, when the wood cutter cried, "Please rescue me too! I have a mother of eighty-three to look after."

Sanzang told Sun Wukong, "Have mercy on him. Let's rescue him."

Sun Wukong freed him, too, and then he used the left over ropes to bind up the demon, who was asleep.

Now Sun Wukong used his stick as a carrying stick to carry the demon out of the cave and took him to where Bajie and Sandy were.

Sanzang called out, "Wuneng, Wujing!"

Bajie said, "Oh no! Here comes the Master's ghost!"

Sun Wukong said, "You stupid pig! This is the Master himself, not his ghost."

Sun Wukong retrieved his hair and the elves in the caves came out of their sleep. They were all slaughtered by Sun Wukong, Bajie and Sandy.

When Bajie saw the demon, still bound up but gradually awakening, he hit the demon with his rake, killing him. It turned out that the demon was a large leopard.

◎ CHAPTER 11 ◎
Producing Rainfall

The pilgrims continued their journey happily, chatting about their adventure and enjoying the scenery on the way. They came to a town, which looked somewhat depressed, with people moving around very slowly, as if consumed by lethargy.

They saw a man who looked like an official and asked him whether there was a problem that was troubling the city.

The man said that he was indeed an official of this city, named Fengxian (Phoenix Fairy), with a public notice to seek anyone who could bring about a shower of rain.

Sun Wukong said, "Bringing rain is easy. I can bring over the

Dragon King to give you rain."

The official asked the pilgrims to go and meet with the chief magistrate of the city. They went, and explained to the chief magistrate that they were from the Tang Empire and were on their way to the west.

The chief magistrate told them, "You are already in the kingdom of the west where the Buddha's residence is located. I have been appointed as the chief magistrate here by the king himself. I have governed this place well, but for three years we have had no rain and people are on the verge of starvation. I hear you are able to help us with this problem. If you can, I would be happy to give you a very generous reward."

Sun Wukong replied, "We are not after rewards. Let me call on the Dragon King."

He chanted the mantra to summon the Dragon King, and immediately the sky was covered with cloud.

Sun Wukong flew up to the cloud, leaving the chief magistrate in awe. In the cloud, Sun Wukong saw the Dragon King, who greeted him.

Sun Wukong said, "I would like to ask you for a foot of rain."

The Dragon King said, "Sir, I have not brought with me the rain-giving device. Besides, you may not know it, but this place is not supposed to have rain under orders of the Jade Emperor."

Sun Wukong said, "What? If that is the case, I will go and talk to the Jade Emperor."

He let the Dragon King go home to his palace in the Eastern Ocean, and flew up to the South Gate of Heaven, and asked to see the Jade Emperor.

He said to the Jade Emperor, "I hear that you have decreed not to give the city of Phoenix Fairy any rain. I would like to appeal to you for reconsideration of this decree, because the people are suffering very badly."

The Jade Emperor said, "Three years ago, the chief magistrate of that city was preparing a festival to pay me a tribute. Then he overturned the offering table in a fit of rage, and spilled all the

Sun Wukong called up to the cloud above, saying "Dragon King!
Show yourself to the people here!" The dragon separated the cloud
and appeared in the sky...

food on the ground. Then he fed his dogs with this food, which was supposed to be for me. That is why I am punishing him for that act. But now that you have come to intercede on their behalf, I shall relent."

Sun Wukong thanked him and called on the Dragon King again, this time with the approval of the Jade Emperor. The Dragon King brought his rain-giver with him, so he gave a foot of rain to fall on the city.

Sun Wukong thanked him, and came down to the city. The chief magistrate knelt down in gratitude. Sun Wukong called up to the cloud above, saying, "Dragon King! Show yourself to the people here!"

The Dragon King separated from the cloud and appeared in the sky, with everyone of the city kneeling and kowtowing.

Sanzang asked, "Now, you say we are in the kingdom of the West. How far is it to the Thunder Temple where the Buddha lives?"

"It is still several thousand miles further."

"In that case we should leave immediately lest we waste our time." And the pilgrims left, with the heartfelt thanks of the chief magistrate and the people.

◙ CHAPTER 12 ◙
SHOWING OFF THE WEAPONS AND
TEMPTING A DEMON

As the pilgrims continued their journey, they talked about their recent adventure.

Sanzang said, "Wukong, you have achieved an important merit. In the Bhikkhu Kingdom you saved the lives of one thousand, one hundred and eleven, but here in the Phoenix Fairy Kingdom, the rain you brought to them has saved many times more. You should be congratulated."

"This is all due to your virtue and the help of many gods," replied Sun Wukong.

As they were talking, they arrived in Jade-Flower City.

Sanzang said, "Look at the way buildings are built and the streets are organized. Look at the way people are dressed and conducting themselves. These people are just as civilized as the Tang people and just as prosperous."

They checked in at a guest house, and Sanzang went alone to have his documents stamped. As he was received by the Jade-flower King, he introduced himself. "I have been sent here by the Emperor Taizong of the Tang Empire, to go to the Buddha and obtain his true teachings. I have been on my journey for almost fourteen years, and I am accompanied by three disciples who have supernatural skills and can perform supernatural feats."

The king, impressed, sent his messenger to invite the three disciples to the palace. As they arrived, their appearances caused panic. The entire court, including the king, were amazed by Sun Wukong who had a monkey's face, and Bajie who had a pig's face, and Sandy, whose face was dark blue.

Sanzang hastily reassured the court, "Please do not be alarmed: my disciples may be very ugly, but they are not only good at heart but have abilities to fight and win over demons."

The king had three sons, who were strong and were well-versed in martial arts. When they heard about the three disciples, they wanted to see for themselves. So they came to the audience hall and asked, "Where are the three disciples of the Tang monk?"

They were not frightened by the appearances of the three, and asked what weapons they used.

Bajie took out his rake and shook it into size. The rake emitted brilliant light.

Bajie said, "If you can lift it, it's yours." The princes tried to pick it up, but it would not budge. They were astounded, and asked, "How much does this weigh?"

Bajie replied, "It weighs five thousand four hundred pounds."

Then Sandy took out his Demon-Quashing Stick, which also became enveloped in divine light, and planted it on the ground, saying, "You can have this too, if you can lift it."

Again, the princes could not move it. Sandy said, "My weapon also weighs five thousand four hundred pounds."

Then it was Sun Wukong's turn. He took his stick out of his ear, shook it into size, and planted it on the ground. Instantly, it started emitting blindingly beautiful rays.

Sun Wukong asked, "Can you move it?"

Of course no one could, and Sun Wukong said, "This weighs thirteen thousand five hundred pounds."

The princes were awestruck, and begged the three disciples to show how they used the weapons.

Sun Wukong took the stick, flew up to the sky, and started to show the various forms of the stick's use. Bajie followed suit, then Sandy.

After an hour of demonstrations, the three came down to earth, where the three princes knelt and begged them to teach how to use the weapons.

Sanzang was not pleased. He scolded his three disciples. "Your vanity has gotten the better of you. This is going to cost us undue delays in our departure."

Still, they had no choice. The three disciples then blessed the princes and bestowed upon them supernatural strength, enabling them to lift one thousand kilograms.

The princes then summoned blacksmiths to produce similar weapons for them. The three weapons were kept in the special foundry, and at night the brilliant lights from them were visible from miles away.

A demon who lived in a cave named Tiger's Mouth Cave seventy miles north of the city noticed this and flew over to the palace to see what the sources of the lights were. He saw the three weapons, and carried them away.

The next day the blacksmiths noticed that the weapons were gone, and alerted the princes.

Bajie said, "It must be because our weapons emitted such magnificent lights that someone was tempted to steal."

Sun Wukong said, "No. these weapons are so heavy that no

human can move them. I believe it is the work of a demon."

The princes said, "There is a Golden-Haired Lion Demon who lives seventy miles north of here. He may be responsible for the theft."

Sun Wukong rose to the sky and, using his vision, he saw where the demon in the north lived. He flew over to assess the situation, and noticed two of the demon's servants heading out of the cave. He went down as a fly to hear what they were talking about.

It turned out that the demon had decided to celebrate the capture of the three weapons by throwing a party, and the two servants were being sent to buy some beef and pork.

Sun Wukong cast a spell to freeze the two servants, and flew back to Jade-Flower City to report what he had found.

He then told Bajie and Sandy, "I will turn into one of the servants and you into another. Sandy, you take on the disguise of a butcher. The three of us can go into the cave, find where our weapons are, and then bring them back."

They bought some beef and some pork, and flew over to the cave. The demon saw them coming in, and asked why they had come back with the butcher.

Sun Wukong said, "The meat cost a bit more than you gave us money for, so we brought the butcher so you could pay him the difference."

As they looked around, they noticed that there was some light coming from one of the rooms. When they entered the room, they found the three weapons lying there. They quickly picked up the weapons and, wielding them, got out of the cave.

The Golden-Haired Lion demon chased them to the outside of the cave, yelling, "You thieves! Give back the weapons!"

The three laughed. "You shameless demon! You are the thief."

The demon and nine other lion demons surrounded Sun Wukong, Bajie and Sandy, but they were defeated by the trio. Somehow, they escaped to the southeast to the Scrawny-Roots Cave where the Nine-Headed Lion lived.

The trio went back to the Tiger-Mouth Cave and killed all the demons there, who turned out to be wolves, foxes, hyenas, and other animals. They also burned down the cave.

The trio then went back to the Jade-Flower kingdom and reported what had happened. The king was both happy and worried; happy that the demon was defeated, but worried that he might seek revenge.

Meanwhile, when he saw the Golden-Haired Lion, the Nine-Headed Lion was surprised. "I was getting ready, he said, "to go to your cave for the celebration of the weapons, and I find you here. What brought you here?"

The Golden-Haired Lion told him that he had picked up the three weapons from the palace, but then he was attacked by the three monks and the three weapons had now been taken back by them.

The Nine-Headed Lion asked who the three monks were. Golden-Haired Lion said, "The first is a monk with the head of a pig, the second has a blue and black face, and the third is a monk with a monkey's head."

The Nine-Headed Lion replied, "You have taken on the wrong kind of enemy. The two others are not too difficult, but the one with the monkey's head, his name is Sun Wukong, and he is very powerful. Well, we have gotten ourselves into this situation. Let me see what I can do."

So the older demon went out of the Scrawny-Roots Cave to fight Sun Wukong, Bajie and Sandy.

The Golden-Haired Lion let his nine brother lions confront the trio, and they fought for half a day long.

Gradually, Bajie was getting tired, and he was hit. As Bajie fell and was captured, Sun Wukong used his hair to make hundreds of copies of himself, and captured two of the lion demons.

Taking the two captured lion demons, Sun Wukong and Sandy returned to Jade-Flower City. Sanzang was concerned about Bajie's safety, but Sun Wukong reassured him, "We have two of theirs. They will not harm Bajie lest we harm these two."

After a night's rest, Sun Wukong and Sandy went back to the

Scrawny-Roots Cave to finish off the demons.

The Nine-Headed Lion told his grandson, "You go out and engage them. I will go to the Jade-Flower kingdom and capture the king, the princes, and Sanzang."

So the Golden-Haired Lion let his remaining lion brothers engage Sun Wukong and Sandy. The Nine-Headed Lion flew over to the palace and revealing his original form of nine-heads, he took Sanzang, the King, the three princes, and shouted, "I got them, I am going back to my cave!"

Sun Wukong and Sandy were undaunted. They succeeded in killing the Golden-Haired Lion and captured all of the lion brothers. When they went back to the palace, they found the queen and ministers crying and panic-stricken because the king and the princes had been taken.

Sun Wukong reassured them, "Do not be anxious. We will get them back in no time. Meanwhile you can go stuff the Golden Haired Lion, or use his fur as a floor rug."

Sun Wukong and Sandy went back to the Scrawny-Root Cave again, but this time the Nine-Headed Lion captured them, using his mouth to bite them. They were taken into the cave and bound up.

The demons were tired, and they lay down to sleep. The king, the princes, Sanzang, Bajie and Sandy were scared, but Sun Wukong laughed. "Don't worry," he said, "I'll set you free in no time."

He shrank his body and slipped out of his bonds, and started to free the rest by cutting the ropes, beginning with Sandy who happened to be nearest to him.

Bajie complained, "Hey, I have been bound up for the longest time. Free me first."

Sun Wukong replied, "Shhh! You are going to wake up the demon!"

Sure enough, the demon awakened, and came to see what was going on. Sun Wukong blew his magic breath to put out the candles, and slipped out of the cave in the dark. But Sandy was not as skilful, and he was discovered by the demon before he could escape from the cave.

As Sun Wukong emerged from the cave, the gods of the mountains came to him. "Sir, the gods of the localities reporting," they cried.

Sun Wukong was a little annoyed. "Why did you wait this long to come to me?" he enquired.

They said, "When you just arrived, you were received by the king of the Jade-Flower Kingdom and we did not wish to disturb you. But now we see that you are having problems with the demons, so we came to report to you."

Sun Wukong asked the gods about the demon's origins, and they told him that the Nine-Headed Demon had been around for three years, and that he came from the palace of God the Saviour of the Afflicted.

Sun Wukong thanked them for this information, and flew up to the East Gate of Heaven.

The guardian gods received him and asked why he had come. Sun Wukong explained that he was having a problem with a demon and that God the Saviour of the Afflicted could help.

The guardians ushered Sun Wukong in and he proceeded to the Eastern Heaven to the Saviour's temple.

The Saviour asked Sun Wukong whether his mission had now been accomplished. Sun Wukong said, "No, but we are already in the kingdom where the Buddha's residence is located."

"Then why are you coming east, instead of going west?"

Sun Wukong said, "I believe that you have a nine-headed lion missing. This lion is causing a lot of trouble. He even captured my Master and the king along with his three princes. Why don't you check to see if you are missing this animal?"

The Saviour summoned the Lion-Tender and asked him what was going on. The Lion-Tender said, "I am to blame. I saw a bottle of divine wine and drank it, and I fell asleep. Meanwhile, the lion stable was unlocked, and one of the lions, the Nine-Headed one, escaped."

The Saviour asked the Lion-Tender when he had drunk the wine, and he told him that it was three days ago. The Saviour said,

"Three days in Heaven is like three years on earth. So it makes sense that the demon has been there for three years" Turning to Wukong, he said, " I am sorry you have had so much trouble. I will fix this for you."

The Saviour, with the Lion-Tender in tow, went down to the Scrawny Roots Cave.

Sun Wukong went ahead to challenge the demon. As the demon came out, the Lion-Tender shouted, "Nine-head! Come back to me!"

The demon saw the Lion-Tender and, behind him, the Saviour himself. He crumbled and prostrated himself, turning into a nine-headed lion.

The Saviour put a magic rope through the demon's nose, and took Sun Wukong's leave. Sun Wukong then went into the cave to rescue everyone.

Sun Wukong, Bajie and Sandy took Sanzang, the king and the three princes, told them to close their eyes, and carried them, flying back to the palace.

The entire court and the country celebrated the end of the demon's scourge. The celebrations lasted for weeks, until the pilgrims finally decided to leave.

Seeing that the people were not willing to let them go, they decided to leave in secret, without informing anyone but leaving behind a note.

◉ CHAPTER 13 ◉
THE FALSE BUDDHA STEALING OIL

The pilgrims were now journeying in the kingdom which included the Buddha's abode. It was pleasant and easy.

They came upon a temple, named the Cloud of Mercy. Sanzang knew this was a good Buddhist temple, and decided to go in to worship and to ask for lodging.

The resident monk knelt when he heard Sanzang tell him that they had come all the way from the Tang Empire, and asked them to participate in the Lantern Festival, the first full moon of the lunar New Year.

The pilgrims agreed, and Sanzang offered to sweep the tower. The Lantern Festival involved each household lighting oil lamps, and there was a competition to see which household had the largest and brightest lamp.

As the Festival approached, there was a chill wind blowing. The monks said, "Here come the three Buddhas – Past, Present and Future. They are here to accept our offering of oil."

Sun Wukong thought this was suspicious, and went up to the sky to see. He saw three Buddha statues coming down to take the oil offering. Sanzang knelt and kowtowed, but Sun Wukong recognized them to be demons.

The demons swiftly picked up Sanzang and flew away. The monks were in a panic and asked Sun Wukong what was going on. Sun Wukong told them, "You are ordinary people, as is my Master, so you are not equipped to tell the difference between demons and people. Now, our Master is captured and we will have to go and rescue him."

Sun Wukong, Bajie and Sandy flew towards the north-east where the demons had gone. On their way, the trio met the four gods assigned to protect Sanzang. Sun Wukong was very annoyed. "Why did you not alert me to these demons?" he asked. "Come and get your punishment!"

The four gods trembled and said, "Please don't hit us. We were too busy trying to protect your Master."

Sun Wukong asked the gods about the demons and the gods told him, "There are three of them. Their names are Avoid Gold, Avoid Heat, and Avoid Dust. They have been here for a thousand years, living in the Mystic Essence Cave on the Blue Dragon Mountain."

Sun Wukong dismissed the gods, and went to the cave.

He shouted, "You filthy oil thieves and kidnappers! Return my Master!"

The three demons came out and, after they had fought for a few hours, the demons summoned their troops, mostly bull-headed and horse-headed, to surround and attack Sun Wukong.

Seeing that the odds were against him, Sun Wukong made a somersault to get out of the situation.

He went back to Bajie and Sandy to tell them what happened. The trio returned to the cave. Changing into a firefly, Sun Wukong flew inside the cave and found Sanzang, all bound up in an empty room.

He went to Sanzang and said, "Master, I am here."

Sanzang said "Wukong, rescue me quickly."

Sun Wukong reverted to his own form and pointed his finger at the rope, untangling it. He then took Sanzang's hand to lead him out of the cave.

But they had been noticed by the demons, who came after them with their weapons. Sun Wukong took out his sticks to fend off the demons, but in the frantic fight that followed, he lost touch with Sanzang.

Sun Wukong managed to free himself from inside the cave, where Bajie and Sandy were waiting outside, and told them what had happened.

Sun Wukong told them, "Most of the demon's troops were bulls and horses. This tells me that he is either from the Underworld or from Heaven. Let me go and find out who can control them."

He went to heaven, to the Western Heavenly Gate, where the guardian gods greeted him. Sun Wukong asked them if they knew any one missing three household animals.

The God of North Star told him, "Those are three rhinos. I believe the four Animal Star Gods can control them."

Sun Wukong asked the Jade Emperor to permit the four animal Star Gods to come and deal with the situation. The Jade Emperor agreed, and Sun Wukong and the four came down to the Mystic Essence Cave.

Sun Wukong challenged the demons who came out to fight him, but when they saw the four Animal Star Gods, they knew they were defeated, and started to run. Sun Wukong and two of the Gods chased after them, and killed one of them.

The two remaining demons ran to the Eastern Ocean, and

then dove into the water. Sun Wukong summoned the Dragon King and asked him to help.

The Dragon King sent his crown prince to lead an army which would surround the two demons and capture them.

Sun Wukong and the two Star Gods returned to the Mystic Essence Cave, with the two live rhinoceros and one dead one.

Bajie said, "I think we can saw off the horns for medicinal use. The dead one can be used to upholster a chair."

◙ CHAPTER 14 ◙
THE FALSE PRINCESS TRIES TO MARRY SANZANG

The pilgrims were traveling in nice weather and eagerly discussing their imminent arrival in the Western Heaven.

They came upon one of the first places connected with the Buddha's activities during his lifetime. It was the Gold-Paved Garden. A rich disciple of the Buddha had wanted to establish a new ashram at a beautiful riverside, but the owner of the land refused to sell it.

The landowner said to the disciple, "You cannot afford this piece of land. It will cost as much as the number of gold coins that will cover the entire land."

The rich man proceeded to cover the land with gold coins, and the owner had no choice but to sell. That is where they established an ashram and called it the 'Gold-Paved Garden'.[4]

The quartet entered the garden, where there was a large temple, and Sanzang knelt and kowtowed to the statues of the Buddha. They were given lodging and food.

At night, Sanzang and Sun Wukong were walking in the garden, when they heard someone sobbing. It was a young woman, sobbing sadly inside a small room.

Sanzang asked, "Young lady, why are you sobbing?"

She replied, "I am the princess of the kingdom of Tianzhu

4   This garden exists to this day, just outside of Varanasi, India. called Sarnath.

(Heavenly Parasol). One night a year ago I was enjoying the flowers in my garden at night, when I was abducted by someone whom I could not see, and was dumped here.

The chief monk took pity on me, but he did not know who had abducted me. To protect me, he put me in this small room, telling the rest of the monks that I was a demon so no one would approach me. I understand his goodwill, so I go along with this role. During the day, I make menacing noises to frighten people, but at night I sob because I miss my parents."

Sanzang asked the chief monk about this the next day.

The chief monk told them, "Yes, that is true. And I have gone to the capital to investigate, but I saw that there was a princess, who looked just like this young lady here. So I do not know what to do."

"Let us go to the capital. I will find out what to do," suggested Sun Wukong.

The pilgrims left the temple and arrived at the capital. After checking in at an inn, they asked around about the princess.

They were told that the princess had reached the eighteen years of age and, of a marriageable age now, was going to choose a husband the next day by throwing a ball from the top of the tower in the main square. There would be thousands of young men hoping to be selected. Sanzang and Sun Wukong decided to go and see.

When they arrived at the square, they were pushed by the crowd towards the centre of the square. After a while, the princess appeared at the top of the tower and an announcement was made.

"Her highness will throw this embroidered ball. Whoever is hit by this ball shall be chosen as the consort."

The princess saw Sanzang and knew he was a sage, so she threw the ball at him, hitting him in the head.

Sanzang was dumbfounded, while thousands of others were deeply disappointed. The palace guards came to Sanzang and took him into the palace, congratulating him.

Sanzang was distressed, and cried out to Sun Wukong, "Help

me! Help me get out of this mess!"

Sun Wukong replied, "Don't worry. You go in, and I will hide myself and go with you, so I can find out whether the princess is a fake."

Sanzang had no choice, and the king was less than pleased to see that the princess's choice was a monk. But since the princess had thrown the ball and hit Sanzang, he could not object.

When he saw the king, Sanzang begged, "Your majesty, I am a monk, and I am not allowed to get married. Please forgive me and let me go."

The King asked, "Where have you come from?"

Sanzang explained, "I am from the Tang Empire, and I have been designated by the Emperor Taizong to journey to the Western Heaven to obtain the sutra of the Buddha's true teaching."

When the king heard this, he was delighted. He was not happy to have a monk for a son-in-law, but this monk was different. He was of noble origin, and he was from the Tang Empire. He ordered preparations to be made for the wedding which was to take place in four days.

Sanzang was in a panic. He told Sun Wukong, who was perching on his shoulder as a bee, "Wukong! Help me."

Sun Wukong chuckled and replied, "Hey, if the princess is a demon in disguise, I will destroy it and rescue you. But if the princess is real, you might as well enjoy her company – the three of us can go to the Western Heaven to get the sutra. We will visit you on our way back."

Sanzang was furious. "Nonsense!" he said. "If you will not help, I will chant the mantra to tighten the ring."

Alarmed, Sun Wukong hurriedly replied, "No, no, no. I will help you. If the princess is a demon, I will kill it; if the princess is real, I will just freeze everyone in the court and rescue you. Now I cannot tell whether the princess is real of a fake because I have not seen her. So you should play along, and when the princess shows up, I will be able to tell."

The day came when the wedding was to take place. There was a banquet, which the princess regally walked in to attend.

Sun Wukong immediately saw that the princess had a demonic glow behind her head. He assumed his true form and shouted, "You shameless demon! What did you do with the real princess?"

Sun Wukong took out his stick and attacked. The fake princess jumped out of the princess's dress and crown, and taking out his weapon, he went up to the sky and fought.

The king and his court were overwhelmed by what they saw. "The princess is a fake! Now the demon has stripped off his dress and is naked? And the divine monk can fly?"

The demon was no match for Sun Wukong, so he escaped in the form of a cold wind to the northeast of the capital.

Sun Wukong chased after him, but lost the demon in a cave. He was afraid that the demon might go and kidnap Sanzang, so he flew back to see that Sanzang was safe. He suggested that Bajie and Sandy be asked to join Sanzang and guard him against the demon's attack.

The court, by now in awe of the quartet, immediately sent a messenger to collect Bajie and Sandy. Sun Wukong told them to guard Sanzang, and flew off to the cave.

Sun Wukong still could not see any demons, so he summoned the gods of the mountain and asked them about the demon he was after.

The gods told him, "This mountain has not seen any demons. There are three caves, and the demon you are chasing may be hiding in one of them. We can tell you the exact locations of the three caves."

Sun Wukong inspected the three caves, and saw one of them covered. He thought that this one must be the one where the demon was hiding, and so used his stick to poke at it.

The demon was indeed hiding inside, and he came out fighting, wielding his pestle. Sun Wukong was about to kill him, when there was a voice in the sky, saying, "Wukong, spare his life."

It was the Moon God. Sun Wukong greeted him, and he explained. "The demon is a rabbit who is kept in the moon palace.

The princess was a lady in waiting at my palace, who eighteen days ago (in heaven, that is equivalent to eighteen years ago on earth) had mistreated the rabbit. She then aspired to earthly pleasures, and had herself born as the princess.

The Rabbit kidnapped her for a year to punish her for mistreating him. I came to collect him because his karma was up, but did not reckon with his trying to marry Sanzang. That's wrong, and I shall punish him."

Sun Wukong thanked the Moon God, and they parted.

Sun Wukong flew back to the palace and reported what had happened. The king asked, "Where is my daughter?"

Sun told him that she was locked up in the Gold-Paved Garden. The king and the queen immediately prepared to go.

Sun Wukong flew ahead of them and told the monks there to prepare for the royal visit. The princess was told, and she bathed to get ready.

When the king and his entourage arrived, they were surprised to see Sun Wukong there. Sun Wukong said, "It took me one moment to fly over, while it took you several hours."

The royal couple saw their daughter, and embraced each other, weeping for joy. Happily, the pilgrims left the kingdom on their way west.

◙ CHAPTER 15 ◙
Tycoon Kou Entertains the Pilgrims

The pilgrims were getting closer to their goal. At the entrance to a village, they saw two old men sitting at a small table, chatting with each other.

Sanzang told his disciples, "Let me go and ask about food and lodging. Do not make yourselves conspicuous lest you scare people."

Sanzang explained to the old men who he was and what his mission was.

The old men told him, "You just have to go a bit further to

find a devout millionaire who advertises that his house is 'open to all monks'.

Sanzang returned and told his disciples, and they proceeded as instructed. Sure enough, they found a big sign saying 'All monks welcome'.

Sanzang went in first to introduce himself. The old man of the house introduced himself as Kou, and he was delighted to hear that Sanzang was from the Tang Empire. He received him and invited the disciples to come in as well.

The appearance of the disciples didn't frighten him. Kou prepared a very generous dinner to feed them, and called his wife to come and greet the pilgrims from Tang.

Kou had two sons, Kou Liang (Beam) and Kou Dong (Keel). Both came out to greet them. After several days of feasting, the pilgrims wanted to leave.

Kou's wife told them, "You have accepted my husband's hospitality for two weeks. You should accept mine for two weeks too." And the two sons said they also wanted to feast with them for two more weeks.

Sanzang replied, "We are grateful for your generosity. But we must fulfill our mission. Please do not think we are ungrateful." And so they left, leaving the wife and the sons somewhat disgruntled.

There was in and around the village a gang of some thirty-five young thugs who had exhausted their money and were thinking of pulling off a robbery. They had heard of the sumptuous feasts the Kou's had been offering the pilgrims, and decided to raid the Kou's.

They burst into the house, sending everyone running and into hiding. The thieves took most of the valuables and gold and money. Old Kou came out and begged the thieves, "Leave some for us."

The thieves had no sympathy for the old man. One of them kicked him in the head, and he dropped dead.

The Kou family saw the father lying dead, and began crying hysterically.

Kou's wife still held a grudge against the pilgrims for not having accepted her hospitality. So she decided to blame the robbery on them.

She told the family, "The four monks are the thieves. Sanzang broke the door, Sun Wukong kicked your father dead, and Bajie and Sandy collected the valuables."

The family immediately reported the robbery to the police.

Meanwhile, as the thieves took the valuables and left, they ran into the pilgrims, and decided to rob them too.

They shouted, "Stand and deliver!"

Sun Wukong sneered at them, and cast a spell to freeze all thirty-five of them.

Taking his hair and turning them into ropes, Sun Wukong, Bajie and Sandy bound up the thieves and then lifted the spell.

The thieves begged for their lives. Afraid that Sanzang might chant the ring-tightening mantra, Sun Wukong decided to take all their loot so he could return it to the Kou's, and let them go.

He shouted to them, "Leave everything you robbed from the Kou's, and run for your lives!"

The thieves ran away like scared animals. The pilgrims were heading back to the Kou's when the police force came upon them and captured them, together with the loot.

Sanzang tried to explain. "Please," he said, "we are not thieves. We have met the thieves and took their loot back and we are on our way to return the loot to the Kou's."

The police chief replied, "That is a clever excuse. We do not believe you, because you are accused by Kou's widow as being the robbers."

Sun Wukong did not use his tricks to relieve the Master, realizing that the Master still had not exhausted his karma of hardships.

The pilgrims were taken to a jail where they spent the night. At about midnight, Sun Wukong escaped, and flew to the Kou's residence, where the family was having a wake.

Sun Wukong went in as a bee, and perching on the coffin, loudly cleared his throat. The family was startled. Kou's widow whispered to her dead husband, "Have you revived?"

Sun Wukong said in old Kou's voice, "I am not reviving. Because you lied to the police and got the four Tang pilgrims into trouble, I am in trouble with the King of the Underworld. You should have realized that these people are protected by all the gods and the fairies, and no one can harm them without paying dearly. You must quickly clarify the situation with the police."

The widow shook with fear and promised to tell the truth. Sun Wukong then returned to the jail, and turned into a towering giant, with his foot on the roof, shouting thunderously.

"You incompetent officials, you rascals!" Sun Wukong roared. "You have imprisoned the four sages wrongfully. They are not the thieves. They were taking the loot from the real thieves to give it back to the Kou's. If you do not release them immediately, I will crush you."

The police chief was frightened, and did not know what to do. But soon the messengers from the Kou family came and told the police chief that the accusation was a mistake and that the pilgrims were not the thieves.

The police chief released the pilgrims and apologized to them. The pilgrims went to the Kou family to pay their respects to old Kou. Sun Wukong left one of his hairs in his form, snuck out and flew down to the Underworld.

There, he was greeted by the King of the Underworld. He told him that he wanted to take Kou back to have him tell everyone that he was kicked to death by the thief, not by one of the pilgrims.

The King of Underworld agreed, giving old Kou an extra twelve years of life.

Sun Wukong took old Kou's soul and returned to the coffin. He put the soul into the body through the nostril, and soon old Kou was moaning in the coffin. The family opened it and they were overjoyed to see old Kou rise and get out of the coffin.

◎ CHAPTER 16 ◎
THE PILGRIMS ENTER THE TERRITORY OF THE WESTERN HEAVEN

Now the pilgrims were in the territory adjacent to the Western Heaven, and the landscape reflected the benevolent influence of the Buddha - trees, flowers, grass, birds, animals, even rocks and mountains looked peaceful and pleasing to the senses.

Filled with the thought that they were near their goal, the pilgrims proceeded with joyful hearts.

On their way, they saw a tower with a golden roof, and Sanzang said, "That's a good looking tower."

Sun Wukong laughed and said, "On our way, you have kowtowed to many temples and towers, even the false ones. Now here is a really divine tower, and you are still sitting pretty in your saddle."

When he heard this, Sanzang hurriedly got down from his horse and kowtowed.

Sun Wukong said, "This is the tower of the God of the Golden Dome. He will guide us to the Buddha's seat."

Soon, the God of Golden Domed Tower appeared. "Lo, you pilgrims, I have been waiting for you for fourteen years, he said. "Kuanyin told me that it might take you two or three years, maybe up to ten, but I was misled. Now it's fourteen years.

Nevertheless, I am here to guide you to the abode of the Buddha."

Sun Wukong replied, "We do not need your guidance. I have been to the abode many times and am familiar with the route."

The God of Golden-Domed Tower replied, "No. You have flown there but you have never walked there; so you do not know the land route. You need my guidance."

Sun Wukong saw the point, and thanked him for his help. As they proceeded, they came upon a river called the 'River to Reach the Cloud'.

The God of Golden-Domed Tower said, "Now I take your leave, as now you can see the abode in the distance."

It was a sight of infinite beauty and tranquility, as well as magnificence. There was a brilliant ray of light emanating from the abode, and all four pilgrims, even Sun Wukong, knelt down and kowtowed.

When they came to the shore of the river, they were awe-struck by its dramatic power and its width.

Bajie asked, "How can we cross this? Let's fly over, taking the Master with us."

Sun Wukong knew better. He said, "You and I can fly. But the Master is destined only to proceed as ordinary humans do, because he still has a human body, unlike us. He could be taken across by us, but that would not count as merit for him."

As they were wondering about how to cross, a boat slowly came from upstream, with a boatman on it. The boatman invited them to get on board, but when Sanzang looked, he saw the boat had no bottom. "How can I get on the boat?" he asked. "There is no floor for me to stand on."

Sun Wukong realized that the boatman was a god sent by the Buddha to help ferry them across this river, so he urged Sanzang to get on board, and everyone got on.

The crossing was very smooth, despite the rough waves. When they were at the middle point of the crossing, they saw a body floating down from upstream.

It was the body of Sanzang. Startled, Sanzang cried, "What is this?"

Sun Wukong explained. "This is your human body. Now you have shed your earthly bondage. You are now a fairy. Congratulations."

Sanzang then said a prayer for the body. Bajie laughed and said, "That's convenient. You say a requiem prayer for yourself."

After the crossing, they entered the realm of the Buddha, and were taken to His presence.

This was a grand occasion, and the Buddha summoned all the important bodhisattvas, Bhikkhus, apsaras, deities, fairies, saints and heavenly functionaries to be present. Kuanyin was also there.

The Buddha said, "I lament the evils, corruption, cruelty, dishonesty, brutality and cynicism that fill the world of Tang, and wish to give all the true teaching to lead them to the road of virtue and peace.

"Sanzang, you were one of senior disciples, banished because you were not paying attention to my teaching one day.

"Now you have proven yourself and endured many hardships and risks to your life to come here. I am pleased. So I will ask Ananda and Kasiapa to take you to the sutra warehouse. You may take the sutra to Tang. There are five thousand, four hundred and eight volumes."

Sanzang kowtowed and thanked the Buddha, and followed the two senior disciples, Ananda and Kasiapa, to the warehouse.

At the warehouse, Ananda asked, "What did you bring as a gift for me?"

Sanzang said, "Your Reverence, I am a poor monk on a long journey. I am sorry I do not have anything for a gift."

Sun Wukong exclaimed, "How can you seek bribes even in the Buddha's realm?"

Ananda smiled and opened the door to the warehouse, letting them take the sutras with them.

As the pilgrims took the sutras, and left the Western Heaven to return to Tang China, the Buddha asked Kuanyin, "How long has it been since they left Tang?"

Kuanyin replied, "It has been fourteen years, five thousand and forty days."

The Buddha said, "The sutras have five thousand and forty

eight volumes. So let them return to Tang in eight days to make the number of days the same as the number of volumes. Now that Sanzang has shed his mortal shell, he can fly with his disciples to China and return in eight days."

The Buddha asked how many hardships Sanzang had experienced. Counting from the banishment of the disciple Golden Cicada, all the way down to the last hardship, they counted eighty.

The Buddha said, "Let him have another hardship to make up the total number of hardships eighty one, that is, nine times nine."

Unbeknownst to them, the sutras that the pilgrims took with them consisted of blank pages. These were probably the more precious sutras. The pages were blank because the true teaching of the Buddha is beyond words. And, naturally, it would not have been understood by ordinary people.

Along the way, the Bodhisattva of the Holy Lamp took pity on the pilgrims, and sent his assistant to make them aware of the blank pages. The assistant flew over to where the pilgrims were walking east, and he stretched his arm from the cloud, pulling the sutras and scattering the volumes around, sending the pilgrims scrambling after the volumes as they flew away.

Suddenly, Sandy cried, "Look, these sutras are nothing but blank pages."

They checked and found all the volumes were indeed blank.

Sanzang said, "I cannot take these back to China. It would be a betrayal of my trust. We must go back to ask for another version with words in them."

So they turned around and returned to the Buddha's abode. They complained to the Buddha, "Ananda asked for a bribe and we did not have it. So, out of spite, he gave us this sutra without words. We would like to appeal to your mercy and request a version with words."

The Buddha said, "Ananda was only testing you. Very well, you can have the sutra with words."

So Ananda and Kasiapa again led them to another warehouse

to get the sutras with words.

Sanzang took out the golden begging bowl and said to Ananda, "I really have nothing valuable, but this bowl was given to me by the Emperor Taizong. I would like to offer it to you as a present."

Ananda accepted it with a smile. Now the pilgrims were ready to leave.

◙ CHAPTER 18 ◙
Returning to Chang-An

On their way back, they arrived at the bank of a river, where they heard a voice calling, "Your Reverence, Your Reverence, come!"

They were surprised, and looked around. There he was, the old tortoise who had ferried them across when they were heading westward.

The pilgrims were delighted, and Sun Wukong said, "Now we are going back to China with the sutras. Help us with our passage."

The old tortoise duly let them climb on to his shell, and started crossing the river smoothly. Halfway, the old tortoise asked Sanzang, "So you have been to the Buddha's abode. Did you ask him about how I could receive his blessing?"

Sanzang was embarrassed. He was too preoccupied with worshiping the Buddha, recounting his journey, collecting the sutras, and mixing with the host of saints, Bodhisattvas, gods, and fairies.

In this rush of activity, he had forgotten that he had promised the old tortoise that he would ask the Buddha about how the old tortoise could gain the Buddha's blessing. He was at a loss about what to say.

The old tortoise realized that Sanzang had not fulfilled his promise. He was annoyed, and simply dove into the water, leaving the pilgrims floating in the water.

The old tortoise figured that Sanzang had not fulfilled his promise, and annoyed, he just dove in the water, leaving the pilgrims floating in the water.

The pilgrims picked up the sutras and flew over to the other side of the river. The sutras were wet through and through, so they had to spread them on the bank to dry them.

After a day, the sutras were dry, and they collected them to pack. One of the volumes got stuck to the rock, and when they took it out, a page was detached from the volume. This unfortunately made the sutras incomplete.

But this was the Buddha's true intention. The world of man is imperfect, so the sutras should also be imperfect.

In four days, the pilgrims arrived in Chang-an, the capital of Tang Dynasty China. Taizong was organizing a Buddhist ceremony to commemorate the journey of Sanzang and to pray for his speedy return.

Sanzang arrived at the entrance and asked to see the Emperor. The Emperor was overjoyed to see Sanzang return, and asked, "Welcome home, Your Reverence. Have you succeeded in obtaining the sutras?"

Sanzang showed him the five thousand forty eight volumes of sutras. The Emperor was very pleased to see that. He offered to write an introduction for it. He would call it 'Introduction to divine Teaching', and also offered to assign a large team of scribes to copy the sutras for wide circulation.

Sanzang said, "The originals should be carefully protected while the copies can be widely circulated."

Taizong agreed. Sanzang went back to his old temple, where his disciples were waiting for him.

They said, "We have been waiting all these years, and yesterday we suddenly noticed that the branches of the tree you had planted were turning west. So we knew you were returning."

CHAPTER 19

MISSION ACCOMPLISHED, FIVE NEW
DEITIES CREATED

Having fulfilled their task, the pilgrims took leave of the Emperor and departed for the Western Heaven to report to the Buddha.

The Buddha said, "Now you have completed your tasks. Sanzang, you were once my senior disciple, banished for inattention to my teaching. But this journey of yours clearly shows your devotion. I hereby bestow on you the title of Sandalwood God of Merits.

'Sun Wukong, you have escorted your Master faithfully and have prevailed over many demons. I hereby bestow on you the title of God of Victory.

'Zhu Bajie, you have served your master well, though occasionally you let your lust get the better of you. I hereby bestow you the title of Altar Cleaner Fairy.

'Sandy, you have served faithfully and honestly. I hereby bestow on you the title of Golden-Bodied Lohan.

"Now the horse. I commend you for your loyalty and perseverance. You will be restored to your former glory. Fly away."

Bajie said, "How come I am just a fairy when Master and Sun Wukong get to be gods?"

The Buddha replied, "Do not complain. You have a huge appetite, and altar cleaning gives you ample opportunity to eat to your heart's content."

Sun Wukong then said to Sanzang, "Now that we have finished our task, it is no longer necessary to keep me in line. I want my golden crown removed."

Sanzang said, "But it is already removed. Try feeling it."

When Sun Wukong touched his head, he found that the

When Sun Wukong touched his head, he found that the crown was no longer there. He was very happy, now he was truly liberated.

crown was no longer there. He was very happy, for now he was truly liberated.

Everyone, from the Buddha down, celebrated this auspicious occasion. All the Bodhisattvas, saints, gods, lohans, and apsaras, sang the praise of the Pilgrims, and as they chanted, beautiful music sounded, and flowers of a hundred colours and fragrance rained down on the crowd.

EPILOGUE

———

"Journey to West" is considered one of China's greatest masterpieces in its popular literature. It is interesting to see why this book of fantasy gained such stature in Chinese popular culture.

It appeals to young and old because of the fantastic adventures, and because of the personalities of the protagonists: the Master for being upright if somewhat stiff and humorless; the monkey for being imaginative and loyal if rebellious; the pig for his sense of humor and cynicism; and Sandy for his stolid nature but solid loyalty.

But it is also a vivid description of Chinese society where there was no rule of law.

While I was delighted that my children enjoyed it in their childhood and later, it was not without some trepidation that I provide this retelling.

Even if one suspends one's disbelief, the stories in this book are full of contradictions. As I was reading it for the first time some sixty years ago, I would find the story curiously unsatisfying when the monkey snuck into a demon's cave, stealthily and unobtrusively. Naturally rooting for him, I would say to myself, "Now you are in the demon's cave and he is asleep. Take out your magic stick and crush him into a meatball!" When the monkey failed to do so, I found it frustrating.

Also, when the monkey said he could not carry his Master

across the river because the Master was flesh and blood, I wondered how demons could carry him so easily to kidnap him.

I must confess that I judged the ethically objectionable behavior of the characters from the perspective of Western values. I was deeply offended by the way laws were so arbitrarily ignored or bent for the convenience of the powerful.

How come the Dragon King had to be beheaded for altering the amount of rainfall, while the underworld minister could get away with altering the length of life for Emperor Taizong?

The punishments meted out for some minor offenses were vastly out of proportion, while in some cases the offenses might have been very serious but were simply forgiven because the offenders were connected to powerful gods.

The society described in the book is the Chinese society of the Ming Dynasty, where corruption and an arbitrary 'justice' system made the lives of ordinary Chinese a living hell. In some measure, this arbitrariness and corruption continues today.

Perhaps this vivid description of Ming China is one of the book's hidden virtues. The reactions of our children were interesting. They enjoyed the stories for their action, and considered the rest as 'silly and childish' without any sociological or moralistic wisdom. Perhaps that is the best reaction and the soundest critique of the story, and this book.

YCP